Along with the anger she saw in Anthony's eyes, there was pain.

A deep, tearing anguish that went straight to her heart. What had it done to him to lose his family as he had? "Anthony, I'm sorry."

"I don't want your sympathy, Melina," he said. "I want you to keep your word. Tell me where Titan is."

What could she say? She hadn't deliberately lied. She hadn't actually told him she knew. "I can't answer that."

His gaze burned into hers. "You said you didn't want to play games, so don't."

He was leaning so close to her that she could see a rim of gold inside the green of his eyes. She brushed a silky, almost sensuous strand of hair from his cheek and tucked it behind his ear. Melina recalled his command. She wanted to do a lot of things with Anthony Caldwell. But playing games wasn't one of them.

Dear Reader,

Winter may be cold, but the reading's hot here at Silhouette Intimate Moments, starting with the latest CAVANAUGH JUSTICE tale from award winner Marie Ferrarella, *Alone in the Dark*. Take one tough cop on a mission of protection, add one warmhearted veterinarian, shake, stir, and…voilà! The perfect romance to curl up with as the snow falls.

Karen Templeton introduces the first of THE MEN OF MAYES COUNTY in *Everybody's Hero*—and trust me, you really will fall for Joe Salazar and envy heroine Taylor McIntyre for getting to go home with him at the end of the day. FAMILY SECRETS: THE NEXT GENERATION concludes with *In Destiny's Shadow*, by Ingrid Weaver, and you'll definitely want to be there for the slam-bang finish of the continuity, not to mention the romance with a twist. Those SPECIAL OPS are back in Lyn Stone's *Under the Gun*, an on-the-run story guaranteed to set your heart racing. Linda O. Johnston shows up *Not a Moment Too Soon* to tell the story of a desperate father turning to the psychic he once loved to search for his kidnapped daughter. Finally, welcome new author Rosemary Heim, whose debut novel, *Virgin in Disguise*, has a bounty hunter falling for her quarry—with passionate consequences.

Enjoy all six of these terrific books, then come back next month for more of the best and most exciting romance reading around—only from Silhouette Intimate Moments.

Enjoy!

Leslie J. Wainger
Excecutive Editor

Please address questions and book requests to:
Silhouette Reader Service
U.S.: 3010 Walden Ave., P.O. Box 1325, Buffalo, NY 14269
Canadian: P.O. Box 609, Fort Erie, Ont. L2A 5X3

In Destiny's Shadow

INGRID WEAVER

Silhouette®

INTIMATE MOMENTS™

Published by Silhouette Books

America's Publisher of Contemporary Romance

Special thanks and acknowledgment are given
to Ingrid Weaver for her contribution
to the FAMILY SECRETS: THE NEXT GENERATION series.

This book is dedicated to the gracious and
talented ladies who told our Family Secrets:
Jenna, Marie, Candace, Linda and Kylie.
It's been way too much fun to call work!

 SILHOUETTE BOOKS

ISBN 0-373-27399-1

IN DESTINY'S SHADOW

Visit Silhouette Books at www.eHarlequin.com

Printed in U.S.A.

Books by Ingrid Weaver

Silhouette Intimate Moments

True Blue #570
True Lies #660
On the Way to a Wedding... #761
Engaging Sam #875
What the Baby Knew #939
Cinderella's Secret Agent #1076
Fugitive Hearts #1101
Under the King's Command #1184
Eye of the Beholder #1204
Seven Days to Forever #1216
Aim for the Heart #1258
In Destiny's Shadow #1329

Silhouette Special Edition

The Wolf and the Woman's Touch #1056

*Eagle Squadron

INGRID WEAVER

admits to being a sucker for old movies and books that can make her cry. "I write because life is an adventure," Ingrid says. "And the greatest adventure of all is falling in love." Since the publication of her first book in 1994, she has won the Romance Writers of America RITA® Award for Romantic Suspense, as well as the *Romantic Times* Career Achievement Award for Series Romantic Suspense. Ingrid lives with her husband and son and an assortment of shamefully spoiled pets in a pocket of country paradise an afternoon's drive from Toronto. She invites you to visit her Web site at www.ingridweaver.com.

FAMILY SECRETS: THE NEXT GENERATION

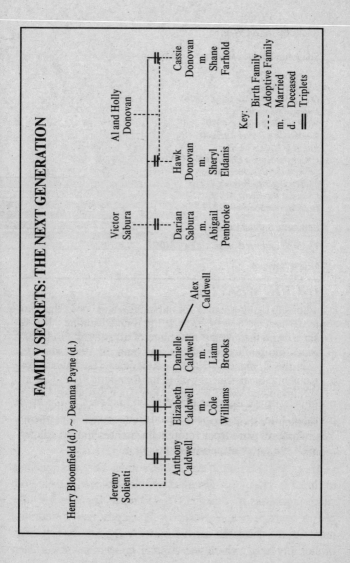

Henry Bloomfield (d.) ~ Deanna Payne (d.)

Jeremy Solienti

Anthony Caldwell

Elizabeth Caldwell
m.
Cole Williams

Danielle Caldwell
m.
Liam Brooks

Alex Caldwell

Victor Sabura

Darian Sabura
m.
Abigail Pembroke

Al and Holly Donovan

Hawk Donovan
m.
Sheryl Eldanis

Cassie Donovan
m.
Shane Farhold

Key:
— Birth Family
--- Adoptive Family
m. Married
d. Deceased
‖ Triplets

Prologue

Benedict fondled the woman's body, feeling the stone warm in his hand. No one knew how old she was. Her previous owner, the late collector who had last possessed her, had claimed her age was ten thousand years. She had been caressed like this for eons; her rough edges had been smoothed by the touch of countless handlers. She was squat and gray, not much longer than the length from his wrist to the tip of his middle finger, but she contained all the essential elements. Yes, whatever prehistoric craftsman had fashioned this figure knew exactly what mattered most in a female.

He rubbed his thumb across the woman's breasts, pausing to flick his nail over a distended nipple. No pert, Barbie doll silicon implants on this girl. These breasts hung in a V like heavy, overripe pears, swollen with the promise of nourishment for the child she carried in her belly. She had no face on her tiny head, which was another point in her favor. Her arms were mere suggestions in the stone, short grooves that angled backward out of the way and would be incapable of putting up a fight. Her thighs were wide, her legs short and sturdy. She had no feet because she would have no need to go anywhere. Her sole purpose was to bear children.

The stone grew slippery from the sweat on his palm. Benedict moistened his lips and rubbed harder. Too bad real women weren't more like this. It would have been so much simpler if Deanna had been like the stone carving, all breasts and womb, no brain. He had entrusted his plans to her body but she had betrayed him. She had stolen the six children who would have given him the future.

She had paid for her crime with her life.

He replaced the priceless figurine in its case. Turning in a slow circle, he contemplated the other treasures that lined the spot-lit alcoves of his inner sanctum. There was a sphere of solid crystal mounted on a pounded copper circlet, a deer hide medicine pouch, a jade amulet, the sword of a Samurai, marble from the Temple of Athena, a fragment of stone from the Pyramid of Cheops… The extent of his collection was too long to list. Every item was reputed to possess mystical powers. And now he possessed them.

That was how it worked. Possess them, possess their power. He was going to need it. His enemies were growing stronger. They had destroyed much of his empire but they would never find him. They didn't understand that with each blow they struck, they pushed him closer to his ultimate destiny.

Benedict climbed the steps to the platform in the center of the room. At the top was a plain square table and high-backed chair fashioned from alder wood. The chair creaked as it took his weight, the dry wood making a noise like a scream. He laughed at the sound. The wood had been taken from a Welsh valley once said to be used by Druids. Whether their old gods liked it or not, the power that lingered in the wood was his now, too. Soon he would be invincible.

He had reinvented himself before. He would do it again. He had begun life as Benedict Payne. After Deanna's betrayal, he'd assumed the identity of uber-criminal Titan. His next transformation would be his last. He smiled and slipped a deck of tarot cards from his suit pocket.

Like the stone woman, the edges of the cards had been worn down from handling. He dealt a pattern for himself on the table and turned over the first card. His smile deepened as he saw the figure depicted on the front. It wore different guises in different decks. At times it was a blue-robed sorcerer, other times it was a rabbit, but its true identity remained the same. The Magician—working in secret, gathering power, using any means to control those around him.

Yes, control was the ultimate power, he thought, tapping the card against his lips. Soon, the world would see the culmination of the plan he had set into motion over three decades ago. He had been patient, watching and waiting for the right time to make his move. Five times he'd almost had Deanna's children within his grasp. Five times they had eluded him.

Yet there was still one left. The firstborn, the boldest, the one who dared to hunt *him*. This time the hunter would become the hunted. The Magician would prevail.

And then the future would be his.

Chapter 1

"If you help me, Fredo, I'll help you." Melina put her hand on his shoulder. She could feel the sharp outline of his bones through his denim jacket. He was trembling. The night carried the taste of autumn, but Fredo's tremors likely weren't due to the cold. "We don't have to go to the local police if you don't want to," she said. "I know someone in the FBI. They would protect you. They could get you somewhere safe."

"You don't understand what Titan's turning into." Fredo shrugged off her grasp and stepped from the sidewalk into the alley where the streetlight didn't reach. "Nowhere is safe. You can't trust anyone."

"Fredo—"

"The feds got all his labs. They destroyed his drugs, his equipment, everything. Half his guys were arrested. It made him flip out."

Wind gusted past the canvas awning of the closed fruit market beside the alley, rattling the strings of dried chilies that hung out front. Melina's skirt swirled against her calves, the wool rubbing over her suede boots with a noise like stealthy whispers.

She looked behind her to check that the street was still deserted. It was. They were far from the popular tourist haunts of downtown Santa Fe. There were no quaint adobe buildings or historic missions here, just modest shops, video places and liquor stores, all of them closed up hours ago. The only movement she could see came from dead leaves and bits of crumpled paper that skittered along the pavement.

Most women would find the situation unsettling, to say the least. It was two in the morning and she was standing at the entrance to a dark alley with a thief. Yet Melina Becker had faced far worse to get a story. She slipped one arm through her purse strap to loop it around her neck and followed Fredo into the darkness. "Do you know where Titan is now? I heard he has a stronghold. When you called me you said you had information."

"All I have for you is a warning. You better stop what you're doing."

She detected a rising note of anxiety in his voice. Her pulse sped up. She must be closer to paydirt than she had thought. "I can't stop yet, Fredo. Couldn't you give me something?"

"You were decent to me once, Melina. That's why I'm trying to do you a favor now. Why won't you listen?"

"I've put months into this story, and I do realize how dangerous Titan is. I promise he'll never know you talked to me."

Fredo laughed, a high-pitched, nervous bark that echoed from the brick walls flanking them. "If you believe he won't know, for sure you don't know Titan at all. Ever since the feds raided his labs he's more paranoid than ever. He scares me. I'm telling you, he flipped out."

"How? What do you mean?"

"He was always weird, but now he's over the edge. He's got a stronghold, all right. It's a regular fortress. He's so paranoid now, he never leaves it."

"Where—"

"Go back to New York. Get out of Santa Fe. Tonight. That's what I'm doing."

Melina reached for his arm. "Just give me something, Fredo. Anything. Tell me where to look."

He turned away before she could touch him, tucking his chin farther into the collar of his jacket. "He's in plain sight, but even if you look, you won't see him. Honest to God, he thinks he's some kind of magician."

"I don't understand. What—"

"I can't go home, but you can." He started walking toward the rectangle of faint light that marked the other end of the alley. "If you don't, you're going to get us both killed."

Melina hurried after him. Her boot heels resounded hollowly from the walls, making it sound as if she were being followed. She took a second to check over her shoulder, but the shadows appeared empty. When she looked for Fredo again, he was already several yards ahead of her. "Titan's here in New Mexico, right?" she persisted, increasing her pace. "You can give me that much, can't you?"

Fredo broke into a jog. "Leave it alone."

"Wait!" Melina stopped short as she barely avoided running into a utility pole that rose close to one wall. "Fredo, please."

He dodged past the dark bulk of a garbage bin and left the alley at a run. The street he emerged on was narrower than the one at the other end. It was dimmer, too, lined with warehouses instead of stores. No light showed around the steel doors that were rolled down and locked for the night. Yet before Fredo was halfway across the street, his thin form was suddenly bathed in white.

There was a series of muffled pops. He jerked and stumbled sideways. Dark splotches appeared on his jacket, spreading over the worn denim like giant drops of water.

But it wasn't raining. That wasn't water. Melina skidded to a stop at the mouth of the alley and flattened herself against the side of the garbage bin.

Fredo crumpled to the pavement. An engine roared from the darkness, and a yellow van barreled down the center of the street. Gunfire flashed from the open passenger window, illuminating a pale, heavy-joweled face. Fredo's body continued to jerk. The van lurched. Its right wheels ran over him with a noise like splintering wood. Without slowing down, it reached the end of the block, turned the corner and disappeared.

For an instant, Melina couldn't move. She felt numb. The bag of chips that had passed for her dinner rose in her throat, making her gag, muffling her building scream. She staggered out of the alley, her legs boneless.

Oh, no. Not Fredo. Poor, hard-luck Fredo. She had just been talking to him. He couldn't be...

You're going to get us both killed.

She moved beside him and dropped to her knees. He was dead still, lying on his back, his limbs bent in unnatural angles and his head twisted to the side. His eyes were open, unblinking and already starting to glaze. There was a pool of blood under his cheek. More blood gleamed in the moonlight from the dark holes and the zigzag pattern of lines that smeared the front of his jacket.

The holes were bullet holes. The lines were tire tracks. Those sounds… Oh God! She swallowed hard. Her fingers shook as she extended her hand. She laid her palm on his chest. "Fredo, I'm sorry. I never meant—"

At the noise of an engine, she twisted to look behind her. Headlights swept across the pavement. The yellow van was coming back.

Melina's mind was reeling from the brutality she had just witnessed. It took her a crucial second too long to process what was happening. By the time she sprang to her feet, the van was mere yards away, the glare of its headlights obscuring everything else.

She tried to jump out of its path, but the soles of her boots slipped in Fredo's blood and she fell. Sticky warmth seeped through her skirt to her knees.

Oh, God. She was going to die. She didn't want to die. Not now. Not when she was so close to getting everything she wanted—

She grunted with the impact. But it wasn't the impact of a one-ton vehicle. A hard, male body slammed into her side, knocking her out of the way an instant before the van surged past.

Tires squealed. The van skidded into a U-turn at the end of the block.

"Let's go!"

Melina looked up. The man who had tackled her was already on his feet. She had a quick impression of dark hair, broad shoulders and the scent of leather, but there wasn't time to absorb more. He caught her under her arms and hauled her upright. "Come *on*!"

She wasn't sure she could have spoken if she'd wanted to. There was no need. Not if she wanted to survive. Hiking up her skirt, she ran with him into the alley.

The van accelerated behind them, the engine whining with the strain. Mortar and fragments of brick sprayed the air as bullets struck the wall of the buildings on either side of them. The stranger grasped her wrist, spinning her to his chest. With one arm clamped around her waist, he lifted her from her feet and backed her behind the garbage bin at the alley's entrance, using its bulk and his body to shield her from the bullets and the ricocheting debris. "Hang on," he said.

She struggled in his embrace. Why was he stopping here? They weren't safe yet. The alley wasn't that narrow. The van could squeeze past the bin and they would be caught. "No. We have to keep going."

He tensed, as if he were gathering his strength. A tremor went through his body, but otherwise he remained motionless.

Tires screeched again, so close, Melina drew in the smell of exhaust and burnt rubber. The van's headlights swung into the alley. She shoved at the man's chest. "We can't stop. They'll—"

Her words were drowned out by an explosion overhead. Melina stretched on her toes to peer past the stranger's shoulder. Sparks showered downward from a transformer atop the utility pole she had almost run into when she'd chased Fredo. The air sizzled as something long and thin flicked through the alley above them, weaving like the end of a whip. It was a power line, Melina realized. It must have been severed by a stray bullet. It crackled in a smoking trail where the tip danced across the ground—and it cut off their only escape route.

Metal screeched as the side of the van scraped along the garbage bin.

The stranger scooped Melina into his arms and ran straight for the live wire.

She screamed, clutching the front of his jacket, her fingers digging into the leather.

The wire coiled, snakelike, hissing and spitting. It came so close, Melina felt a prickle of energy shoot through her nerves. She shuddered at the sensation and clung to the stranger. At the last possible second, he veered to the side, ducked safely past and set her back on her feet.

The wire swung directly into the front grille of the van that followed them. Bolts of blue-white brilliance arced along the metal. The engine died, along with the headlights. The van coasted forward a few feet but didn't clear the steel bin. It stopped, caught between the bin on one side and the building on the other, the doors wedged shut. Sparks shot out from beneath the hood as the current passed through it and found a direct route to the ground. The sparks were followed by flames.

The stranger grabbed her elbow, wrenching her around. He tugged her forward. "Run! It's going to blow!"

Melina didn't need any more encouragement. She sprinted with him toward the other end of the alley. For a suspended moment, all she could hear was their pounding footsteps, the noise of their breathing and the hammering of her own pulse. One beat. Two. There was a crackling *whoosh*. She glanced over her shoulder. The van erupted in flames. One more heartbeat and the gas tank exploded. The alley was engulfed in a fireball.

The shockwave caught them before they could reach the street. The man lunged for her, wrapping his arms around her as they were lifted into the air. He twisted so that he took their combined weight on his back when they hit the ground, then quickly reversed their positions, sheltering her beneath him as embers and pieces of burning wreckage bounced from the walls and the pavement around them.

It seemed to go on forever. Melina tucked her face against his neck and squeezed her eyes shut. Her retinas burned with an afterimage of the fireball. Her ears rang. Her knees stung.

And her nerves were humming as if she were still too close to that live wire.

She struggled to draw air into her lungs. She tasted smoke and ozone…and warm male skin. Her lips tingled where she touched the stranger's throat. A shiver shook her body. The hair at the nape of her neck stirred.

"He rolled off her. "Are you hurt?"

She shook her head and opened her eyes. He was kneeling at her hip, a large, dark silhouette against the fire that crackled behind him. She could see the outline of his square jaw and caught a glint of gold at his ear but she couldn't see his face. The fire was the only illumination—the streetlights beyond the alley had gone black.

He leaned over to run his hands along her arms and down her legs. He lingered at her knees. "I don't think that's your blood on your skirt."

"No. It's Fredo's. I just was talking to him. I can't believe—"

"I saw what happened. I'm sorry. Was he a friend of yours?"

"I didn't even know his last name. Oh, God, he—" Her voice broke.

He slipped one arm under her back to help her sit up. "Can you walk?"

She swallowed hard before she could speak again. "Yes, I'm fine. I'm just…winded. What you did back there…" She sounded scared. Well, she *was* scared, and she felt sick. But at least she was alive. "Thank you."

"You're welcome. Sorry if I hurt you when I grabbed you."

"We both could have been shot. And that wire—"

"We got lucky."

"I have to call an ambulance. For Fredo." She groped for her purse. The strap had twisted around her neck but it hadn't broken. She pulled the purse to her lap, undid the clasp and shoved her hand inside. "I need my phone."

"No, you don't." He got to his feet and held out his palm. "There's nothing anyone can do for him now. Or for his killers."

In her heart, she knew he was right. She had been at enough accident and crime scenes to recognize death when she saw it. Fredo was gone. She squinted at the burning wreckage of the van. Unless they had escaped out the back doors, the people who had killed him were dead, too.

Could she have saved the people in the van if she had gone back to help them? Probably not—everything had happened too fast. If she had tried, she would be dead now, either from electrocution, the explosion or from one of their bullets.

She fought back a wave of nausea. God, this was a nightmare.

"Come on, Miss Becker." The man leaned over, caught her hand and tugged it out of her purse. "Time to leave before we have more company."

The slide of his skin against hers sent a strange tickle up her arm, distracting her. She had started to rise before she realized what he had said. She tried to yank her hand free. "How do you know my name?"

He firmed his grasp and pulled her the rest of the way to her feet. "I'll explain later. You need to get somewhere safe."

"What's going on? Who are you?"

"My name's Anthony Caldwell."

She tried to kick her brain into gear. The name wasn't familiar—she was sure she had never met him—so how did he know her?

There was a sudden bang and a flare of light from the wreckage. The alley and everything in it was bathed in red. For the first time, she was able to see her rescuer's face.

Once again, Melina couldn't seem to draw air into her lungs. The man's expression was as unyielding as his grip on her fingers. His features were all harsh lines and sharp angles, too austere to be termed handsome. His hair was thick and raven-black, pulled ruthlessly back and caught by a band at the nape of his neck. A thin gold hoop pierced his left earlobe. He looked hard, uncompromising. Untouchable.

Yet his gaze…oh, those green eyes snapped with power that shot right through her body, jolting her nerves to vivid awareness, sending her racing pulse into overdrive, reaching deep inside where she hid the pain….

She trembled. She felt as if she were being drawn forward. It took all her strength to keep from swaying into him. What was happening here?

The flare of light died. Oily smoke rolled over them. A dog barked somewhere in the distance above the crackle of the flames, jarring her back to reality.

"You have no reason to fear me, Miss Becker," he said. "We're on the same side."

Melina yanked her hand free of his and stepped back. Her pulse still pounded. Traces of awareness trickled down her spine and hardened her nipples. Her nipples? She couldn't be aroused, could she? Not now. What was wrong with her?

Her reaction to this man had to be shock, that's all. Or adrenaline. She had to get herself under control. She had to think logically, objectively. Set aside her emotions and put the facts together. That was what she did best. That was who she was.

But who—and what—was he?

Anthony Caldwell was a complete stranger. She definitely had never met him before, or she would have remembered. Any woman would have remembered a man who caused a reaction like *that*.

She shoved her hand back into her purse. Her fingertips brushed the edge of her phone. This man had saved her life, but that was the only thing about him she knew for certain. The prudent thing to do now would be to call the police. "You said we were on the same side. What does that mean?"

"We both want the same thing."

She turned the phone in her hand until her thumb was positioned over the keypad. "And what's that?"

"Titan."

This wasn't how Anthony had wanted to play it. He did his best work in the shadows. He had never intended to meet Melina Becker face-to-face. It would have been simpler to follow her until he had the opportunity to take what he needed. But the man who called himself Titan had been a step ahead of him. Again.

Because of that, yet another soul had died.

Anthony's knuckles whitened where he gripped the steering wheel. How many deaths were on the bastard's hands now? How many more would there be before Anthony stopped him? Would any of them have happened if he had been stopped twenty-eight years ago, after the first one?

He kept the Jeep steady despite the burst of rage that shook him. The anger was nothing new. He couldn't remember a time without it.

He spotted the oval green-on-white sign that was the trademark of the Grand Inn chain, and turned into the parking lot. Out of habit, he backed the Jeep into a spot so that he could get out quickly, then shut off the engine and looked at his passenger.

She probably thought that clenching her hands in her lap that way would hide the tremor in her fingers. It must be important to her not to show weakness. Anthony could understand that. For a woman who had witnessed a murder and had narrowly missed becoming a victim herself, she was holding up well.

He had expected no less. Melina was the lead crime reporter for the *New York Daily Journal*. She hadn't gotten to the top of her field by being a coward. It had taken some nerve to fly halfway across the country and walk into a deserted alley in the dead of night to meet a source. Almost as much nerve as it had taken for her to get into this Jeep with him.

Then again, he knew she would do anything to get the man she knew as Titan. They had that much in common.

She turned her head to meet his gaze. Her auburn curls were backlit by the floodlight over the motel office, giving them the appearance of a halo. The curve of her cheek was softly feminine, gleaming like satin. Her lips were full and shaped in a classic bow, and he couldn't help remembering how good she had felt in his arms.

Had she sensed the sexual current that had flowed between them back there in the alley? Its strength had taken him by surprise. It had been all he could do to bring it back under control, but he'd had no choice. He couldn't afford the distraction. This was the wrong time, the wrong place and definitely the wrong woman.

Her gaze glittered, not with interest but with challenge. "I didn't tell you I was staying here, Mr. Caldwell."

"You didn't need to. The *Daily Journal* always puts its people in the Grand Inn chain. They're both owned by the same company."

"How do you know that?"

"I looked it up on the Internet. Now you need to pack your things. I'll answer your other questions once we get you out of here." He opened his door and stepped to the ground. He had to grit his teeth against a wave of dizziness. It had taken more out of him than he'd thought to blow that transformer and snap the high tension wire.

"Just a minute," she said. "You said we would talk about Titan. That's why I came with you. I'm not going any farther until—"

He slammed the door on her protest and rounded the hood to the passenger side. He paused until the dizziness had passed, then flung open her door and held out his hand. "We don't have much time, Miss Becker. I couldn't be the only one who figured out you're staying here. Someone in Titan's network must have learned about your meeting with Fredo tonight. They don't leave loose ends."

Her gaze darted past him as she scanned the parking lot. She drew her lower lip between her teeth. It was an unconscious gesture, another chink in the brave front she was trying so hard to project.

Anthony felt a sudden urge to pull her into his arms and protect her the way he had before. Instead, he withdrew the hand he had offered and gripped the edge of the door. He had to maintain his focus. Hers wasn't the only life at risk. "I'm staying at the Pecos Lodge. It's built around a courtyard and is more out of the way than this place. I'll book you a room there under another name."

"I could go to the police."

"Yes, you could, but you already chose not to," he said, mentally replaying the cell phone call she had made from his Jeep. "Why didn't you give your name when you called to tell them about Fredo's murder?"

She returned her gaze to his face. "Fredo said I shouldn't trust anyone. That could mean Titan has an informant on the local force."

"Then why did you trust me?"

"What makes you think I do?"

"You came with me."

"I would go with the devil himself if it got me to Titan."

Anthony was familiar with the signs of obsession—he recognized them in himself. That Melina's obsession stemmed from professional reasons rather than personal made no difference. He would use it to his advantage. "There's another reason why you didn't go to the police."

"Oh? And what's that?"

"You don't want them to get between you and your story." He glanced at his watch. "I'll give you five minutes to pack. Then I'm leaving, with or without you."

She gathered her skirt to one side, swung her legs out of the Jeep and hopped to the ground. She led the way across the parking lot to her room in silence. As soon as they were inside and he had closed the door behind them, she turned to face him. "Look, I came this far with you because you know something about Titan. And I'm going along with your suggestion about checking out of this motel because I agree with you about that. It would be safer to change location on the off chance Titan learned I met Fredo. But let's get one thing straight."

"What?"

"I don't take orders, Mr. Caldwell." She put her fists on her hips and drew herself up. "And as much as I appreciate the way you saved my life, I won't be bullied."

She was tall for a woman, and the suede boots that hugged her calves had good-size heels. Because of that, she didn't need to tilt her head much to meet his gaze. It reminded him of how well their bodies had fit together when he'd been holding her—

Concentrate, he told himself. "It was never my intention to bully you, Miss Becker. I'm merely stating the most logical course of action."

"No, you were trying to push me, and it won't work. Yes, I want my story, but you must want something from me. It couldn't have been coincidence that you happened to show up in that alley tonight. You must have been following me since I left this motel. What is it? What do you want?"

She shouldn't have put it that way, he thought. What would any man want when he was at a motel in the middle of the night with a woman who made his blood hum the way it did now? He brought his index finger to her cheek. He stopped short of touching her, yet he could feel her warmth reach out to him, drawing him closer, making him yearn for the time to explore where this could lead.

But they didn't have time, and he couldn't afford this. The sooner he got what he came for, the safer everyone would be. He dropped his hand. "I already told you."

"Right. You said you want Titan."

"He has to be brought to justice."

"Absolutely. We agree on that much, but you didn't answer my question. What do you want from me?"

"I want your files."

Her eyes widened. She took a step back. "You can't be serious."

"I need the information you've gathered. Your notes, your files, your list of contacts. You're closer than the police are to learning where Titan is. Combined with what I know, that will lead me—"

"Whoa. I should have seen it. You're a reporter. That's how you know so much about me and the *Journal*. What paper do you work for?"

"I'm not a reporter. I don't work for anyone but myself."

"Prove it."

"My questions should prove it. I'm not interested in what Titan has done, I only care about where he is now."

She studied him, as if trying to read the truth on his face. "Well, whatever you claim, you've got some nerve thinking I'd give anything away. I'm not telling you where Titan is. This is *my* story. I've been tracking him for months and I intend to be there when he's arrested."

"You can't plan to continue. You were almost killed tonight. They won't give up."

She turned away. There was a pale green carry-on bag on a suitcase stand beside the door. She picked up the bag and took it to the desk in the corner. "I don't give up, either," she said. A laptop computer sat on the desk, surrounded by disorderly piles of handwritten notes. She unplugged the laptop and slipped it into a pocket on the outside of the bag, then gathered the papers and stuffed them in, as well. She zipped the pocket closed and faced him, her chin lifted and her shoulders squared. "And just in case you're thinking of stealing this stuff, don't bother."

That was exactly what he'd been thinking. It would have been the simplest solution, after all. That was why he'd been watching her room earlier tonight—he'd planned to enter when she was asleep and help himself to what he needed. But when he had seen her go out, he'd decided to follow her instead. "Miss Becker... Melina."

"Because it wouldn't do you any good," she continued. "I use the computer mostly for research and for sending finished copy to my editor. And I use my own brand of shorthand for my notes." She tapped her temple. "Most of what I know is in here."

"That's all the more reason for you to be concerned about your safety."

"I am concerned. That's why I'm packing." She placed the bag on the bed. Her gaze dropped to the bloodstains on her skirt. For a moment she wavered, clenching her hands the way she had in the Jeep.

It was obvious to Anthony she was still struggling to control her emotions. He took a step forward, but she recovered quickly and turned to the dresser. It was just as well. He probably shouldn't touch her again.

Moving mechanically, she emptied the dresser drawers and the room's small closet. With the skill of a habitual traveler, she rolled the garments smoothly—there weren't many—and squeezed them into the middle compartment of the bag. She walked to the bathroom. "If you're not doing a story, then what's your connection to Titan?" she asked over her shoulder. "Did you work for him?"

Anthony followed her. The bathroom was small and didn't appear to have a window, so he stopped in the doorway. "I'll answer that question if you tell me what you know."

"That isn't the way it works." She used her forearm to sweep the belongings off the counter beside the sink into another pocket of her bag. "You should be giving me information, not the other way around."

"And you shouldn't be risking your life for a story."

"My work *is* my life, Mr. Caldwell," she said. "And I'm going to break the news about Titan. What he did tonight to Fredo is only the latest in a string of crimes that's more extensive than anyone believes." She hitched the strap of the carry-on over her shoulder and brushed past him.

He turned to keep her in sight. "You don't have to convince me of that, Miss Becker. His thugs attacked and almost killed my friend."

She paused at the foot of the bed to look at him. Some of the antagonism eased from her expression. "Why?"

"Because my friend wouldn't tell them where to find my sisters and me." He moved toward her and reached for her bag. "Here. I'll carry that for you."

She curled her fingers around the strap. "No, thanks."

"You still don't trust me?"

"No, but if Titan hurt your friend and is threatening your family, I can understand why you would want to see him brought to justice."

Anthony didn't respond. If she ever discovered what he really planned to do with the bastard, she would be even less inclined to trust him. He walked to the door and put his hand on the knob. "The five minutes are up. Time to go."

Melina gave the room a final survey, then moved to join him. She put her free hand on his arm. "Why would Titan be after your family?"

"Where is Titan hiding?"

She hesitated briefly, her lips thinning, then sighed and gave a crisp nod. "All right. If it turns out you're telling the truth, we might be able to make a deal."

He looked at where her fingers rested against his jacket sleeve. Her nails were trimmed short and bare of polish, her grip firm, yet there was a delicate femininity in the shape of her hand. Her touch couldn't penetrate the leather, but he sensed it just the same. "What kind of deal, Melina?"

"You might have information about Titan that I could use."

"And in return?"

"In return for an interview, I promise to call you before I break the story." She patted his arm. "Aside from the FBI, you'll be the first one to know where he is."

It wasn't nearly enough, but it was a start. He took her hand. The contact teased through his palm and raised the hair on his arm. At her intake of breath, he lifted his gaze. Her lips seemed closer to his than before. Had she swayed toward him? Had she felt it, too?

Anthony released his grip and forced himself to look away. He knew what he wanted. He tried to tell himself it wasn't this.

Melina Becker was a means to an end, that was all. Anthony didn't have the time or the right to indulge his cravings with her. He had to control this connection between them. He had no choice.

For Anthony's destiny had been determined twenty-eight years ago. He had been three years old when he'd watched Titan commit his first murder.

Back then, Titan had called himself Benedict Payne.

And back then, Anthony had called him father.

Chapter 2

"I have a new lead, Neil." Melina pushed down on the handle of her hotel room door with one hand while she held her cell phone to her ear with the other. She swung open the door, snatched up the *Santa Fe Examiner* that lay on the threshold and bumped the door closed with her foot. "It's going to take some more time to check it out."

"How much more time, Melina?"

Tucking the newspaper under her phone arm, she straightened her sweater as she walked back to the bed. It was a relatively long walk. The proportions of the rooms in the Pecos Lodge were far more generous than those at the Grand Inn. They were more distinctive, too. The Pecos had a Southwestern flavor: red and black Navajo-style patterns brightened the bedspread and curtains, warm varnished pine planks made up the floor, and the window was set into a thick plastered arch. It was nice, but she knew she wouldn't linger. She seldom did.

"I'm interviewing him this morning, so I need another day. Maybe two."

"That's what you said last week."

"I know, but this is promising, Neil. No one else is on it." She laid the paper flat on the bed and scanned the headlines.

"Maybe no one else is on it because there's nothing to *be* on. Titan is just another drug dealer. He's news, but not big news."

She turned the pages and continued to skim the articles as she squatted down to grope beside the bed for her boots. "We've had this discussion before, Neil. Titan has a bigger agenda, I'm certain of it."

"What happened to the lead you were chasing—the thief you interviewed last year? What was the guy's name? Pablo? Paco?"

The newsprint blurred. Melina left her boots on the floor and sat on the edge of the mattress. "His name was Fredo. He's dead."

"What? How?"

"Titan had him killed. I saw…" She breathed in slowly through her nose, trying to push her horror away so she could recall the events objectively. Almost six hours had passed, yet she still felt like throwing up when she remembered the sound of the van running over Fredo's body. She brushed the folds of her skirt. She had thrown out the one she'd worn last night. "I was there. He was shot. The people who did it are dead, too."

"Are you all right?"

"Yes, I'm fine."

"Did you get pictures?"

"No, Neil. I did not get pictures."

"You don't need to shout."

She did some more nose-breathing, striving for calm. Neil

Tremblay wasn't as insensitive as he sounded. He was just doing his job as her editor. She switched her phone to her other ear. "Sorry."

"Did you get a statement from the police at the scene? Are they finally admitting it was Titan?"

"I didn't wait for the police. There was too much going on at the time. Afterward I called in a tip anonymously." She looked at the paper. "So far there's nothing about it in the local news. It's probably too early. I'll follow up on Fredo's murder and on what I learned from him when I finish this interview with my new lead."

There was a silence. "You should have been more forthcoming with the police, Melina," he said. "You still have nothing solid to run."

Neil was using his reasonable voice, the one he adopted when he was about to say something she didn't like. She pushed herself off the bed and paced as far as the window. She fingered the geometric pattern at the hem of the curtain. "We've discussed this before, too, Neil. I want to hold off running anything until I can cover Titan's arrest. My contact at the FBI has been ducking my calls, so I'm sure they're closing in. I want to be there when they do."

"I admire your determination, but you have to understand my position. I've given you all the leeway I can and still have nothing to show for it."

"This new lead could pay off big," she began.

"That's what you said when you flew to North Carolina in September, and again when you flew to Texas last month. Nothing came of those leads, either. It makes me wonder whether you're using this story as an excuse to keep traveling."

"Neil—"

"If it was only up to me, I'd give you carte blanche, you

know that. But I have to answer to the board and I can't continue to justify your expenses."

"Are you cutting me off?"

"Don't put it so harshly, Melina. This is for your own good. It's time to reassess our priorities. We should direct our energy to more worthwhile pursuits."

"Neil, this is worthwhile. I have the inside track with a friend of one of Titan's victims."

"Great. Write it up as a human interest piece and we can run it in the Sunday supplement."

"He can give me more than that. It seems that Titan is after this guy's family. I want to find out why."

There was a stuttering creak on the line. Melina recognized the sound of Neil's chair. She pictured him leaning back behind his desk, the Manhattan skyline beyond his window a dramatic backdrop, his gaze directed at the ceiling. He did that a lot.

She pushed aside the curtain to look at the mountains in the distance. She didn't know what the range was called, but the skyline sure was different from what she was used to. "Two more days, that's all I'm asking."

"And then?"

She hesitated.

"Will you give me your answer when you come home?"

"My answer about this story?"

"No, about us."

Oh, damn. Melina turned her back on the view and sank down on the windowsill. She didn't want to go into this now. "I can't promise that, Neil."

This time his silence was longer. When he spoke again, his voice had dropped. "I miss you, Melina."

"Neil…"

"I know we agreed not to discuss it until you got back."

The chair creaked again. "But you're still thinking about what I said before you left, aren't you?"

"Yes, I think about it," she said.

"Good. You can have your two days. Let me know what flight you're taking. I'll meet you at the airport the day after tomorrow."

The call ended as it had begun, with business. Melina should be pleased that Neil had relented about the expenses, but the victory was a small one. The larger battle was awaiting her on her return to New York.

She placed the phone on the windowsill beside her, then bent forward, dropping her face into her hands. *You're still thinking about what I said before you left, aren't you?*

Marriage wasn't something she liked to think about—she hadn't seriously considered it for eight years—but this was the third time that Neil had proposed.

He had popped the question in his office with the same ring he'd offered the first two times. It hadn't exactly been romantic, but she had been in a hurry to get to the airport, and he kept the ring in the top drawer of his desk.

There were many points in his favor. He was a nice guy. Mature, respectable, emotionally stable and financially comfortable. They had countless things in common, from their fondness for jazz to their interest in foreign films. They had a terrific working relationship and they enjoyed each other's company. Their dates weren't passionate but they were pleasant. She genuinely liked him, and she was certain he would make a great father. Those were all sensible elements to build a solid marriage on. If she set aside her emotions and thought logically...

Right. Set aside her emotions, use her brain. Seek the truth. That was what she did best. That was what being a good reporter meant.

But this wasn't a story she was contemplating. This was her life.

My work is my life. That was what she had told Anthony only a few hours ago. And it was. It had given her a structure to cling to when the rest of her world had fallen apart. Chasing a lead across the country, walking into dark alleys, getting shot at by criminals didn't frighten her half as much as taking another leap of faith with her heart.

Would her feelings be any different if Neil had intense green eyes instead of comfortable brown? Would she be logically weighing the pros and cons of commitment if Neil had thick black hair that he wore in a bandit queue, and a defiant gypsy hoop in one ear? Would she be hesitating like this if he had a tall, lean body that moved with the pulse-skittering, sexy grace of a prowling wolf?

Groaning, she crammed the heels of her hands against her eyes. What was wrong with her? Anthony had nothing to do with her relationship with Neil. He was a source, that was all. A source she still didn't completely trust. A source who could be extremely useful because he had a personal ax to grind with Titan.

He also had a strangely stimulating effect on her. When he was near, everything seemed more vivid, as if her senses were somehow more acute. Granted, the circumstances last night had been exceptional and that could have influenced her perception, yet Anthony Caldwell wasn't an ordinary man. He projected an impression of energy, a feeling of leashed power.

That was what drew her. There was far more to Anthony than met the eye. It was only natural that, as a reporter, she would want to discover what made him tick, what secrets he kept. And it was totally understandable that, as a woman, she would respond to that…that… She fumbled for a word. How could she describe it? What *was* it about that man that made him so different?

Whatever it was, it was inconvenient. He hadn't told her anywhere near enough after he'd brought her here last night. She would have to push him harder during their interview. She only had two days to get results. Otherwise, she would have no excuse left not to return to New York.

Excuse? The thought made her groan again. Was Neil right? Was she finding reasons to keep traveling?

"Melina?"

At the deep voice, she snapped her head up. As if she had conjured him out of her thoughts, Anthony stood less than two yards away.

Her heart did a painful thump. It wasn't only from surprise. His gaze probed into hers and sent a tickle of awareness all the way to her bare toes.

He wore the same clothes as he had the night before. Black jeans encased his long legs and rode comfortably loose on his slim hips. A black leather bomber jacket hung open over a shirt that had likely started out black, as well, but was faded to a washed-soft pewter. The sober tones suited him—even though he stood squarely in the light that poured in from the window behind her, he gave the impression of being surrounded by traces of shadow.

"Melina, are you all right?"

How long had she been staring? she wondered belatedly. She surged to her feet. "What are you doing here? How did you get in?"

"We agreed to meet at eight," he said. The gold at his earlobe glinted subtly as he tipped his head behind him. "When I knocked on your door, it swung open. I thought I heard you moan, so I came in to make sure you were okay."

"I didn't hear any knock."

He scowled. "You obviously didn't hear me come in, either. You have to be more careful. Titan's people don't give second chances."

She looked past him. The door to the corridor was closed now. She remembered undoing the security chain when she had picked up the newspaper from the threshold. She had been talking to Neil so she hadn't bothered to rehook the chain. She also hadn't paid any attention to whether or not the electronic lock had engaged.

Her carelessness jarred her. "Thanks for your concern, but as you can see, I'm fine. And I believe I already mentioned to you how I don't take orders."

"It was advice, Melina."

"We won't quibble over semantics," she said, deciding it was time to take control of the situation. She stepped forward, expecting him to move aside. "I'll meet you in the restaurant downstairs."

He didn't budge. "I'll walk down with you."

She wished she had taken the time to put her boots on—she could have used the psychological advantage of the extra three inches. Not that she felt threatened by Anthony's presence, which was odd, considering his size. He had to be at least six foot two, maybe three, and he'd already demonstrated how easily he could manhandle her. Back in that alley, he had picked her up and lugged her around as if she weighed nothing.

So why *wasn't* she nervous? He had appeared uninvited in her hotel room, she'd known him for less than six hours and she didn't entirely trust him. Source or not, why didn't she simply step around him, grab her boots and leave?

Those were good questions. She didn't have answers for them, other than to chalk up her lack of fear to a gut feeling.

Her gaze dropped to his throat. She noticed his pulse beating at the base of his neck where he'd left his shirt collar unfastened. She caught a hint of his scent, the musk of warm male skin, and she remembered how she had felt when he'd sheltered her with his body.

A few dark hairs showed at the top of his shirt. She had a sudden urge to test their texture with her fingertips, to unfasten more of the buttons and slip her hand inside and run her palm over his bare chest and drag her lips across the swells of his muscles and—

She didn't realize she had moved nearer until her toes came up against the hard leather of his shoes.

She blinked and leaned back. When had she leaned forward? And when had she lifted her hand? Her fingers were only inches away from his top shirt button. She snatched her hand away and pressed her fingertips to her mouth. The touch made her shudder—her lips were tingling.

What on earth had just happened?

Melina didn't know what to say. She felt ridiculous. How could she explain reaching for him like that? He must think she was coming on to him. All right, she found him attractive, even compelling, but she was a mature, rational woman. She wasn't ruled by her impulses. She clenched her jaw and looked up.

God help her, she wanted to reach for him again.

"On second thought, Melina," Anthony murmured, turning away, "I'll meet you downstairs."

There were only a dozen people in the hotel dining room—November seemed to be a slow time of year for the Pecos—so Anthony had his pick of the tables. He chose one at the far end, near the terrace doors, where the ventilation system and the music that played through the speakers in the wall would mask any conversation. The spot also provided him with a good view of all the exits and the courtyard beyond the terrace, as well as everyone in the room.

He draped his jacket over the chair back, ordered coffee, then angled himself so he could study the other guests over the rim of his cup. Beneath the wrought-iron chandelier that hung in the center of the beamed ceiling, four men in suits sat at a round table. Businessmen, from the look of them, he decided, likely no threat. A young couple, possibly honeymooners, were at a table secluded behind a clay planter full of cacti. A small, middle-aged woman with a colorful fringed shawl draped around her shoulders sat by herself in a corner. The rest of the patrons were seated in pairs or alone, all of them occupied with their meals, none of them particularly suspicious.

Still, Anthony remained alert, observing their reactions as Melina entered through the archway from the lobby. He looked for anyone who paid too much attention, or was trying to seem as if they were paying no attention at all. He was confident no one had followed Melina and him when they had left the Grand, so they should be safe here for a while, but he couldn't afford to let down his guard.

And he couldn't afford to get distracted, either. What was happening to his control? Maybe it was fatigue. Or maybe it was Melina. The mere sight of her walking across the room toward him was making his pulse race.

She had a straightforward, no-nonsense stride, her slender legs making quick work of the distance to the table that Anthony had selected. She likely had no idea how tantalizing she looked, with her hair tumbling in rich curls over her ivory sweater, and her skirt swaying in rhythm with her hips. Her boot heels clicked delicately on the wood floor, a sweetly feminine sound. Her chin was lifted, her fingers were wrapped around the strap of her shoulder bag and there was no smile on her face—she was obviously prepared for business. Yet, except for the honeymooner, she drew the regard of every man she passed.

Anthony wiped his palms on his thighs and rose to hold out her chair.

She seemed startled by the courtesy—startled enough to look at his face.

Oh, hell, Anthony thought. She wasn't helping his concentration. The moment her gaze met his, her eyes darkened. A flush pinkened her cheeks. Beneath her sweater, her breasts lifted with her quickened breathing.

He'd wondered about it last night, but after what had happened—or almost happened—in her room a few minutes ago, there was no longer any doubt in Anthony's mind. It was obvious to him that Melina was as attuned to the sexual connection between them as he was.

The strength of the connection likely puzzled her—she would have no way of understanding the source. Few people outside his family knew the full extent of his special, psychic ability. Fewer still knew about its peculiar side effects.

Anthony's ability was a legacy from his mother's Gypsy heritage. He could sense and control energy fields. That was how he'd caused the transformer in the alley to overload, and how he'd guided the live wire into swinging in the direction he'd wanted. It was how he'd deactivated the electromagnetic lock on Melina's hotel room door a few minutes ago when he'd heard her moan. Normally, he was extremely precise in his manipulations. Sometimes, though, the excess power he gathered in order to exercise his talent…spilled.

In the right circumstances, the effects of the stray energy were the same as arousal—accelerated pulse, increased sensitivity to touch, raised sexual awareness. Not everyone sensed it. When they did, Anthony did his best to tamp it down.

He hadn't been very successful tamping anything down when it came to Melina. The effect had never been this strong or this swift before.

He was careful to avoid touching her as he pushed in her chair, yet a trace of her perfume reached him, anyway. It was a mixture of floral and musky tones, soft and sensuous, making his nostrils flare. For a greedy moment, he inhaled. He thought about sweeping aside her hair and pressing his nose to the pulse point behind her ear.

She wouldn't object, not if he opened the connection fully. The fact that he could smell her perfume meant her body heat was already elevated. They fit together well. And he'd been so alone for so long….

But he couldn't do it. Damn, he was crazy to consider it. The safety of his family was at stake. He wouldn't risk it for what would only be a fleeting pleasure, a temporary relief. He knew what he wanted from Melina. How many times did he have to remind himself that it wasn't this?

He returned to his chair, picked up his coffee and drained the mug. The liquid was no longer scalding, but it was hot enough to burn his tongue. He concentrated on the prick of pain. It was almost as effective as a cold shower. He reined in his power as well as his thoughts.

Melina cleared her throat and busied herself with her purse. Her hair swung forward, hiding the blush on her cheeks.

She looked embarrassed, as well as confused, Anthony thought. That was understandable. He judged she wasn't the kind of woman who normally got carried away by her passions; several times he'd seen her try to suppress them. She had the right idea. It would be easiest for both of them if they didn't acknowledge this…complication.

"If you don't mind," she said, withdrawing a small note-pad from her purse, "I'd like to get started right away."

He glanced around the room to verify that no one was sitting close enough to overhear. "Fine with me. That's what we're here for."

"Exactly," she said. There was a small earthenware vase of dried wildflowers on the table. She pushed it aside and set her notepad in front of her. Her hands weren't quite steady. She took a pen from the pad's spiral spine and clicked it a few times with her thumb.

He spotted a waiter approaching. "Breakfast is on me, Melina," he said.

"Thanks, but this is my interview, so breakfast is on the *Daily Journal*."

"You must have a generous boss."

"Yes. We work well together."

Something in her tone caught his attention. Before he could pursue it, the waiter arrived to take their orders. The moment he left, Melina flipped through her notepad to a clean page and made a scribble at the top. "All right, Anthony. You claim your friend was attacked by Titan's people."

He thought of the last time he had seen Jeremy. The man he had known for almost twenty years had been unrecognizable. He'd been swathed in bandages, hooked up to machines and fighting for his life. "Claim? There's no doubt there. I know they did it."

"Because they wanted information about you and your sisters. Is that right?"

He nodded. "My sisters and I used to work for Jeremy Solienti, the man who was attacked. I still do."

"The first thing I'd like to know is why Titan is interested in your family. Was this the prelude to an extortion attempt?"

"He didn't want money. He wanted us."

Melina looked up. "But why?"

It had taken Anthony months to figure out the answer to

that question. He decided to give her only part of it. "To understand that, you have to know Titan's real identity."

Melina's fingertips whitened as she squeezed her pen. "This had better be on the level," she said.

"It is."

"I've been tracking this guy since June, when he started moving his drug network from Europe to North America." She lowered her voice. "Interpol had nothing on his background. He seemed to appear out of nowhere with his one name. He's a fanatic about secrecy. No one I've talked to will tell me who he is or where he came from, so how do you know?"

Anthony saw the spark in her eyes. He had a moment's regret that it was because of her story, not him. But this was what she was here for. "Tell me where he is," he said.

She frowned. "I promised to call you when I'm ready to break my story. You can be there when he's arrested."

"Not good enough. I need to know now. Every minute he's free is too long."

"That's not the deal we agreed on."

"We're making a new one."

She tossed her pen down. "Don't play games with me, Anthony."

"It's no game. I know who Titan is. I saw him commit his first murder. How much is that worth to you?"

She braced her forearms on the table and leaned toward him. "Who is he?"

"Where is he?"

"Fine. I'll tell you what I know as soon as you tell me who Titan is."

Anthony probed her gaze, trying to discern whether she meant to keep her word. It was difficult to gauge—she had her defenses back up and firmly in place—but he was fairly certain he'd pushed her as far as she would allow.

She didn't respond well to his bullying. He couldn't help admiring that. She reminded him a little of his sisters that way. He dipped his chin in agreement and waited until she had retrieved her pen. "Titan's real name is Benedict Payne," Anthony said. "He's an American. Fifty-eight years old. His last known address in the United States was in North Carolina."

Melina listened, her expression a mixture of concentration and excitement. "Wyatt, North Carolina?"

"That's right."

"I went to Wyatt because I heard the FBI were investigating there. I didn't find anything about Titan, so I thought it was a dead end."

"Most of the relevant records were destroyed. You would have needed to know what to look for to connect Titan with Payne."

"And what would that be?"

"Around thirty years ago, Benedict Payne worked at a fertility clinic in Wyatt run by his older sister, Agnes. He had been expelled from college for selling drugs, so she gave him the job to keep him out of trouble. Not because she cared, but because she didn't want him drawing any more attention from the cops. She had her own illegal schemes going."

"That's some family." Melina made some more scribbles on the paper. "You're giving me great material, Anthony. Please, go on."

"Agnes Payne is dead now."

"Tell me more about this Benedict Payne."

"He had a wife. Her name was Deanna Falaso."

"Falaso. Is that Italian?"

"Romanian. She married him to get a green card. He tricked her into believing it was love."

"That sounds like Titan. Do you know where Deanna is now?"

The memory sprang full-blown into Anthony's head. The argument, the screams, the choking scent of gardenias from the clothes in the closet, all of it as vivid as the night it had happened.

"Stay here with your sisters, Tony. Be a good boy and don't make a sound until Mommy comes back. Promise me you'll take care of them, okay? Stay here, no matter what."

Ruthlessly, he took control of the memory. He'd suppressed it for most of his life, but it had resurfaced in its entirety two months ago, when he'd been in Wyatt himself. His mother's death remained as raw in his mind as the day it had happened. It was only one part of the truth he had learned. He had yet to come to terms with any of it.

He tightened his fists on the table, feeling the familiar rage stir. Anger had been his constant companion throughout his life. He hadn't understood its source until two months ago, when he had fully remembered the night it had started.

He was angry at Benedict, the man who had pretended to be his father. He was angry at fate. Most of all, he was furious with himself, haunted by the helpless guilt he felt for being unable to save his mother.

"Anthony?"

"She's dead. He murdered her."

"When? Can you give me more details?"

"Yes, I can give you details. It was summer, a hot night, and she was wearing a ruffled sundress. He'd beaten her, so there was blood on both of them. He had taken off his jacket and rolled up his shirtsleeves. The veins on his arms bulged like snakes as he strangled her with his bare hands." Anthony leaned back in his chair, rubbing his hands over his face, trying to contain the rage. He couldn't let himself be drawn into it now. "It was twenty-eight years ago. I was three at the time. He never knew I saw it."

"Oh, my God. That was the murder you said you witnessed."

"Yes. I had blocked out the memory of it until—" He crossed his arms over his chest. "I went to the house in Wyatt where it happened. It came back to me then."

"Why were you in the house, Anthony?"

"I used to live there. Deanna had six children. Two sets of triplets. I'm the firstborn."

Melina set her pen down. She looked at him for a while, her gaze brimming with sympathy. "You saw Titan kill your mother."

"Yes. Afterward, he left the country and assumed a new identity to avoid the law."

"Then that means Titan is…"

Anthony shook his head fast before she could complete the sentence. That was something else he'd only found out two months ago. The one piece of good news. "He isn't my biological father. He's sterile. No blood of his runs in my veins. My siblings and I were fathered by a donor. I have the files that prove it."

"Oh, Anthony. You were so young when your mother was killed. What happened to you and the other children?"

"I don't know where the younger triplets ended up. My two brothers and my youngest sister were infants at the time. My other two sisters, Danielle and Elizabeth, and I were taken into the foster care system. Some social worker changed our last name to Caldwell so Benedict couldn't trace us."

The terse statements were accurate, but they didn't come close to describing the devastation that had been wrought to what had been a close family. Like the murder, Anthony's memory of the younger triplets had been blocked out for most of his life, too. Losing his infant siblings on top of losing his mother had been too much for his mind to handle.

"I can't imagine how awful that must have been for you."

"Benedict Payne is going to pay for his crimes, whatever he decides to call himself."

"Yes. He will. Absolutely. But after all this time, why would he want to find you and your sisters if he isn't your biological—"

"That's all I'm going to tell you, Melina. I kept my half of our bargain. I told you who Titan is and where he came from." No longer able to restrain himself, Anthony stood and walked to her side. Gripping the back of her chair with one hand and the edge of the table with the other, he leaned down to bring his face to hers. "Now it's your turn."

"Anthony…"

"Tell me." His muscles hardened. His voice dropped to a rasp. "Tell me where to find the son of a bitch."

Chapter 3

The lights in the dining room flickered, then brightened. Melina felt her skin prickle, as if a surge of electricity had passed through the air. She rubbed her arms and looked at Anthony.

Had she thought she wanted to know what secrets he hid? Had she been curious about what he kept leashed beneath the surface? She was no longer so certain. The control he usually maintained over his gaze had slipped. What she saw made her pulse pound.

There was anger. Of course, there would be. He had just described in detail his mother's murder at the hands of Titan. Benedict Payne, she corrected herself. That was his real name. She should be delighted over that piece of information. What a scoop revealing Titan's identity would be. She had no doubt that Anthony was telling the truth. Whether it was her reporter's instinct or another gut feeling, she was certain he was sincere.

Yet along with the anger in Anthony's gaze, there was pain. A deep, tearing anguish that went straight to her heart. His grief struck a chord in her. To lose a parent was painful at any age. She had been twenty when she had lost both of hers, and she had been left so vulnerable, she had been driven to make some horrible mistakes. But for a toddler to witness a murder and then to lose half his family…

What had that done to him? What scars had it left?

She wanted to hold him. It had nothing to do with those sexual impulses he'd stirred before. This was a yearning as basic as the desire for simple human contact. She wanted to reach up and stroke the tightness from his jaw and cradle his cheeks in her hands. She wanted to pull his head to her breasts and comfort him. "Anthony, I'm sorry."

"I don't want your sympathy, Melina," he said. "I want you to keep your word. Where is the bastard?"

Oh, God. What could she say? She hadn't deliberately lied. She had never actually told him that she knew.

"Melina?"

"I'm sorry," she repeated. "I can't answer that."

His gaze burned into hers. The lights flickered again. "You said you didn't want to play games, so don't."

He was leaning so close to her that she could see a rim of gold inside the green of his eyes. A lock of hair had pulled loose from his ponytail. It swung against his face, the soft strand an unexpected contrast to the harsh rise of his cheekbone.

She touched her index finger to the loose hair. It was as soft as it looked. Silky, almost sensuous in the way it curved against her nail. She brushed the strand from his cheek and tucked it behind his ear, then ran her fingertips around the curve to his earlobe. The gold earring flicked gently against her thumb. She slid her thumb down the side of his neck, trailing her fingers over the line of a tendon. His skin was warm and taut, the texture intriguingly male.

He straightened abruptly.

Melina was left with her hand in the air. She looked at it blankly for a moment, then twisted to face the table and groped for her notepad.

It was on the tip of her tongue to apologize again. She didn't. Because, for the life of her, she didn't know what to say. How could she explain that mindless caress? How could she excuse it? She would be lying if she claimed she didn't want to touch him.

Dammit, this was so awkward. Why was this happening? He was a source, that was all. He was a potential gold mine of information. With his help, she could build the article she had begun about Titan into Pulitzer Prize material.

But to do that, she had to get Anthony's cooperation. "Your story moved me," she said. "I didn't mean anything by—" she lifted her hand and let it drop "—by what I did just now."

Anthony returned to stand beside his chair. He put his hand on the jacket he'd draped over the chair back, as if he was debating walking out.

Awkward didn't come close to describing the situation, Melina thought. She wished she knew what was wrong with her. "I don't know where Titan is—I mean, Benedict Payne. Not for certain. That's why I can't tell you. But I do know where I'm going to look. Hear me out, okay, Anthony?"

He sat.

Melina took a few moments to steady her breathing before she went on. "The FBI has smashed the Titan Syndicate drug ring and raided all the labs he had established. They had thought they would find him in one of them, but he got away."

"Benedict's drugs were only a means to an end," he said. "It was a moneymaking scheme. He has a bigger agenda."

"Yes, I've believed that all along. He has a base of operations that's independent of his drug business. I suspect it's in this state."

"Why?"

"There are a few reasons," she said. "Here's the simplest— the Titan Syndicate has done some business in every state *except* New Mexico."

"The area of New Mexico is over one hundred twenty thousand square miles. How do you plan to narrow that down?"

"Fredo told me he couldn't go home. I think the reason has to do with Benedict, so that's the next place I intend to start looking. Fredo's hometown."

"And what is Fredo's hometown?"

"I'll answer that in exchange for the rest of your story."

He stared at her, his gaze snapping. The music that had been playing unobtrusively in the background of the room was suddenly interrupted by shafts of static.

"It's basically the same deal as before," she went on. "Only I'll want more from you than just one interview. Your involvement with Benedict before he became Titan completes the picture. You know more about his character than I do. If you tell me everything that you know, I'll be able to combine it with the information I have and we can both get what we want a lot sooner."

"Melina—"

"This is what I do for a living, Anthony. I'm very good at digging up the truth and putting clues together. The sensible choice for us would be to team up. You can tag along with me while I work."

There was another burst of static from the speakers. "I can 'tag along'?" he repeated.

"All right, we could be partners."

He leaned toward her, his body rigid with tension. "Define partners."

Her heart thumped. She was honest enough to admit to herself that it wasn't only from the prospect of getting his story. The width of the table lay between them, yet she felt the force of his gaze make the back of her neck heat and her breasts tingle. But she should ignore that. She *had to* ignore that. "It would be strictly business," she said quickly. "We can pool our knowledge and our talents."

He continued to look at her. "Bringing Benedict to justice isn't a matter of business for me," he said. "It's personal."

"Yes, I understand that now. The sooner we start working together, the faster we'll both get what we want. Fredo said Benedict is too paranoid now to leave his stronghold, so once we locate that, we locate him. Then we'll call in the authorities and—"

Before she could finish, there was a commotion at the other side of the room. Chair legs scraped across the floor, voices lifted in question. She turned to look just as someone screamed.

A young couple stood in the doorway of the dining room, apparently stopped on their way out. Melina had noticed the pair when she had arrived. She had assumed they were honeymooners—they had been smiling, so wrapped up in each other that the man had propped his elbow in his plate of eggs. Neither was smiling now. The man had his arms around the woman, her face pressed protectively to his chest.

"Stay here," Anthony ordered. Seconds later he was on his feet and heading across the room.

Melina grabbed her purse, shoved her notebook inside and followed.

A crowd was gathering in the lobby near the elevators. Their attention appeared to be directed toward something on the floor. Melina couldn't see what it was until she reached the edge of the ring of onlookers.

At first she thought she was looking at a pile of clothes. The edge of a glossy postcard poked out from one of the folds—it looked like a picture of a thatch-roofed cottage set in a green countryside. But why would someone dump dirty clothes in the lobby? And they were dirty. She could see dark smudges on the denim garment that lay on top.

But then Melina saw the hand.

It wasn't a pile of clothes, it was a body.

A body dressed in a denim jacket that bore bullet holes and tire tracks.

Anthony shifted into high gear and jammed the accelerator to the floor. The mountain range in the distance inched closer as the Jeep hurtled down the narrow blacktop, its square frame vibrating in the wind. The vehicle wasn't built for comfort. The stiff suspension transmitted every flaw in the pocked pavement into teeth-rattling jolts, but Anthony was too impatient to slow down.

Melina hung on to the grab bar over the door, her feet planted hard against the floor. Her green carry-on bag was in the back seat beside his duffel. This time she hadn't argued when he'd told her to pack. She understood the danger they were in. He could see that she was upset, and she had every right to be. She was also adamant that she wasn't going to give up.

"The turnoff to Antelope Ridge should be coming up soon," she said. "You'd better hope there isn't a speed trap."

He glanced at his mirrors as if he was checking for flashing red lights behind them. He didn't want to explain to Melina he would have felt the radar impulses long before the police would have spotted him.

Their destination was a town in the rough countryside northeast of Santa Fe. It was miles off the interstate and rated only a small dot on the map. It would be a good place to lay low for a few days, but they weren't coming here to hide, they were coming here to hunt.

Antelope Ridge was Fredo's hometown. This is where Melina wanted to begin their search for Benedict's stronghold.

"I feel bad about leaving Fredo again," she said. "It doesn't seem right."

"The staff at the Pecos will make sure his body is treated with respect, Melina. That's all we could have done. It wouldn't have been safe for us to hang around any longer."

"I realize that, but the whole thing is so…gruesome."

"It was a warning from Benedict." He reached into his jacket and pulled out the postcard he'd managed to lift from the body. "This scene of a cottage in the German countryside is the Titan Syndicate's calling card. Jeremy described it to me. Apparently my sister got one just like it."

"How did you take that from Fredo without anyone noticing?"

"That's not important. It was meant for you, anyway." He flipped it over and held it out to her. "There's no writing on the back, but the message is clear. Benedict wants you to quit investigating him."

She took the card by one corner and studied it. "It's such a peaceful picture, it makes the whole thing creepier. But I'm not giving up."

No, she wouldn't, Anthony thought. Once again, he felt a stirring of admiration for her grit. "How did you meet Fredo in the first place?"

"He tried to sell me a hundred-dollar Rolex. Instead of calling the cops, I interviewed him for a story on habitual thieves.

Afterward, I gave him some money and got him a job at a grocery store, but he quit after a week." She twisted over the seat to store the postcard in her bag. "Whatever his faults, he doesn't deserve what happened to him."

"Something else Benedict will answer for," Anthony muttered.

"How did Benedict's men get Fredo's body from in front of the alley before the police got there? I didn't delay all that long before I phoned them."

"You made the call eleven minutes after we left the scene."

"He was lying in plain view in the middle of the street."

"A dark street in a deserted neighborhood."

"Maybe Fredo's suspicions were correct and Benedict has bought off someone on the Santa Fe police force."

"Even if he does have someone on the force, there would be no telling which patrol car took the call. It's more likely that there was nothing for the police to see when they arrived."

Melina shivered. She clasped her hands in her lap. "How could that be?"

Anthony reached out to turn up the heater despite the sunshine that poured through the windshield. "Benedict's men must have escaped through the rear doors of the van before it exploded."

"I thought of that possibility last night, but decided it was too remote."

"The van they were driving was likely stolen. They could have stolen another vehicle, possibly a delivery truck, from one of the warehouses on that street and picked up the body. Eleven minutes plus however long it took the cops to get there would have given them enough time for that."

She turned to face him. "If it was a delivery truck, they could have faked a delivery to get Fredo into the hotel. Anthony, we should go back."

"No. Too risky."

"It might be quicker. We could start with the hotel and find out what deliveries they had. Or we could check the warehouses, see if a truck was stolen and trace it from that end."

"Wouldn't do any good. They would have ditched it by now. The Titan Syndicate wouldn't have left such an obvious loose end." He glanced at her. "It's not too late. If you went back to New York and put out the word that you're off the story, then Benedict would have no reason to come after you."

"No."

"Think about it for a minute, Melina."

"No. I told you already, I don't give up. And I'm not ready to go home, especially now. We *must* be close to Benedict. Otherwise, he wouldn't have given us that warning." Her voice firmed. "We're in this together now, Anthony, whether you like it or not."

He already knew that. He hadn't truly believed she would go home, but his conscience had made him try to persuade her one last time.

It would be safer for her if she gave up…but it would be better for him if she didn't.

The partnership she had proposed earlier made sense. They would get further if they pooled their information and their abilities. Melina would make a good ally. There were strong, logical reasons to keep her with him.

Then there were other, less logical reasons. There was the way she had touched him when he'd stood over her chair in the restaurant. His entire body had sensed the gentle stroke of her fingers on his neck. He could feel her presence beside him now as vividly as sunshine. The connection was getting stronger by the minute. He would be lying to himself if he pretended he didn't want to feel it again.

Yet even before she had touched him, he'd felt the caress

of her emotions. The sympathy in her gaze had steadied him, drawing him back from his anger. It was odd. Although his psychic abilities allowed him to link with his sisters on occasion, he was no empath.

"I don't understand how Benedict could have known I was at the Pecos," Melina said.

Anthony wrenched his thoughts back on track. "Neither do I. You didn't tell anyone, did you?"

"Just my editor. And there's no way that Neil would give out that information."

"What about someone else at the paper?"

"That's unlikely. Maybe we were followed when I checked out of the Grand Inn."

"No. I made certain of it."

"Someone could have put a tracking device on this Jeep while it was parked outside."

"Impossible. Any device would need a power source to transmit data. I would have noticed."

"How would you know?"

"I do regular scans of my surroundings."

"You do scans? Why? How?"

Anthony kept the Jeep pointed down the highway and opened his mind, directing his awareness to search for any trace of foreign energy. He probed the underbody first and found nothing. The area under the hood was more difficult, since the field generated by the engine and the vehicle's electrical system provided background noise, but it was clean, too. He completed the sweep by probing the interior. Satisfied there was nothing that didn't belong, he returned his full attention to driving. "Trust me, I just do."

Melina was silent for a while. "Anthony, you said you work for your friend Jeremy Solienti."

"That's right."

"What kind of work do you do?"

He considered how to reply before he spoke. "We're what you would call troubleshooters."

"What does that mean?"

"Jeremy runs a private business that's based in Philadelphia. You could think of it as a consulting firm. When a client comes to him with a problem, we try to solve it."

"Is that where you live? Philadelphia?"

Yes. I have an apartment there, but my work can take me anywhere."

"Did you learn about scanning for tracking devices as part of your job?"

Incredibly, Anthony felt his lips quirk. How long had it been since he'd felt the urge to smile? Melina's inquisitiveness stemmed from more than her occupation—she had a remarkably active mind. Her intelligence was one of the most attractive things about her. "I've had to learn many skills over the years."

"Including learning how to remove evidence like the postcard that was in plain view of a dozen bystanders?"

"That particular skill does come in handy."

"Is your profession the reason you didn't want to go to the police?"

"You mean, am I involved in something illegal? Is that what you're getting at?"

"Yes. Are you?"

"Would it make any difference?"

There was another silence. "Yes, it would, but I don't believe you are, Anthony. You seem more like the type of person who would bend laws rather than break them."

The smile pushed at his cheeks. He felt unreasonably pleased by her assessment. "My work is varied. I take assignments that often involve some gray areas of the law, but sometimes it's necessary when the law itself has failed."

"For example?"

"Returning an item to its rightful owner. Tracing a missing person. Acquiring some particular information of interest."

"That's very vague."

"It was meant to be. But in answer to your other question, I don't want to go to the police about Benedict for the same reason you don't. I believe I can do a better job without them. They would shut me out of the investigation."

"I know what you mean. My source on the FBI hasn't given me anything in months."

"Who's your source?"

"An agent who is interested in Titan."

"That's very vague."

She gave him a sidelong glance. "It was meant to be."

His cheek twitched. She gave as good as she got.

"Is this vague profession of yours the reason you know so much about running away and dropping out of sight?"

His smile winked out before it could finish forming. No, he thought. He had learned about keeping out of sight a long time ago.

"Stay here with your sisters, Tony. Be a good boy and don't make a sound until Mommy comes back...."

He'd tried to do what she had said. He'd held on to Dani and Elizabeth, hiding with them under his mother's dresses that hung in the closet, doing his best to protect them and keep them safe. But it had been dark and hot, and the hems of the dresses kept sticking to his face, and his sisters were crying and his mother was screaming and he couldn't breathe in that tiny, tiny space....

Anthony inhaled fast, stemming the panic before it could set in. He fixed his gaze on the horizon, anchoring himself in the here and now. No one could feel hemmed in in countryside like this. The sky was huge. The air was fresh. It was too cold to take the top off the Jeep, but the square design surrounded him with windows. That was why he'd chosen it, so he could see he wasn't enclosed.

He hated small spaces. Knowing why he hated them didn't make it easier. It only added to his list of reasons why he hated Benedict Payne.

"Anthony?" A light weight settled on his sleeve. "Are you okay?"

His hands cramped on the wheel. He eased his grip and flexed his fingers. "I'm fine. Thanks."

She squeezed gently and withdrew her hand from his arm. "We'll find him. Once he's behind bars, your family will be safe."

He looked at her. There were so many things he could say, but none of them were about Benedict. *Touch me again. Let me see the warmth in your eyes. Let me hold your body next to mine and escape into what's building between us....*

He said none of those things. Instead, he nodded once and returned his gaze to the horizon.

The tang of incense hung in the air, making columns of hazy white where the spotlights tunneled through the darkness. Benedict ran his fingertip over the cool surface of the crystal sphere. The interior was dark. It didn't reveal its secrets to him. He hadn't been gifted with the talent to read the future there as Deanna's family could. There were psychics and fortune-tellers in that group of Gypsies. It was the only reason he'd married her.

She should have been grateful to play a part in Benedict's master plan. Without him, she would have been nothing. He had talked her into fertility treatments, he had selected the special sperm to breed superior children. The first three had displayed talent. The infants had been too young to test properly, yet even at a few months of age they had shown promise. He had already begun to devise the best way to train them when Deanna had ruined it all.

No, not ruined it, Benedict corrected himself. Deanna's interference had delayed his plans, that was all. He had done well for himself in the years he was Titan. He was in a better position now to reap the benefits of his genius. All he needed was to acquire the remaining child....

Benedict's breath hissed out. The crystal sphere was no longer dark. A bloodred glow pulsed within its depths.

He grasped the ball between his hands, bringing his nose to the crystal surface in his eagerness to see inside. Yes! *Yes!* The mystical power of this place must be starting to work. He'd been right to build his headquarters here.

The glow condensed before his eyes, forming itself into a rounded form. It looked like a ball. No, it was more like a...a bulb.

Benedict twisted to look behind him. The red light over the door of his inner sanctum was flashing. Someone was signaling him from outside. He looked back at the sphere. It wasn't a vision that he saw in the depths; it was a reflection of the light bulb on the surface, that was all. A trick. An illusion.

It never occurred to him that the mistake was his.

He snatched the crystal sphere from its base, lifted it over his head and hurled it to the floor. It shattered against the rock.

The light continued to blink. Benedict kicked aside shards of crystal and walked to the door. He pressed his thumb to the lock, swung the door open and stepped into the anteroom. A puff of incense followed him. As soon as the inner door swung shut, he climbed the four steps to the outer door, thumbed the lock and emerged in the corridor.

It took a few seconds for his eyes to adjust to the light. He had left the walls and floor of his inner sanctum natural, wanting nothing to insulate him from the power of this place, but much of the complex boasted white marble floors, plaster walls and a cleverly designed lighting system that made the windowless hallways as bright as day.

"Sorry to disturb you, sir."

He looked at the men who stood before him. Gus and Habib had worked security for him during the early years of the Titan Syndicate in Europe. They could be relied on to carry out his orders—they were two of his most innovative confederates.

Benedict focused on their clothes. They were wearing coveralls with other men's names on the breast pockets. "Where did you get those?"

"They were in the back of the truck we stole," Habib replied. He tugged at one cuff—the sleeves were ridiculously short for his lanky frame. He was usually very fussy about his appearance.

"And those cuts on your face?" Benedict asked, looking from one to the other.

"They're nothing," Gus said quickly. Crooked lines of scabs creased his pale, basset-hound jowls. He rubbed his right eyebrow. Most of it was missing, as if it had been burned off.

Benedict scrutinized them closely. They were banged up, but they were still on their feet. Good. Whatever injuries they had suffered weren't serious enough to interfere with their duties. He started walking toward the lab. "Since you're here, I assume you completed your task."

They fell into step behind him. "Yes, sir," Habib said. "We took care of Fredo."

"Excellent. He had outlived his usefulness to us even before he tried to leave."

"He only got as far as Santa Fe."

"We made sure he's dead," Gus chimed in. "He won't be talking to anyone else."

Benedict stopped and whirled to face them. "Anyone *else?*"

Habib waved his hand. There was a strip of gauze around his palm. "He met that reporter from New York. They spoke for only a few minutes. If he did say anything to her, she won't be talking."

"Ah, so you eliminated her, too. Good work."

Gus cleared his throat. "We weren't able to kill her. We gave her a warning instead. It scared her spitless. She took off so fast—"

"You made a mistake," Benedict said. "You should have killed her. Melina Becker is becoming more of a nuisance than the FBI. Where did she go? Where is she now?"

"Habib was driving," Gus said. "He lost her."

"The truck we stole couldn't keep up with her friend's Jeep," Habib said. "And they left so fast we didn't have time to pick up another car."

Benedict spoke through his teeth. "What friend? Don't make me drag the story out of you piece by piece."

"The reporter had a man with her," Habib said. "He was tall, dressed all in black. He had a black ponytail like one of those martial arts guys. I'm not sure, but I think he's got some kind of earring, too. He didn't look like a cop."

Benedict stared at Habib. As he sorted out the disjointed description of the reporter's companion, his anger transformed to excitement.

A tall man who wore his dark hair in a ponytail and who had a gold earring. The description matched the one that two of his late confederates had given him several months ago. They had tried to acquire Anthony for him in Philadelphia and had failed.

Could it be true? Could the oldest of Deanna's children already be this close?

Benedict's excitement grew. He licked his lips and rubbed his thumb over his fingers as if he were back in his inner sanctum, holding the pregnant stone woman. There was no time to waste. The preparations were almost complete. Soon he would be able to set the final phase of his plan into motion.

It was beginning to happen just as he wanted. The power of this place must be working, after all.

Chapter 4

The one-story, cinder-block building that housed The Oasis Bar had been painted turquoise once, but weather and time had reduced the paint to peeling strips of faded color. It squatted on the outskirts of Antelope Ridge, across the highway from a gas station and hard against the chain link fence of a construction company. The neon sign over the door buzzed in a glow of violet and gold, like a pale reflection of the sunset that streaked the horizon.

Melina paused in the gravel parking lot, the hem of her skirt brushing against her calves. She was thankful for the warmth of her suede boots. The night wind that swept in from the mountains carried a foretaste of frost that was different from the dampness of November in the city. Everything out here seemed to be done on a large scale. The office towers of Manhattan were impressive, but when it came to sheer grandeur they couldn't compare to the rugged landscape that surrounded her. She held her jacket closed at her throat and inhaled deeply. There was the scent of dust and a faint trace of wood smoke.

"The place looks rough. Better let me handle this."

There was also the scent of leather and of Anthony. She exhaled on a sigh and looped her purse strap over her shoulder. "I've been in worse places. Remember, I'm a New Yorker. I can take care of myself. It might be better if you wait for me in the Jeep."

He cupped her elbow. "No way."

"Anthony, I've done this kind of thing before. You don't have to—"

"Tag along?"

She looked at him. His jaw was clenched. She wanted to stroke away the tension with her fingertips. She tightened her hold on her purse. "You might want to lighten up a bit. You don't want to scare everyone away before I get to ask any questions."

"The way you look, no man's going to pay attention to your questions."

It was a backhanded compliment, so she didn't acknowledge it. She didn't want to acknowledge the pleasure it gave her, either. "Don't go getting all macho here. We're partners, remember?"

"Fine. Let's go." He started forward, guiding her past the row of pickup trucks and motorcycles that were angled in front of the building.

The moment they entered the barroom, Melina was thankful for Anthony's presence. She had been wrong—she hadn't seen anyplace as bad as this.

The walls were bare cinder block; unlike the outside, no one had attempted to add any color in here. With only a few dim overhead bulbs for lighting, the gray cement was a lifeless smudge. On her left there was a bar made of plywood. It had a splintered hole in the front panel the size of a large boot. There were a few mismatched tables near the front window to her right, some made of wood, some with chrome legs and linoleum tops. A pool table crowded the back wall in front of a jukebox with cracked glass. It was playing Elvis's, "Don't Be Cruel." The tune seemed bizarrely perky.

The patrons were as grim as the decor. The men were dressed roughly, some in plaid shirts and jeans, others in dingy green work clothes. They slouched over the tables or bent over their pool cues or leaned a shoulder against the wall with the air of someone who just didn't give a damn. Except for Melina, there were no women present.

Well, this was what she had wanted. It was her experience that one of the best ways to get information about a crook in a small town was to find the seediest bar and the drunkest patron. The Oasis Bar certainly qualified as seedy.

Anthony draped his arm around her shoulders and brought his lips close to her ear. "Better let me do the talking."

She wanted to disagree—she was accustomed to being in control—but the brush of his breath on her ear sent a wave of heat through her body. The awareness was getting stronger, but as she had been doing all day, she did her best to ignore it. She had more important issues to worry about.

"Two Millers," Anthony said, stopping at the bar. He had to raise his voice to be heard over Elvis.

The bartender was almost as tall as Anthony, and at least twice as heavy. A faded Sun Devils sweatshirt stretched over his belly. He took two bottles from a cooler behind him, opened the caps and plunked them down on the bar. He didn't offer either of them a glass, for which Melina was grateful. She wouldn't want to stake her health on the hygiene of this place.

She wiped the lip of the bottle with her thumb and took a sip as she turned to regard the room. If there had been any conversation before they had come in, it had stopped at their entrance. Every face was turned toward them. So much for subtle. She was trying to decide who would be the best one to approach when the jukebox suddenly went black. The music cut off in the middle of a chorus.

The man closest to the jukebox went over to it and thumped it with the side of his fist. When nothing happened, he thumped it a few more times.

"Cut that out," the bartender shouted. "You're gonna break it."

"It's already broke," the man replied, hitting it again. "You owe me a quarter."

Anthony squeezed Melina's shoulder, then withdrew his arm and moved to the center of the room. "I'm looking for an individual named Fredo," he announced. "Anyone know him?"

Melina almost dropped her beer. She knew Anthony was short on patience, but what did he think he was doing?

One of the men who had been playing pool straightened up from the table, his cue stick still in his hands. "Lots of men named Fredo around here, mister."

"He's about five-six, looks like an underfed weasel and runs like a girl."

The man by the jukebox guffawed.

Anthony walked over to him. "You know who I mean."

"Maybe."

"I want to talk to him."

The man propped his forearm on the jukebox and leaned past Anthony to look at Melina. He gave her a grin. "Yeah, well, I'd like to talk to the redhead over there."

The jukebox lit up. The music started anew, louder than

before. Melina couldn't hear what Anthony said to the man in front of him. Whatever it was, it had an instant effect. The man straightened up with a jerk, his face pale, his jaw slack, as if he'd received an electric shock.

As much as she disliked being left on the sidelines, Melina decided to remain at the bar and let Anthony handle this his way. He appeared to be making progress. She approved of the way he didn't pretend to be Fredo's friend—these people would never buy that. It was also wise to pretend Fredo was still alive. Less than a day had gone by since he'd been killed, so chances were the news might not have spread. In addition, if anyone here learned how he had died, they would be even less likely to admit that they knew him.

She wondered once again about the nature of Anthony's "troubleshooting" work. He seemed to know his way around difficult situations. She didn't know why she believed him when he claimed he wasn't doing anything illegal. More gut feelings?

He wasn't a man who sought confrontation, yet he didn't back away from it. He would have learned to be tough early in life—after his mother's brutal murder, he would have had no other choice. Although the foster care system was full of generous and caring people, it wasn't perfect. There were all too often cases of abuse and neglect. It was understandable that he had become a man who preferred to keep to himself and to be in control. It would have been his way to cope with the life that fate had given him.

There was so much she still didn't know about him. She had only scratched the surface. The more she learned, the more questions arose. It made her wish they didn't find Benedict right away so she would have the chance to spend more time with Anthony.

She lifted the bottle and took a hurried mouthful of beer. What was she thinking?

"Hey, honey. Wanna feel my balls?"

She swallowed quickly, trying not to choke, and turned to see who had spoken.

While she had been watching Anthony, one of the pool players had moved toward the bar. She hadn't heard him approach over the noise of the music. He had left behind his cue stick, and instead he held a pair of colored balls in his hand. He grinned slyly as he rubbed them together.

Melina glanced at the balls. "No, thanks. It looks as if you're having too much fun playing with them yourself."

His grin stiffened and he leaned closer. "Your friend asked about Fredo. If you're nice to me, maybe I'll tell you something."

"What's your name?"

"Kenny."

"All right, Kenny. I'm listening."

"Not here." He nodded toward the door. "Outside. In private."

Melina was fairly sure he was lying. But what if he wasn't? The crude way he approached her might have been an excuse, a cover story, for the benefit of his buddies. She set her bottle on the bar, took a firm grip on her purse and led the way to the door.

Only a narrow streak of violet on the horizon was all that was left of the sunset. Melina deliberately positioned herself a few feet from the door, in the glow of the overhead sign where she would be visible through the barroom window. She glimpsed Anthony's tall form near the jukebox, so she judged he should be able to see her, too, just in case he wondered where she had gone. "All right, what can you tell me?"

"How do you know Fredo?"

"I met him in New York a year ago."

"Yeah, I heard he was trying his luck there for a while. He came back here last winter."

"Why?"

Kenny ran the curve of one billiard ball down her jacket sleeve. "He needed more stuff to sell to some big-time collector."

This didn't sound credible, she thought, easing a step sideways. From what she had seen of Antelope Ridge when she and Anthony had arrived this afternoon, it was a small town that had seen better days. There were vacant storefronts in the modest downtown, and the houses, though neat, were leaning toward shabby. There probably wouldn't be a lot of Rolexes like the one Fredo had tried selling to her. "What kind of stuff?" she asked.

"Some old Indian stuff. He said he found it."

"What was it? Where?"

"That's all I know, honey." He moved closer, rubbing the ball along her hip. "Now how about being nice to me?"

She moved nearer to the door. "I appreciate the information, Kenny, but—"

"I like redheads. Redheads with long legs." He dropped the balls on the ground and brought his knuckles to her thigh. "What you got under that skirt, honey?"

Melina glanced toward the window. She could no longer see Anthony. Okay, she had told him she could take care of herself, so she'd better start. She reached into her purse and withdrew the folded bills she kept in one of the compartments for emergency cab fare. "Here's thirty bucks, Kenny. Buy your friends some more beers on me."

"Yeah, good idea." He plucked the money from her fingers and stuffed it in the back pocket of his work pants. "We'll all have a party."

While he was busy with the money, Melina slipped her hand back in her purse and felt around until she found the slim cylinder on the bottom. Her heart was pounding. She would prefer not to resort to pepper spray, but she wasn't going to be any man's victim. Not again. If he made another move to touch her, she was going to let him have it.

All at once, the lighted sign over the door let out a sizzling crackle. Kenny twisted his head to look up. The glass that covered the light bulbs cracked. A flare of blue-white shot out from one corner, straight toward his face.

He shielded his face with his forearm and jumped backward. The flare died as suddenly as it had come up. Swearing loudly, he staggered into the wall and slapped his hands over his eyes.

Melina was already moving away from the light when she was seized from behind. Strong arms encircled her, pulling her back against a solid chest.

It all happened within a split second, but she didn't need that long to recognize the man who had come up behind her. She left her pepper spray in her purse and gasped in relief. "Anthony!"

"Are you all right, Melina?"

She could hear the concern in his voice, she could feel it in the tremor that hummed through his frame. She pressed back into his embrace, blinking hard to get rid of the afterimage that danced in front of her eyes. "I'm fine. My, God, did you see that light? What happened?"

Kenny groaned and stumbled against the wall. Flecks of blue paint drifted to the ground. He rubbed his eyes while he continued to spew an unbroken string of oaths.

"Something must have shorted out in the sign," Anthony said. He shifted his hold, clamping one arm around her waist. He started for the parked Jeep. "We should leave."

Pebbles skidded beneath her boots as she tried to dig in her heels. How could Anthony sound so casual about that…that miniature lightning bolt? "Wait. We should go back and help

Kenny. He said that's his name. He was closer to that light than I was. He could have been blinded."

"The flare wasn't bright enough to do permanent damage. His vision should come back in a few minutes."

"How do you know that?"

"The voltage in those bulbs wouldn't be high enough to hurt him. It just dazzled him."

There was a burst of music. Melina twisted to look behind her. Kenny was staggering through the door to the bar, one hand shielding his eyes. "Something must be wrong with the power here," she said. "Look at the way that jukebox cut out and then started up."

"It probably does that all the time. If there's a problem, the electric company will sort it out."

"But—"

"We're done here, Melina." He ended the discussion by pulling her up on his hip. He half carried her the rest of the way across the parking lot.

They were leaving. Melina realized it was the wisest choice. Kenny's friends would see to him if he needed help, and there probably wouldn't be anything more she and Anthony could learn about Fredo here. She knew she was safe, yet her pulse was continuing to accelerate. She felt little bursts of energy, just as she had when they had been close to that live wire in the alley. Could it be from the faulty wiring in the bar…or was it because Anthony was lugging her around again?

She grasped his arm, trying to loosen his hold. The muscles under his sleeve were like iron. She had trouble catching her breath. She tried to focus her thoughts. "He told me about Fredo."

"We'll talk about that later."

Heat spread from her hip to her thigh where she rubbed

against him. With each stride he took, a shot of awareness throbbed through her body. "Anthony, put me down."

He reached the Jeep, yanked open the passenger door and lifted her onto the seat.

The impact sent a swift jab of pleasure between her legs. She pressed her knees together and clenched her jaw. This was embarrassing. Crazy. How could she be feeling excited?

Anthony got behind the wheel and gunned the engine. Gravel sprayed from the tires as he left the parking lot. He turned onto the highway and headed toward town.

Melina watched his thighs as he worked the clutch. His muscles flexed in smooth ridges beneath his jeans. She touched her tongue to her lips, picturing how he'd look without the barrier of denim—

Stop it! she told herself. She curled her nails into her palms, trying to distract herself.

The interior of the Jeep had cooled while they had been in the bar. Melina could feel the bite of cold air on her nose, yet she tasted sweat on her upper lip. Her jacket was too heavy. She unfastened the buttons.

"Don't," Anthony said. His voice was strained.

She shuddered as her arms brushed the front of her breasts. They felt swollen. Sensitive. Longing to be touched. "What?"

"Leave your jacket on, Melina."

"I'm too hot."

"Open a window. The breeze will cool you down."

"How many times do I have to tell you that I don't take orders?"

Anthony slammed on the brakes, shifted gears and steered the Jeep off the highway.

She gasped at another jab of pleasure as they bumped over the shoulder of the road. She braced her palms against the dashboard, trying to hold herself steady, hoping to stop the reaction that was spreading through her body.

It was no use. She couldn't control it. What on earth was wrong with her? Or was it him?

In the light from the instrument panel, Anthony's face looked as harsh and unyielding as the first time she had seen him. With disbelief, she realized that had been less than twenty-four hours ago. How could it be him? She barely knew the man.

She looked away quickly, focusing on the rocks and pin-yon trees that loomed in the headlights. He wasn't following any trail that she could see. "Where are we going?"

"We aren't going anywhere until we get some things straight." He hit the brakes harder and jerked the wheel, sending the Jeep into a skidding circle. It came to a stop with its headlights pointing over the tracks in the dirt they had made on the way in. Puffs of dust drifted through the beams.

Her hands slipped from the dashboard. She wiped them on her skirt. She bit her lip to hold back a moan as the fabric slid over her sensitized thighs.

He killed the lights and turned off the engine. "Melina, you put yourself in danger tonight. I won't let you do it again."

She tried to concentrate on his words, but the sudden dark-ness made her more conscious of his presence than ever. She heard the creak of his leather jacket and the soft rasp of denim against denim as he shifted on his seat. His scent enveloped her as seductively as the night.

"You had no reason to go into that bar," he continued. "You should have let me handle those men. It was foolish to risk your safety."

He was scolding her, she realized. *Scolding* her. That was why he had brought her here—he wanted to lecture her. "I'm twenty-nine years old, Anthony. I've been taking care of myself just fine for years and I don't need you to tell me what to do."

"What would you have done if I hadn't seen what was going on through the window and come out the back way? That man was twice your weight."

"I admit I was grateful you were there, but I was about to use pepper spray, anyway. It's top-of-the-line and it's rated to stop bears, so it would have stopped Kenny. But that's beside the point. You have no right to give me orders or to reprimand me."

"I'm trying to protect you."

"I don't need or want your protection. I want your story. I thought we were clear about that."

"Yes, we're clear. I know what you want. You know what I want."

"Then let's get out of here. We're wasting time. We have to find someplace to spend the night. We should go over what we learned."

He hit the steering wheel with the heels of his hands. "Don't you think I know that?"

His sudden spurt of temper made her breath catch. The veneer of control he kept over his emotions was cracking, just as it had in the restaurant this morning. There was anger in his actions and frustration in his voice. She should be afraid, yet she wasn't. She still didn't believe that Anthony would harm her. "Then why are we still here?"

He didn't reply. He hit the wheel again, then twisted to face her.

Her eyes had adjusted to the darkness. Moonlight glinted from the gold at his earlobe and bathed the angle of his jaw in silver. His eyes were hidden in shadow, yet she could feel the force of his gaze. She laced her fingers together, telling herself not to reach for him. She took slow, shallow breaths, trying not to smell him.

It was useless. The awareness of him was in her blood, pulsing into every hidden, intimate spot in her body. Her legs quivered. Her breasts felt so full, they ached.

Ignore it, she told herself. He's a source. A temporary partner. Nothing more.

He leaned closer. So did she. His breath puffed across her mouth. She parted her lips. Waiting. Ready. Oh, so ready. Please. *Please!*

He groaned and thrust his fingers into her hair, grasping her head between his hands. "I'm sorry, Melina," he whispered. "I never should have let it go this far."

What did he mean? Their argument? Or this…thing between them?

Oh, God. Did he know what she was feeling?

He pressed his forehead to hers, holding her steady, keeping their lips a safe distance apart. His fingers moved in her hair, his breath feathered over her cheek, but those were the only caresses he allowed. He held her in silence until her heartbeat gradually slowed. The heat eased from her blood, as if she were drawing away from a flame. Traces of it remained, like a fading afterimage, but the driving, mindless ache had dimmed.

She was the first to pull away. The instant she did, he released his hold and sat back against his door.

She swallowed her protest. This was good. Really. Things were already awkward. The quarrel they had just had was bad enough and could damage their working relationship. It would have been so much worse if he had kissed her, right? *Right?*

Without another word, he started the engine and drove back to the highway.

Melina rolled down her window, closed her eyes and hoped the cold breeze would work.

Chapter 5

Anthony pushed the loose-weave curtain aside to study the street below. Dawn had broken over an hour ago, but there wasn't a rush hour in Antelope Ridge. The only traffic he saw was a dusty pickup truck and a school bus. The bed-and-breakfast he and Melina had found after they had left the bar the night before was a large two-story adobe house that had once belonged to the town's doctor. Like the rest of the town, it had seen better days.

Still, they were lucky to have found the place. It was private, with a large yard and ample space for parking behind the house so the Jeep couldn't be seen from the street. The spry, white-haired widow who was the proprietress was grateful for their business—only one other of her six guest rooms was occupied. The rooms she had given Melina and him were done in the same Southwest style as the ones at the Pecos, although they were half the size. At least the bed was big and comfortable. Too bad the walls weren't thicker.

Melina's room was next to Anthony's. He'd been conscious of every creak in the floorboards as she had moved around in the night. It sounded as if she got as little sleep as he did.

That incident in the Jeep had been too close. Where was his self-control? She had no idea what was going on, so it was up to him not to let it get out of hand. But when he'd felt her hair curl around his fingers and heard the catch in her breath, he'd been one stray thought away from letting nature take its course, and to hell with the consequences.

But he wasn't free to do that, was he? Until Benedict was stopped, no one in Anthony's family would be safe. Nor would Melina.

The sooner they finished this, the better.

He let the curtain fall back into place and turned to look at Melina. She was sitting cross-legged in the center of the patchwork quilt that was spread over his bed, her notepad on her lap. She was wearing an olive-colored turtleneck and loose-fitting cords, so she was covered from her chin to her toes. She had tied her hair back with a flowered scarf and hadn't put on any makeup.

If she thought that made her unattractive, she was wrong. Just seeing her on the big, pine four-poster where he'd lain awake trying not to picture her beside him was playing havoc with his concentration. Yet meeting in this room was the sensible choice—they couldn't afford to be overheard discussing Benedict, especially if she was right and his stronghold was in this area.

Anthony walked to the door, checked that the hallway was empty, then resumed his post at the window. With Melina's room on one side and an outside wall on the other, they should be able to speak freely. "According to the man I talked to at the bar, Fredo's last name was Guzman. He was raised by his grandmother. She died a few years ago and he had no other relatives."

"That could be why Fredo went to New York," she said. "If his last relative died, he would have nothing to keep him here."

Anthony heard a businesslike distance in Melina's tone. She hadn't met his gaze once since she had entered his room. He didn't like it, but he knew she was doing the right thing. He leaned against the window frame, drumming his fingers on the sill. "His grandmother's house is gone. It burned to the ground after she died. Fredo had no other fixed address in town, so there wouldn't be anyplace we could search for more clues about him."

She made an entry in her notebook. "What else did you learn?"

"He was a petty thief, but he wasn't into drugs."

"No," she said. "He wasn't into drugs when I met him, either."

"If Fredo didn't do drugs, and his crimes were too minor to interest the Titan Syndicate, then what connected him to Benedict?"

She tapped her pen against her lips. "Kenny said the last he knew, Fredo was trying to sell what he called 'old Indian stuff.'"

"Artifacts?"

"That's probably what he meant. It couldn't have been regular Indian pottery, since there's too much of that around for it to be worth anything on the black market."

Anthony picked up the high-scale map he'd acquired yesterday and rolled it out on the mattress. He held on to the edges to keep it flat and pointed his chin at the shaded areas.

"There are several pueblos and Indian reservations within thirty miles of Antelope Ridge. I've heard that this entire region has been occupied for more than seven hundred years, so I wouldn't be surprised if there are undiscovered caches of artifacts around. Fredo might have found one."

Melina put her weight on her hand and leaned forward. She twisted her neck, trying to read the map upside down. "There aren't many roads. Judging from the countryside we went through when you took the Jeep off the highway—" She paused and looked at him sideways. The way they both leaned over the map, her head was only inches from his. She pressed her lips together and sat back on her heels. "It, uh, seems pretty rough."

"It's rough but not impenetrable. And if a thief like Fredo managed to stumble over something genuine, he wouldn't take it to a museum."

"No, he wouldn't. He'd try to sell it as fast as a hot Rolex."

Anthony straightened up. The map rolled shut with a snap. "That's the connection, Melina. Benedict would have wanted the artifacts."

"Kenny mentioned Fredo knew some big-time collector, but why would Benedict be interested in Indian history?"

"He's interested in power. And he's obsessed with psychic phenomena. If he believed those artifacts possessed any trace of either one, he would have wanted them."

"Whoa. Back up a bit here. What's this about Benedict and psychic phenomena? This is the first I've heard about it."

Anthony debated how much to tell her. Only as much as she needed to know, he decided. "Benedict has always been interested in the supernatural."

"Like ghosts?"

"Whatever could give him power. I remember there were Ouija boards and decks of tarot cards at the house."

Melina leaned back against the bed's headboard. "Well, now it makes sense."

"What does?"

"Something Fredo told me before he died. He said Titan had always been weird but lately he'd flipped out. Those were his words. He said Titan was over the edge. He must have meant this psychic stuff."

Anthony felt a sensation of foreboding. Benedict had been careful to keep his obsession private. To reveal it now must mean he was feeling extremely confident…or increasingly desperate. Either possibility made him more dangerous than ever. "What else did he say?"

"That Titan thought he was a magician."

"The Magician is one of the most powerful figures in the tarot deck," Anthony said. "He uses secrecy and illusion as a means to manipulate and control."

"Secrecy and illusion," Melina repeated. "That fits, too. Fredo said Titan was in plain sight but I wouldn't see him." She drew up her legs and hugged her knees. "If we were talking about anyone else, I wouldn't take the supernatural nonsense seriously, but given Benedict's track record of brutality, this obsession of his could make him even more dangerous."

"I agree." Anthony looked at the way she had curled up protectively. It was good that she was intelligent enough to be frightened. Too bad she was too stubborn to be sensible. "Melina," he began.

She held up her palm. "I know what you're going to say, so don't bother."

"If you went home now…"

"I thought we straightened this out last night, but maybe we need to talk about what happened after we left the bar. It might be good to clear the air."

He wanted to do more than clear the air. He wanted to close

the space between them and finish what he hadn't allowed them to start. Instead, he shoved his hands in his pockets. "Nothing happened."

"You hauled me to the Jeep and lectured me about being careful. I wouldn't call that nothing."

She wasn't talking about their almost-kiss, he realized. She was still ignoring the sexual current that had spiked between them. She was more concerned with her...what? Her independence? Her pride?

For some reason, that irked him. "You're angry because I *protected* you?"

"I'm not angry. I realize you meant well, and I appreciate the way you helped me when Fredo was killed. But if we're going to avoid problems in the future, you have to respect the fact that we're partners. I thought I had made that clear, but the first chance that came up, you tried to get me to leave."

"I apologize if I offended you by attempting to keep you away from harm."

"You're missing the point."

"No, you're not seeing the big picture. If I decide the risk is too great, I'll do whatever is necessary to make sure that you're safe."

She swung her legs over the side of the mattress and stood. Her cheeks glowed with color, and several locks of hair had corkscrewed away from her scarf. She parted her lips, then hesitated, as if reconsidering whatever retort she had been about to make. "I don't want to argue again, Anthony. We do have to work together. I have to remind myself your attitude is because of your sisters."

The change of subject took him off guard. "What?"

"Danielle and Elizabeth. And your friend Jeremy. Knowing they could be in danger from the man who killed your mother must be stressing you out. It's making you overprotective." She moved toward him, halting beside the post at the foot of the bed. "I realize you have a lot of personal feelings tied up in this search for Benedict. You have every reason to want him brought to justice."

"I never pretended otherwise."

"That's right, you haven't. So it's understandable that you're going to get emotional at times." She rested one hand on the bedpost and regarded him for a while. "And you probably like to be in control because of your childhood. That would have been one way to deal with the trauma you went through."

"It sounds as if you have me all figured out."

Her lips tilted in the hint of a smile. "You? Hardly. I have a feeling it would take a lot longer than two days to figure out Anthony Caldwell."

He moved to the corner of the bed where she stood, keeping the post between them. "And what about you, Melina? Why is it so important for you to feel in charge?"

"It's my story. It's natural that I'd want to do things my way."

"It's more than that. What happened to you, Melina? You have passion, yet you keep it locked inside. Did something happen in your childhood?"

"I had a storybook childhood. Two great parents and a wonderful home. I never went through anything like the tragedy you did."

"What made you learn to control your emotions?"

"I need to be objective to do my job."

He suspected that wasn't the whole truth. By the set of her jaw, he could see she didn't intend to tell him the rest. Yet he wasn't ready to let the subject drop. He grasped the bedpost, placing his hand below hers. "Do you ever let them go?"

"What?"

"Your feelings." He slid his hand upward until their fingers touched. "Your passion."

Her gaze dropped to his mouth. She didn't reply.

"Don't you get tired sometimes?" he asked. "Tired of having to push your needs aside so you can do what's right? Aren't you tempted to forget your job and your obligations, and seize the pleasure of the moment?"

The color in her cheeks deepened. He could see the flutter of her pulse behind her ear.

He touched his thumb to the knuckle of her little finger. "Is there anything else that happened yesterday, after we left the bar, that you think we should talk about?"

She returned her gaze to his. "No."

"Melina…"

Although her eyes had darkened, she looked at him steadily. "I'm not as emotionally involved as you are, Anthony, but I have a lot riding on this story, too. I've put my personal life on hold. I've invested months of my time, and so much of the *Journal*'s money, that it's either going to make my career or end it. I won't go home—I can't go home—until I can reveal the truth about Titan."

Tension hummed between them. Anthony was tempted to push. It would be so easy….

She pointedly lifted her hand away from his and stepped back. "So what I *need* is information. And the only thing I want to talk about now is finding Benedict."

Anthony slid his palm over the place where hers had been. The wood was still warm from her hand. He hadn't used one twinge of his power this morning, yet he felt almost as connected to Melina now as when they had been caught in the force of his power's backwash last night.

"Tell me more about this interest Benedict has in the paranormal," she said. She snatched her notebook from the bed and retrieved her pen. "That might be an angle worth pursuing."

He let his hand fall to his side. Obviously, the subject of their relationship was closed. It had never really had a chance to open.

She was right to keep her distance. Of course she was right. Anthony shouldn't feel disappointed. He should respect her strength. If they ever did acknowledge the connection between them, there would be no going back.

He walked to the window to check the street while he gathered his thoughts. Yet again, he considered how much he should tell her. He wasn't accustomed to sharing anything—as she had said, he preferred to be the one in control. Yet Melina needed to know more of the truth if she was going to help him. "It's more than just an angle. It's why Benedict married my mother."

"I don't understand."

"Her family came from Romania. She had Gypsy blood. Benedict believed she carried psychic power in her genes, so he thought her children would, too."

"Oh, good God," she murmured. "Seriously?"

"That's why he talked her into fertility treatments at the clinic where he worked." Anthony regarded her over his shoulder, gauging her reaction. "He wanted to possess her children the same way he had Ouija boards and tarot decks. Just as he would collect artifacts."

"*Possess* her children?" she repeated. "Innocent children. That's unthinkable."

"Before he was expelled from college, he studied genetics. He thought he was being scientific."

"More like he was being delusional. Is that why he was trying to get information about you and your sisters? Did he actually believe you had the potential for psychic abilities?"

"That's right. Benedict abandoned us when he fled the country. He wants to reacquire us now."

"This is too incredible. Maybe you misinterpreted his motives."

"There's no mistake, Melina. I've read the notes he left in my mother's records from the fertility clinic. That's how I learned the truth. He documented his theories in her file. He wanted to experiment with all six of us."

The color drained from her face. "Experiment?"

"To train us as psychics."

"Then Fredo was right. The guy is over the edge. Who knows what he's capable of doing?" She paused. "I can see why you're so anxious to keep him away from your family. This is horrible."

Too restless to stand still, Anthony paced to the door. The room suddenly felt too small, too enclosed. He rubbed his forehead. "Benedict went after Danielle first because she was the most vulnerable. She wouldn't let me protect her. I had tried to keep her safe while we were growing up, but she resented it when we got older. Just like you, she saw my concern as being controlling and overprotective. We had a lot of arguments until she and her son moved away."

"Away? You mean out of Philadelphia?"

"She moved to Chicago. She hasn't spoken to me in two years. I only heard she and my nephew had had a run-in with the Titan Syndicate when Jeremy told me after it was over."

"I'm sorry, Anthony. I didn't mean to touch a sore spot."

"What?"

"When I called you overprotective. I hadn't realized you were estranged from your sister."

A sore spot? It was more like a gaping wound.

Not a day went by that he didn't think about Danielle and wonder how she and Alex were. Hearing about her second-hand only added to the pain. Yet he was the one who had cut off the psychic connection between them. He'd been angry that she'd quit the team.

But this was no time to dwell on that. He gestured impatiently. "My feelings are immaterial. Jeremy told me she took my nephew to a private island in the Mediterranean where they'll have round-the-clock protection, so they're safe. That's all that matters. My other sister's new boyfriend has the resources to see to her security, so Benedict won't get to Elizabeth, either. But I still haven't been able to warn our other three siblings. I don't know where they are. I didn't even know for sure they existed until I went to Wyatt and remembered that night—" He stopped and inhaled deeply, focusing on the patch of sunlight that angled across the wall. The room wasn't too small, he told himself. He wasn't enclosed. He could breathe.

The bed creaked as Melina sat on the edge of the mattress. "That must have torn you up inside, to lose so much so suddenly."

He waited until the panic receded before he went on. "I had blocked them out of my memory, like my mother's murder. After we went to our first foster home, my sisters remembered the babies, but we were told they were mistaken. I'm assuming the other triplets were either handled by another social service agency or were adopted."

"Is there any way to find them?"

"There isn't much to go on. The memories that came back to me after I went to Wyatt are hazy, more feelings than anything else. All I found in my mother's medical records is their names, but there's no way to know if they still have them. My brothers were named Darian and Hawk. My youngest sister was named Cassandra. They probably would have been given a different surname, the same way Danielle, Elizabeth and I were."

"You're right. That isn't much."

"That's why I've been concentrating on finding Benedict before he finds them. It's the only sure way to protect them all."

"All that misery over some superstitious belief," Melina said. "Somehow, it makes everything more tragic."

He looked at her. "I take it you don't believe in the paranormal?"

"No, of course not."

"Many people do."

"I deal in facts, and I've never seen any proof of supernatural powers." She hesitated, and her gaze went to the gold hoop in his ear. "What about you, Anthony? Do you think there could be any truth to what Benedict believes about your Gypsy heritage?"

He almost told her then. Hell, he wanted to *show* her. He was tired of pushing his needs aside. He did want to forget his obligations. He wanted to seize the pleasure of the moment with her....

Promise me you'll take care of them, okay?

His mother's words slid through his thoughts, knocking him back on track, as they always did. He went to where he had left the map, unrolled it and bent his head to study the print.

"You didn't answer my question," she said.

"If I had inherited any psychic ability, Melina, you can be damn sure I would be channeling every ounce of it into finding Benedict."

There was a patio made of red brick behind the house, separated from the gravel parking area by a black wrought-iron fence. It was sheltered from the wind by an overgrown yew hedge and was pleasantly warmed by the sun. Melina decided it was a good place to make her calls—she couldn't get a clear signal inside the house. Yet she could feel her hand tremble as she held her phone to her ear. It wasn't from cold; it was from nerves. Was this how Fredo had felt before he had died?

If even half of what Anthony had told her was true, the Titan story promised to be bigger than Melina could have imagined in her wildest dreams. The professional thing for her to do at this point would be to step back and verify as many facts as possible. Anthony had said he'd seen notes in his mother's medical records. For starters, she should demand to see the entire file. Then she should fill in some more pertinent background by questioning him about what else he remembered of Benedict from his early years.

But she didn't want to hurt Anthony by probing further into his personal tragedy. She'd seen pain on his face again today. She had thought his pain had stemmed from witnessing his mother's murder and losing his siblings, yet there was so much more to it.

How did he feel, knowing he had been born to fulfill some madman's superstitious delusions? The very idea stirred Melina to anger. Children weren't possessions, they were gifts. They needed to be loved, they deserved to be cherished. There had been six of them—three babies and three toddlers. That house in Wyatt where they once had lived should have overflowed with the sounds of life, but they had never had the chance to be a family.

And what about the heartache Deanna must have felt? Anthony had said his mother had believed she was in love, but her love had made her vulnerable. That was what love did. It had allowed a man to use her, to betray her trust and to end her hopes and dreams in an outburst of violence.

Melina shuddered. Was she thinking of Deanna, or of herself? The circumstances had been different, yet at the core there were similarities. Eight years ago she had been used and her own dreams about children had been shattered in an instant by a man she had believed she loved….

The phone crackled. Melina pulled her thoughts back to the present in time to hear a woman's voice come on the line. "Special Projects Unit. Harriet speaking."

"Harriet, this is Melina Becker. I'm calling for Agent Brooks."

"One moment, please. I'll transfer your call."

"You already transferred me twice. Just tell me if Liam's there—"

The line clicked. The receiver filled with a dull hiss. She was back on hold.

Melina lowered the phone and terminated the connection. There was no point eating up any more of her minutes. This runaround had nothing to do with the switchboard—her FBI contact still wasn't taking her calls. Liam either had nothing new, or he had information he considered too important to share with the press. Either way, she wasn't going to get anything from him today.

She crossed the patio, tapping the phone against her leg. How close were the authorities to arresting Titan? Did they know that Titan was Benedict Payne? That information would be valuable to them. Would she be betraying Anthony's confidence if she informed them of what he had told her?

That was a silly question. She intended to *publish* what he had told her, didn't she? That was her job. That was why she was asking him so many questions. It was the only reason they were together.

The only reason? She reached the fence that bordered the parking area and wrapped her free hand around one of the arrowhead shapes that ran along the top. She hung on until the cold metal bit into her palm. She realized she couldn't afford to lose her professional detachment on this story, yet how could any woman spend time around Anthony and remain indifferent? It would be like trying to stand close to a fire and not feel heat.

There hadn't been much opportunity to sort out the facts she had been learning, let alone reflect on them. Anthony didn't ask for sympathy. He didn't accept it when it was offered—he'd said flat out that his feelings were immaterial. He was a complex man with many layers. A fascinating man. A lonely man.

Did he realize how much he was revealing about himself to her through his actions? He seemed to think it was his responsibility, and his alone, to keep his family safe from Benedict. He even wanted to protect the younger sister and two brothers he only recently realized existed.

He was so…intense about everything he did. The way he drove, the way he talked with no wasted words, the way he did what he thought best without waiting for anyone's permission or worrying if he offended. All of it arose from his passionate sense of purpose.

Passionate. Oh, yes. That described Anthony. She focused on where her fingers wrapped the top of the fence, and she thought about the big, pine four-poster bed in Anthony's room.

It seemed as if she couldn't spend more than ten minutes in his company without having her thoughts stray in that direction. Thank heavens the acute sexual awareness from the night before had faded. Yet there was still a connection. It was as if she were being drawn to him on a level she was unfamiliar with. Could it really have been only two days since they had met?

It took her a moment to realize her phone was ringing. She put it back to her ear. "Melina Becker," she said.

"Melina! Where are you?"

It took her another few seconds to recognize the voice. "Oh, hi, Neil."

"Didn't you get my messages?"

She had. She had been putting off responding to them. "Sorry, I've been busy."

"I called your hotel but they said you had checked out. Are you still in Santa Fe?"

She hesitated. It wasn't that she didn't trust Neil, but there were many other people who were involved with production of the *Daily Journal*. It might be safer not to take the chance of revealing more than necessary. "I didn't mean to worry you, Neil. Things have been crazy here."

"I hope that means your new lead is paying off."

"Yes. I'm getting great material."

"Terrific. What time will your flight be getting in tomorrow?"

"What?"

"I've got meetings scheduled pretty solid all day, but if you get in after seven I should be able to swing by the airport and pick you up myself."

"Neil, I'm not coming back tomorrow."

There was a silence. Melina listened for the creak of his chair but heard nothing. "Neil?"

"You said two days tops."

"I was wrong."

"I see."

He had switched to his reasonable tone. She had always disliked it, she realized. It was too civilized a way to express his displeasure. If she had tried to put Anthony off like this, he wouldn't be accepting it so calmly. He would get loud. He would probably hop on a plane, come to where she was calling him from and haul her into his arms and—

"Okay. How much longer will you need?"

Melina knew it was stupid to feel disappointed. She liked Neil because he *wasn't* passionate. He was comfortable. He let her walk all over him—

No, that wasn't fair. He was simply a nice man. "Maybe another week."

"I don't know if— Hang on, I've got a call on my other line."

"No, don't put me on hold, Neil. I—"

There was a click and then a blank hiss. It was too late. She was back on hold again.

She lowered the phone and switched it off. In truth, she felt relieved the conversation was over. And she felt guilty for being relieved. She focused on the ringless fourth finger of her left hand. She had told him she would think about his proposal, but she hadn't thought about Neil once since they had spoken yesterday morning.

That was the kind of relationship they had. It wasn't intense and consuming, it was easygoing. Friendly and undemanding. Safe.

You have passion, yet you keep it locked inside.... What made you learn to control your emotions?

In all the years she and Neil had worked together, he had never once asked the question that Anthony had.

Would Neil have believed her if she'd answered with the same lie she had told Anthony?

"Was it bad news?"

The voice startled her. Melina lifted her head and saw that she was no longer alone on the patio. A small, dark-haired woman was walking toward her from the direction of the house. She held a muffin in one hand and clutched a fringed shawl around her shoulders with the other.

This wasn't Mrs. Rodriguez, the owner of the bed-and-breakfast, whom Melina had met the night before—a lively, white-haired, seventy-something widow. So she assumed this woman must be the other guest Mrs. Rodriguez had mentioned. "Not really," she replied. "Just some work issues."

Gold bracelets tinkled at the woman's wrist as she took a dainty nibble of her muffin. There were streaks of silver in her black hair and lines of middle age on her face. Her green gaze was full of lively interest. "I didn't mean to intrude, but you seemed distressed. Would you like to talk about it?"

"That's very kind of you, but it's nothing." Melina gave her a smile and looked at the swirling red, amber and gold pattern on the wool that covered the stranger's shoulders. "What a lovely shawl. It's so colorful."

"Thank you. It's one of my favorites. It reminds me of autumn, the season of endings."

What an odd thing to say, Melina thought. She detected a faint accent in the woman's voice. Something from central Europe, she guessed. "Are you here on vacation?"

"Unfortunately, no. There is still much I must do before I can rest." She tilted her head. "You say your phone call was not bad news, but you squeeze your phone as if you might break it."

Melina slipped the phone into the pocket of her pants, then flexed her fingers. "I guess I don't like being put on hold."

"No one does. It is not fair to either party. One should make a decision to either go forward or to end things. Only then will you be free."

Perhaps it was her accent that made the comment seem more meaningful than it was meant to be, or maybe Melina's ambivalence over Neil's proposal was making her paranoid. Whatever the reason, it sounded as if the woman was trying to make a point about Melina's treatment of Neil.

Had she been listening while Melina had been talking to him? Perhaps, but even if she had eavesdropped on the conversation, she couldn't have heard enough to deduce what was going on between them, not unless she was psychic....

Melina caught herself before she could get carried away by her imagination. After what Anthony had told her about Benedict, it was little wonder that she had the paranormal on the brain. Still, it was ludicrous to suspect that this friendly, middle-aged stranger who was nibbling a muffin in the morning sunlight had some kind of, well, special telepathic power.

The woman finished off her breakfast, brushed the crumbs from her fingers and headed for the edge of the patio. "I must go. I hope you find what you are seeking."

Melina started. Again, it was a comment that seemed to carry more meaning than it should have. "What do you mean? What do you think I'm seeking?"

She drew her shawl more tightly around her shoulders. "Why, your heart's desire. That is what we all seek, is it not?"

Chapter 6

The clouds that had started gathering in the west at noon were continuing to build, growing darker as they thickened, cloaking the mountain range on the horizon with shades of indigo blue. It was late in the year for an electrical storm in this area, but Anthony knew one was coming. He felt a whisper of energy brush across his face. An echo of distant thunder tickled down his spine. Off-season or not, it promised to be a big one.

"There's a left turn coming up," Melina said. She traced her finger along the map she had spread out across her knees. "The Antelope Pueblo should be about eight miles south."

He gave the clouds one final assessing glance, then geared down to make the turn. He was cutting things close. He shouldn't risk being caught in the storm with Melina, yet he didn't want to waste any more time.

Over the past five days, they had systematically visited

every reservation, pueblo and hunting outfitter within thirty miles of Fredo's hometown, questioning anyone who might be familiar with the backcountry. So far, they hadn't met anyone who admitted to knowing Fredo. They hadn't learned of any new construction or recently discovered Indian artifacts in the area, either.

Had they been wrong to concentrate their search here? The link they had established between Fredo and Benedict was still only speculation. If Benedict had built his stronghold nearby because of the artifacts that Fredo might have sold him, surely some evidence of it should have surfaced by now. How could a fortress go unnoticed? What about the construction materials that would be needed, the increased activity and the influx of strangers? Surely someone would have noted something out of the ordinary.

On the other hand, what if there had been construction, but people had been paid to keep quiet?

Melina rolled up the map and twisted to put it on the backseat. "We're running out of options. I hope we have better luck at this pueblo than at the others."

He drummed his fingers on the steering wheel. "So do I. Whatever we find, we need to start back within the hour."

"Why? It's only three."

"The storm is going to hit before dark."

She looked out her window. "You mean those clouds? A bit of rain isn't going to hurt us."

It wasn't the rain that concerned him. It was what might happen if he and Melina were too close to the lightning. With that much stray energy in the air, he'd have a hell of a time controlling his own.

He stole a glance at her profile. Etched against the backdrop of deep blue clouds and the sandstone cliff that rose in the distance, she looked uncharacteristically fragile. Fine worry lines bracketed her lips. The delicate skin under her eyes was tinged with strain. Beneath her jacket and cords, her body was stiff with tension.

The past few days had been hard on her. He knew she was more accustomed to chasing down leads in the canyons of Manhattan than in this trackless wilderness. But she had worked without complaint, trading in her high-heeled boots and fashionable skirts for sneakers and sturdy jeans, accompanying him on these excursions by day while she continued to use her computer to research Benedict through the Internet by night. There hadn't been time for anything else. Since that first morning in his room, she had done her best to keep their relationship professional.

Not that there was any chance of switching off the attraction between them. It was always there, like a haunting melody that swelled or ebbed but never disappeared.

Yet it was surprising how well they worked together. Anthony had to admit that many of Melina's ideas were sound. She was an intelligent, compassionate woman who had an impressive strength of will. It was a fascinating combination. It almost made him wish for an excuse to linger long enough for the storm to break.

He scowled and focused on the road. What was he thinking?

"If this doesn't pan out, we could try contacting the local colleges next," Melina said.

"Why?"

"Maybe someone from their geology or native studies departments is doing a project in the area."

"That's a possibility. We could ask if they noticed anything unusual."

She pulled her feet onto the seat, wrapping her arms around her legs. "Anthony, this all could be a waste of time. What if

I sent us in the wrong direction? What if Benedict isn't even in New Mexico?"

"We're not finished yet."

"I had hoped we would have found something by now."

"Is your editor making demands?"

"Neil isn't the demanding type. As a matter of fact, I haven't spoken with him for days. We're in a…holding pattern."

He looked at the way she had curled up protectively. She tended to do that when she was anxious. He had to fight the urge to take her into his arms and comfort her. He should stick to business, just the way she did. Keep the conversation impersonal.

But she looked so troubled, he couldn't simply ignore it. "Are you worried about losing your job?"

"I should be. I don't know what I'd do without it. I love my work." She leaned her chin on her knees. "It sounds simple, doesn't it? It's the *work* that I love."

"What's going on, Melina? It's more than our lack of progress locating Benedict that's bothering you, isn't it?"

She hesitated for so long, he thought she wasn't going to reply. When she did, it was with a question of her own. "Have you met the small foreign woman who's staying at Mrs. Rodriguez's?"

A pulse of energy stabbed through Anthony without warning. He jerked. The Jeep swerved to the edge of the road. He yanked on the wheel to stop the skid.

Melina gasped and clutched the grab bar. "What happened?"

"Sorry. Must have hit a pothole," he muttered, trying to sort it out.

Where had that pulse come from? Was it the storm? It hadn't felt like the tickle of distant lightning, but it had been so brief, he couldn't be sure where it had originated. He checked his speed. For once, he was within the limit. If it had been a radar pulse, there wouldn't be a problem, but he didn't think any cops would bother with a speed trap out here. The area was too sparsely populated.

"If you're getting tired, I can drive for a while."

"I'm fine." He tried to remember what they had been talking about. "A small foreign woman at the bed-and-breakfast? I don't remember anyone like that."

"I only talked to her once, but something she said got me thinking."

"About what?"

"My job," she said. "What I want. Knowing when to let go."

"Let go?" He looked at her. "You're not giving up on Benedict, are you?"

"No, of course not. Getting this story is what I really want. That's what she would call 'my heart's desire.'"

"Who? That woman?"

"She has an odd way of putting things. She made me think about my priorities. I—" She gasped. "Anthony!"

Another pulse hit him, harder than before. The Jeep swerved as the steering wheel slid through his hands. A truck going the other way honked as it passed, missing him by scant inches. Shaken, Anthony pulled off the road and waited for the surge to subside.

What the hell had that been? It wasn't lightning—the storm was in the west. This had come from the north. And it had been distinct enough for him to rule out radar.

He glanced at Melina. She still had a tight hold on the grab bar and was looking at him quizzically.

He killed the engine and opened his door. "I'm going to check the tires. We might be getting a flat."

He got out, braced his palm against the front fender and leaned over. There was nothing wrong with the tire. He needed to stop so he could check out that power. He opened his mind and searched for an echo, a trace, anything that would tell him what it was.

There. To the north, no longer a surge, more like a background hum. The signal had weakened with distance, yet it bore the deep signature of an exceptionally strong source. The Antelope Pueblo was still several miles to the southwest, so it couldn't have originated there. Besides, none of the pueblos he had seen so far had any equipment that could have produced energy like that.

He straightened up to take stock of their surroundings. The road ran along the floor of a wide canyon here, making it impossible to see what lay beyond the canyon rim. According to the map, there were no roads or settlements immediately north of this spot. The land was a forbidding maze of cliffs and gullies.

There was nothing out there that could account for what he was feeling.

Thunder rolled in the distance. The hair on his arms rose. He could sense the gathering charge in the air from the oncoming storm.

The lightning was already drawing close enough to sharpen his perception. That was probably why whatever power source lay to the north had hit him so hard.

"How does it look?" Melina moved around the front of the Jeep. "Do we need to change it?"

She was talking about the tire, he realized. He kicked it with the side of his foot. "No, it's fine. Before we go farther, I'd like to take a detour and check out what's on the other side of this canyon."

"Why?"

"I caught a flash from something over the ridge."

She moved beside him to follow his gaze. "I don't see anything."

"It was there. It shouldn't have been."

"Hang on. I'll get the binoculars."

While she climbed into the Jeep to retrieve his binoculars from the back seat, Anthony closed his eyes so he could better concentrate on the power source.

It was definitely electrical in nature. The energy wave was distorted by the rock landforms it must have traveled past, so it was difficult to judge how far away it was. He focused on the pattern, fixing it in his mind so he could follow it.

A light touch settled on his sleeve. "Anthony?"

He blinked.

Melina was standing beside him, the binoculars dangling from her hand, her gaze filled with concern. "Are you sure you're okay?"

He could feel the warmth from her fingers strum his nerves. Her scent curled around him as her hair whipped freely in the strengthening wind. He tried to hold himself steady, yet faint bursts from the approaching storm quivered between them, drawing him closer. He lifted his hand to her hair, letting her curls flutter against his palm in a whispering caress.

She moistened her lips. The concern in her gaze shifted to longing. The change wasn't gradual, it was instant, as if a switch had been flipped. Which it had.

He slammed the lid on his power. It was madness to risk spending time looking for that energy source now. He was already feeling the effects of the lightning. The spillover from his talent was only going to get worse. Melina wouldn't understand it. He should get them out of here before the storm hit.

But he *couldn't* leave. What if that source had something to do with Benedict? Anthony was only able to detect that distant energy because the storm was enhancing his perception. If he didn't follow it now, he might not get another chance to find it.

He had restrained himself from touching Melina for almost a week. For the sake of his family, he could hold back for another few hours, right?

And even if he couldn't...

The possibility made his pulse speed up. He closed his fingers around the curl that teased his palm. No matter what else might happen, he was going to grasp this opportunity. It might never come again.

A river of tumbled boulders, some the size of small cars, loomed in front of them, blocking their way. Melina barely waited for Anthony to stop the Jeep before she flung open her door and hopped to the ground.

She didn't care about the wind that funneled through the canyon. She ignored the threatening rumble of thunder in the west. She took no notice of the pebbles that shifted under her sneakers or the sliding steps she had to take to keep her balance. All she cared about was getting out of that vehicle and putting some distance between her and Anthony.

But she didn't get out fast enough. The impact with the ground sent vibrations up her legs to her thighs, releasing a bubble of pleasure.

She leaned over and grasped her knees, drawing in deep breaths. *Get control of yourself,* she ordered. *This is crazy. Nuts.*

"Melina!"

The sound of his voice made her shiver with awareness. She tried some more deep breathing as she stumbled toward the closest boulder. The daylight was rapidly fading. The storm clouds were bringing on an early dusk.

"Melina, where are you going?"

She spun to face him, pressing her back hard against the rock. But the movement thrust out her breasts, making them ache, making her yearn for Anthony's touch. She swallowed a sob. "Give me a minute, okay?"

He stood beside his open door. He made no move to approach her. "Come back to the Jeep. The storm's getting close and I want you to be safe."

She would have laughed at that, except she suspected making any sudden movement with her chest would only worsen the discomfort in her breasts.

Safe? In the Jeep? Where she was close enough to smell him, to hear the rasp of denim on denim when he moved his legs, to watch the tendons flex in his hands, to feel the rumbling throb of his heartbeat in her bones?

The past few hours had been torture. Sweet, terrible, delicious agony. Since they had left the road, every rise they had bumped over, every tilting climb they had made, each bend in the winding, unmarked route Anthony had taken had triggered a flash of sexual pleasure.

Not enough to satisfy. Only enough to tease and build and deepen and heighten…

It was like the awareness she had felt that night they had gone to The Oasis Bar, only a hundred times better. No, worse. Her body was humming with a driving desire to touch him, kiss him, feel his skin slide over hers and taste his breath on her lips.

Why now? She'd been able to keep her distance for five days. She'd almost been able to convince herself that the other time had been a fluke, a consequence of stress, or maybe an embarrassing accident of overactive hormones.

Oh, God. What was wrong with her? Except for these cravings, her mind was clear. In fact, her thoughts were snapping as vividly as her senses, as if her entire being was suffused with some mysterious energy.

"The rain's going to start soon," he said. "You should take cover."

She glanced past him to the clouds. They stretched in an ominous wave, black on the bottom, churning gray on the top, smothering the sky with violence.

But she wasn't getting back in that Jeep right now. She wanted time to let this reaction subside. Some rain might be just what she needed. As long as the rain was cold.

Lightning danced between the clouds. Another flash of sensation trembled through her body, setting off a renewed burst of need. She flattened her hands against the boulder, focusing on the rough surface beneath her palms. Even that seemed more vivid, as if she could feel every minute variation in the rock. She returned her gaze to Anthony.

He didn't flinch as thunder crashed close enough to vibrate the ground. He stood tall and straight, as if he didn't feel the wind or fear the lightning. With his dark hair and black clothes, he could have been an extension of the storm, wild, untamed, filled with energy that strained to be released.

Anthony wasn't fighting the storm's power, she thought, he was…drawing from it.

She bit her lip. Her imagination was getting as out of control as her hormones. This was her partner, the man she had worked beside for a week. They weren't here on a pleasure trip. They had work to do.

"We've been going back and forth for hours," she said. "We must have passed the spot where you saw that glint of light by now, don't you think?"

"Distances can be deceptive out here."

"Are you certain you detected anything in the first place? I didn't."

The wind tugged a lock of hair free from his ponytail. It lashed his cheek. He didn't appear to notice. "I'm certain."

"Well, how much farther do you plan to go?"

"I want to see what's on the other side of this canyon," he said. He gestured toward the tumbled rocks. They led to a wide split in the cliff wall that sloped upward in jagged stages. "I'll try climbing up there."

Lightning flickered again. Melina's nipples tightened so hard, they stung. She tried not to wince.

He moved to the edge of the fallen rocks and hoisted himself up on the first one. "I won't be long."

She turned to watch him climb, admiring his controlled grace as he went from one rock to another, testing his handholds and his footing, his arms and legs working in perfect harmony. She had once compared his movements to a prowling wolf. There was a predatory edge to him, more than a hint of the untamed. Was that why he could stir up these primitive feelings in her? "Anthony, wait!"

He looked down just as lightning flashed beyond the cliff. The hoop in his ear gleamed, giving the illusion of a glow in the air around him.

She moved to a smaller rock that was beside the boulder she had been leaning on, and pulled herself on top of it. "I'm coming with you."

"Melina, no."

"It doesn't look that steep."

"No, it isn't, but—"

"Don't you dare tell me to wait here where it's safe." She clambered onto the next rock and worked her way toward the side so she could follow the route he had taken. It wasn't all that difficult. She just had to regard the boulders as round steps. "We're partners, remember?"

"This is no time to argue, Melina. It's going to be dark soon. It really would be best for both of us if you stay here."

"I won't hold you up. And I'd like to see for myself what's up there."

He continued to watch her as she climbed toward him. Despite the shadows that were closing around them, his gaze appeared a more brilliant green than she had ever seen it before. His jaw was clenched, as if he was fighting the urge to argue…or perhaps battling the impulse to kiss her.

Melina ground her teeth. This was business, she reminded herself. They were looking for Benedict. It was for her story, for the work that she loved.

Twenty minutes later, they reached the flat land on top of the cliff. Melina had to stop to catch her breath. Her heart was pounding. Her legs were trembling. It wasn't only from the climb. The strange sense of awareness was expanding, as if layers were peeling away or doors were opening or barriers were crumbling, and everything was so intense she wanted to fling out her arms and embrace it all.

Full darkness had fallen, yet the landscape was alive, lit by strobes of lightning. The rolling clouds crashed over a low mountain range in the distance. Dust swirled across the cliff top, scouring the scattered pines. A gray blur of rain advanced like a curtain toward them. It was a spectacular, primeval scene.

And there wasn't one sign of habitation in sight. No buildings, no lights, nothing.

Anthony turned in a slow circle, as if he were surveying the area. "We're close," he said.

"I don't see anything."

"It's there. To the northwest. A mile, maybe two."

She squinted in that direction. A mile? There was nothing to the northwest except a shadowed cleft that was probably the edge of another canyon. Besides, how could he see anything through the shadows and that curtain of rain? She glanced at his face.

His eyes were shut. His jaw was clenched. He appeared to be lost in concentration, just the way he'd looked two hours ago, after he had driven off the road.

Alarmed, Melina touched his hand.

The contact with his skin sent a shock through her arm. It zinged to her breasts and down her stomach, releasing a flood of sexual heat between her thighs. She gasped and staggered backward.

Anthony's eyes flew open. He grabbed her by the shoulders, yanking her away from the cliff's edge. "Careful!"

Tendrils of pleasure spread from where he touched her. Tingles rose along her neck to pulse in her earlobes. She shuddered.

He released his grip and snatched his hands away. "Dammit, Melina, I can't keep this up much longer. The storm's too close. You should have stayed with the Jeep."

She stared at him, trying to make sense of his words. What couldn't he keep up? "I don't understand."

"No, you don't. That's why you have to go back."

"What's going on? How can you be looking for Benedict's stronghold with your eyes closed? How do you know it's nearby?"

"I don't have time to explain."

"Did you see something and just not tell me? Is that it? Are you trying to cut me out?"

"Melina, no." Lightning flashed. "I'm trying to protect you."

"Don't start that again. We had a deal. I—"

Her words were cut off by a clap of thunder. The ground trembled beneath them.

And somehow, she ended up against Anthony's chest, her arms wrapped around his waist, her fingers digging into his leather jacket. Her lips were pressed to the base of his throat and her right leg was hooked around his hip.

She didn't know how it had happened. She hadn't remembered moving. But she stayed where she was, incapable of pulling away.

Somewhere in her logical, rational mind, a part of her was screaming out a warning. This was wrong. It didn't make sense. But the rest of her had never felt more certain of anything. Yes. This was right. This was where she wanted to be. This was where she belonged, with this man. This was all that mattered.

"Melina." His voice was strained, as raw and as elemental as the sound of the wind. "Leave now."

"No." She opened her mouth to breathe in the taste of his skin.

His body shook. "Melina, don't."

The taste wasn't enough. She tipped up her face, grabbed his head and pulled his mouth down on hers.

Chapter 7

The world dissolved in a sensual blur. On one level Melina was aware of the approaching storm, of the wild, empty landscape around them, the Jeep that they'd left on the floor of the canyon and the criminal they had come here to find. Yet all of that faded, submerged beneath the impact of Anthony's kiss.

It was a kiss like none she had experienced before. She absorbed the warmth of his lips, she felt the moisture of his tongue, but there was so much more than the physical sensations. Something flowed between them, a connection, a current. Sex. Desire. As pure and free as the storm.

It took the strength from her knees.

He caught her before she could fall, wrapping his arms around her back. Not breaking the kiss, she hooked her other leg around him and locked her ankles behind his waist, clinging to him shamelessly. No, that wasn't right. There was no room for shame. No room for anything but this driving need.

More lightning cracked, close enough to raise the hair on her arms. The thunder that followed made her ears ring. A tremor went through Anthony's frame. She felt it echo in every sensitive place in her body, pushing her close, oh, so close to the edge. She whimpered, rubbing against him, wanting it to stop, never wanting it to end.

He lifted his head. His hair whipped against her cheek. "Melina, we can't stay here."

She opened her mouth over the side of his neck, pressing her teeth to his skin.

"We need to take cover." He grasped her legs to ease them away from his waist. "The storm's going to break."

She clamped her legs around him more tightly, refusing to be dislodged. Her eyes stung with tears. She didn't care. She had to get closer. After two hours of torment she had no more restraint. She had to join with him now, this instant, or surely she would go mad. She tilted her hips, trying to fit more snugly against him.

Through the barrier of their clothing, she felt the outline of his erection. He wanted her. That was plain. Her thighs quivered. Her sex throbbed. Yes. Oh, please. Now. *Now!*

"Melina…"

She pounded her fist against his back. "Damn you, Anthony. Don't leave me like this!"

"Do you think I want to? I know what—"

His words were lost in a blinding flash, followed a split second later by an explosion of noise.

Melina screamed with frustration. Tears coursed down her cheeks. She felt like crawling out of her skin. It was as if each bolt of lightning was making the craving worse. She was helpless to explain it, powerless to end it. How could she expect Anthony to understand when she didn't?

Before the vibrations from the thunder ended, Anthony

peeled her off his body and set her on her feet, keeping one arm behind her back to steady her. He grasped her chin. His gaze sizzled through hers. "I warned you, Melina."

She had trouble drawing breath to speak. It was all she could do to stay upright.

"Remember that afterward, all right?" He moved his hand to her hair, his touch gentle despite the roughness in his voice. "I didn't plan for this to happen."

She leaned her cheek into his palm and nipped his thumb.

"Damn," he whispered.

She swirled her tongue over the tip of his thumb and drew it into her mouth.

He opened her jacket, undid her blouse and slipped his fingers beneath the edge of her bra. He stroked his wet thumb over her bare nipple.

The pleasure was so intense, she cried out. She was close, so close, oh, yes. *Yes!* He did understand.

"Trust me, Melina," he said, lowering his hand to her waistband. Tingles shot outward from every inch of skin he touched, making her moan. He unfastened the front of her cords and slipped his hand inside. "I'll make it better."

Better? *Better?* She was going to die. She couldn't possibly endure one more second. It had gone past the point of pleasure and was building into pain.

He kissed her, sliding his tongue into her mouth at the same instant he moved his fingers.

A bolt of brilliant blue-white burst in her vision. Wave after wave of release pounded through her body. It was swift and brutal and too much, oh, too much….

Her lungs heaved. Her vision went black. The last sound she heard was her own scream.

Anthony sat cross-legged on the sandstone outcropping and listened to the water trickle from the overhang above him.

The rock sloped gently into the side of the canyon here, forming a shallow cave at the back of the ledge where he had kept watch through the night.

He was lucky to have found this spot. It was set far enough into the cliff wall to provide shelter from the weather yet still exposed enough so he didn't feel enclosed. The rain had stopped more than an hour ago. The remnants of the storm had moved off to the east. The glow in the clouds wasn't from lightning, but from the approaching dawn.

He looked at Melina. In the dim light from the fading stars, all he could see was the dark outline of her shape as she lay curled against his knee. Wrapped in his jacket, her arm folded beneath her head for a pillow, she appeared achingly vulnerable. He touched the bend of her elbow. A faint echo of the power that had sparked between them yesterday teased his senses, but like the thunderstorm, most of it was spent now, too.

Anthony had known the connection with Melina was unusually strong, but he hadn't anticipated how strong. It had been more intense and more immediate than anything he had experienced before. He had scarcely touched her when the force of her climax had made her pass out. She had still been unconscious when he had carried her here. She had stirred briefly when he had draped his jacket around her but she hadn't wakened up fully.

He stroked her arm with his fingertips. Rest was the best thing for her. She would be exhausted. On top of the shock of her sudden release, she had sustained a state of extreme physical arousal for too long and her body needed time to recover. Add to that the fatigue and the stress she had been fighting all week and it was no surprise that she was still asleep.

He should be feeling guilty over what he'd put her through. She wouldn't understand it. Considering her pride, she would probably blame herself for her loss of control. Yes, he should feel guilty.

He didn't. He felt cheated.

How long had it been since he'd allowed himself to connect with a woman this way? He couldn't remember. The only thing he was sure of was that he had never known anyone as responsive as Melina. She had deep passions. In other circumstances, she would have been an extraordinary lover.

He moved his fingertips to her cheek. After the intimacy they had shared, it would be easy to open the connection again. Why not do it? Why not use her as he'd allowed her to use him? Things were going to change when she woke up. There would be no more need to hide his ability, no going back. Depending on how she reacted, the truth might end their partnership.

Yet that was the risk he'd been willing to take when he'd chosen to use the storm to track Benedict. This might be the last opportunity for him to take the relief he had denied himself last night.

He felt tiny crystals of dried tears on her skin. He brushed them off, remembering her desperation as the storm had broken. All she had wanted from him was relief. Like thirst that had to be quenched or an itch that had to be scratched, the sexual craving she had been suffering from had needed to be satisfied.

Was it crazy to wish it could have been more? To wish that it could have lasted throughout the night, that it could have been genuine?

He leaned over to place a kiss on her temple, then rubbed his nose against her hair, drawing in her scent. He wanted Melina to look at him with desire that wasn't the result of some freak side effect of his talent. He wanted her to want *him*. He wanted the freedom to indulge himself in her warmth, to forget his responsibilities, to escape from his destiny for another few hours....

Muttering an oath, he straightened up, breaking the contact with Melina. No. He couldn't let his resolve weaken. He was here for one purpose and one purpose only. Until it was over, he didn't have the right to want more.

He rose to his feet and walked to the edge of the overhang. Placing his fist against the stone, he turned his face to the darkness and opened his mind.

As it had been the last three times he had tried, the space around him was empty, the pulse was gone. He had lost contact with the energy source that he had been following when he had opened the connection with Melina.

In a moment of weakness, he had chosen her over Benedict.

He couldn't let that happen again.

Melina woke up to the sound of dripping water. She wondered dimly where she was. Was the faucet over the bathroom sink leaking again? Was she in her apartment? In a hotel? She opened her eyes to daylight and tones of sepia and gray. Were the walls in this hotel made of unfinished adobe? Strange place. The ceiling was low enough in the corner to resemble a cave. She yawned, drawing in the smell of damp stone and Anthony's leather jacket.

At his scent, a tickle of reaction chased through her body, kicking her pulse. Images flitted across her brain. Strange scenes, crazy feelings. Lightning on a cliff top. Anthony's gaze hot on her face, his hands on her body, her throat aching from her scream—

She squeezed her eyes shut. Oh, God. Please let it be a dream. It had to be a dream. Either that or she was going insane.

She moved her hand tentatively. Anthony's jacket was

wrapped around her from her chin to below her hips. Her knuckles brushed the edge of her own jacket and her cords. She was still fully dressed. She shifted her legs, then stifled a groan. She ached. Everywhere. As if she had run a marathon. Or attacked her partner in a sex-crazed frenzy.

She curled her knees to her chest. A pebble rolled under the side of her foot. She was lying on a rock, she realized. She wished it would swallow her.

"How are you feeling?"

For a cowardly moment she wanted to pretend she was still asleep. How could she face him?

"I know you're awake, Melina. I can hear the change in your breathing."

Anthony's voice came from behind her back. Okay, she could delay having to look at him for a while longer. She moistened her lips. She tasted salt, dust and a hint of musky spice that she immediately recognized as a trace of Anthony's kiss. A jab of memory made her breath catch.

His kiss. It had gone through her entire body. She hadn't known feelings like that were possible. Sure, she was attracted to him. Strongly attracted to him. She had been for a week and it showed no signs of going away. She was drawn to his magnificent body. His brooding strength intrigued her, his intelligence and his passion challenged her, yet that didn't justify what she had done...or what she had practically begged him to do.

There was a soft, scraping noise, then the sound of footsteps. When Anthony spoke again, it was from directly in front of her. "Melina?"

She clenched her jaw and opened her eyes.

He sat cross-legged on the rock. His hair was loose. It was the first thing she noticed. Except for the strands that had occasionally escaped his ponytail, it had always been tightly controlled. Now it brushed his shoulders in thick, untamed waves, dark and sensual, making her fingers tingle with the urge to plunge into its softness.

She curled her legs to the side and pushed herself up to sit. His jacket fell from her shoulders to the ground. She picked it up and held it out, focusing on a spot past his ear. "Where are we?"

He took his jacket from her hand and laid it across his lap. "We're on the other side of the plateau we climbed yesterday."

She latched on to the excuse to delay meeting his gaze for a while longer. She turned to look around.

The view was breathtaking. They were high on a wide ledge of reddish-brown rock. Drops of water fell from the rim of an overhang above them to splash onto a tilting ramp that appeared to come from the top of the plateau. It was a gentle slope compared to the steep canyon wall they had ascended the day before. A series of narrower ledges fanned downward from this one like a natural staircase, tapering out on the floor of a wide, rocky valley a hundred feet below. Another cliff rose out of a forest of pine on the far side of the valley, gleaming more gold than red in the morning sunlight. The sky was a crisp, endless blue.

She glanced at the clump of bushes on the next ledge down. This delay wasn't an excuse, she thought as she worked her way down to them to make use of the privacy they provided. When she returned, Anthony was sitting where she had left him, his forearm propped on his raised knee.

He flicked a pebble toward the valley. He watched it arc through the sunlight until it was out of sight. "Melina, we need to talk."

She chose a spot that was as far away from him as possible before she sat.

They did need to talk. He was right about that much. She

had to say something if she wanted to salvage their working relationship, but she didn't know where to start.

How could she possibly apologize for her conduct? She was the one who had made it clear she wanted to keep their partnership strictly business. She decided to give herself time to settle her nerves by beginning with a neutral topic. "It looks as if the storm cleared up."

"The rain started right after you fainted," he said. "It turned the rock slippery. I didn't want to risk carrying you back down the boulders to the Jeep so I brought you here, instead. I hope you're not too sore from spending the night outside."

Melina pressed her nails into her palms. Sore? Yes, but it wasn't only because of where she had spent the night. *The rain started right after you fainted.* Before yesterday, she had never fainted in her life. She had never climbed a cliff or spent the night on a rock ledge. She had never crawled up a man's body and rubbed herself against his groin, either.

And she had never, ever, had an orgasm powerful enough to knock her out.

Oh, God! Heat flooded her cheeks. She hugged her knees to her chest. "Thank you. For bringing me here. I'm sorry that I…"

Her apology refused to form. How could any woman be truly sorry for an experience like *that,* regardless of how it had happened? If she regretted anything, it was the fact that it had been over so fast.

She cleared her throat. "Anthony, I really don't know what to say about my behavior."

"It's all right. I understand."

"No, even I don't understand, so you couldn't know what happened."

"I'm the one person who does know." His jeans gritted against the rock as he moved closer. He put his hand on her shoulder. "I respect you too much to see you beat yourself up over this, Melina. You deserve to know the truth."

A tremor went through her at his touch. It wasn't anywhere near as strong as the last time, yet it was enough to stir an echo of response. She shrugged off his hand and slid backward. "Respect? Anthony, I acted inexcusably. I threw myself at you."

"I'm not complaining. I enjoyed…catching you."

"Anthony—"

"Don't blame yourself. It was the storm. The energy in the lightning. That's what you felt. It was out of your control."

"I can't blame the weather. I've been in storms before and never…" She shook her head. "This is so awkward. I'm not sure how to get past it."

"Melina, look at me."

She couldn't. She dropped her face into her hands. "I can't believe what I did."

"You didn't do it alone. That's why it happened, because there was already a connection between us. I was channeling the storm's power, but it was too much for me to control. We were swept up in the backwash."

His attempt at an explanation only added to her confusion. It sounded like some kind of New Age nonsense. She would have thought Anthony was too levelheaded for that. Channeling the power? Okay, for a moment yesterday she'd had a fanciful thought that he was drawing in the wildness of the storm, but that had all been part of the craziness.

"Set aside your disbelief and think about it, Melina. This wasn't the first time it happened. Remember how you felt after we left the bar last week? I had gathered my energy to disable the jukebox and then to overload the lightbulbs in the sign. I realized you picked up on it. You just didn't know what it was."

She rubbed the heels of her hands against her eyes. Her

mind was spinning. Gathering his energy? What on earth was he talking about? His tone was so reasonable, it made what he was saying all the more fantastic.

"You probably felt it the first time we met when I knocked out the transformer in the alley."

"Anthony—"

He caught her wrists and drew her hands away from her face. "You were short of breath. Your pulse accelerated. Your senses felt heightened. Remember?"

Yes, of course she remembered. It had been so strange, so instant, so...inexplicable. She looked at where he gripped her wrists. Something tickled her skin, like a series of tiny shocks.

"What you felt were the physiological side effects of my stray energy," he said. "In certain circumstances, it mimics sexual arousal."

Mimics? There was nothing false about the tingles that were chasing up her arm. She suppressed a shudder. "I don't know why you feel it necessary to come up with a story like that but—"

"It's the truth."

She tugged against his grip. "Let go of me, Anthony."

Rather than releasing her, he guided her to face him and twined his fingers between hers. "Melina, I was born with the ability to manipulate energy fields. I can sense power sources. I can disrupt or reroute electric currents by channeling the energy. I've been doing it since we met. You must have noticed it."

"That's impossible."

"If we were near a phone or some lights I could demonstrate my ability for you, but you've already seen it. Many times. Think, Melina. Use that reporter's brain of yours and put the facts together."

"I am. They don't make sense."

"Does this?" He reversed her hand, lowered his head and dipped his tongue into the center of her palm.

Delight rocketed from her fingers to her toes, setting off bursts of sharp pleasure in every body part along the way. Her heart raced. Her lungs spasmed.

The next thing she knew, she was sitting on his lap, her hands tangled in his thick, glorious gypsy hair. She had no idea how she got there.

He rubbed his hand over her back. "I opened the connection just now. That's what you felt."

She was startled into meeting his gaze. There was a power in the green depths that she hadn't seen before. No, that wasn't quite true. She had caught glimpses of it. Many times. She hadn't seen it fully until lightning had crashed around them and he'd held her in his arms.

I warned you, Melina. Remember that afterward....

That was what he'd told her in the storm. She hadn't understood then. She wasn't sure she did now. Had he *known* she would react that way? Had he realized she would lose control?

She scrambled off him and retreated to the back of the ledge where the overhang was the lowest. Oh, please. Let this be a dream, too.

He twisted as if he was about to follow her, then glanced at the rock that sloped above her head and stayed where he was. "It's a side effect of my talent, Melina. A reaction to the stimulation from stray energy. Don't blame yourself."

"Your talent," she repeated.

"Psychic talent."

"That's only superstition. There's no such thing. I've never seen proof."

He raised one eyebrow. "Do you want another demonstration?"

She didn't know how to reply. Did she honestly not want

to feel pleasure like that again? Side effect or not, what woman in her right mind would complain about stimulation like that?

A woman in her right mind? Was she actually starting to believe this nonsense?

Yet there was no rational explanation for what was happening between them. The feelings couldn't be genuine, could they? They had only known each other for a week.

He'd told her to think. Put the facts together. Yes, that was her job. What she was good at.

But she had trouble thinking about anything when he sat there watching her, his taut, rangy, black-clad body silhouetted against the sunlit valley that stretched beyond the ledge. His midnight hair stirred softly in the breeze, his morning stubble darkened the hollows of his cheeks and accentuated the lean, sexy lines that framed his mouth. His gaze was bold and steady and just a hint wild.

Oh, he was a splendid specimen of a man. There was nothing supernatural about his appeal....

Or was there?

How many times had she sensed something different about him? Leashed power beneath the surface. Shadows that surrounded him. Coincidences. Weird details. Right from the start.

When they had been running from Fredo's killers, Anthony had stopped in the alley and waited, as if he had expected that transformer would explode. And how had he known that live wire would disable the van?

Wasn't it too convenient how the jukebox in the bar had cut out when he'd wanted to speak? And how about the bolt of light from the sign outside that had seemed to be aimed at Kenny?

And why had the lights at the Pecos Lodge dining room flickered when Anthony had been angry?

No, this was crazy. There must be some other explanation that she hadn't yet seen. There was no such thing as psychic power. It was bad enough that Benedict was obsessed with the supernatural….

Melina's spinning thoughts congealed with a thump. She pressed herself hard against the rock at her back. Benedict. He was obsessed with supernatural power. He had chosen his wife and had bred six children for the sole purpose of gaining that power. Melina had thought he was deluded, but what if he was right? *What if he had succeeded?*

She folded her arms over her chest, suddenly chilled. She rocked herself back and forth. On top of everything else, this was too much to take in. The scope was too huge to grasp. "I want to go back to town, Anthony."

"Melina—"

"Now. I need—" Oh, God. She didn't know what she needed. A bath? A toothbrush? A stiff drink? Work. That was it. She would focus on her job. It had gotten her through worse. "I need my computer. I want to do some more research. I'll contact those colleges. We talked about that yesterday."

"You still don't believe me."

"How can I?"

"Why would I lie?"

"Stress? I don't know. None of this makes sense."

"I've told you the truth, Melina."

"If you really have psychic powers, then why go through this charade of searching for Benedict? Why don't you look into a crystal ball or something and *tell* me where he is?"

"My talent doesn't manifest itself that way. All of us have different strengths."

"Us?"

"My sisters have their own talents. Elizabeth is a teleki-netic. Danielle's gift of luck helps her sense potential danger. I don't know what strengths the other triplets have or how well they learned to use them. My talent happens to be energy fields. That's what I was tracing before the storm. I sensed an energy source out here where it shouldn't have been. It could have been Benedict's stronghold."

It was all so fantastic, she didn't know what to deal with first. "I thought you said you saw a light."

"No, I said I caught a flash. I meant energy. You assumed I meant light."

"Really? Then where is it?"

"I'm not sure. I lost the signal."

"How convenient."

"Why are you so angry, Melina?"

Why? Because she would rather be angry than terrified. She had to regain control. Of herself and of her emotions. Of the things she knew were logical and reasonable.

She crept forward until she had enough space to get to her feet without having to duck her head. She busied herself with brushing the dust off her clothes. "We're done here, Anthony. I'm leaving."

He shrugged on his jacket and rose to his feet. He had to move farther toward the rim of the ledge before he could straighten to his full height. "You're right, it's time to go. I'll drive you back to town. I don't want you with me when I fin-ish tracking down that source."

"Finish— Wait a minute. Do you mean you're going to come back here? Without me?"

"Melina, I already put you at more risk than I should have. What happened last night should prove that."

"Well, if you're worried that I'm going to jump you again,

don't be. I'm a logical, rational woman. I have no intention of repeating—"

He caught her by the waist and spun her to his chest.

"Anthony, what are you doing?"

He backed her against the side of the cliff. "Do you hear that?"

All she could hear was the pounding of her pulse. Her forehead nestled under his chin. She inhaled the familiar smell of his neck and her body immediately softened.

"It sounds like a helicopter." He cupped her head, holding her in place.

His touch felt so good, she started to lean into his hand. Damn. She couldn't let this happen again. She bit the inside of her cheek, using the pain to help her concentrate. She heard it then, the chugging of an engine. "Okay, so there's a plane or something. That's no reason to grab me." She brought her palms between them and pushed.

Trying to push Anthony was as useless as trying to push the rock cliff. He didn't move. "It's coming from the northwest," he said. "That's the last place I felt the energy source."

She lifted herself on her toes to look past his shoulder. Metal and glass gleamed in the sunlight. The rhythmic noise of the engine grew louder. A small black helicopter was skimming over the cliff top on the other side of the valley. It was heading toward them. "Let go of me, Anthony," she said through her teeth.

"We'll wait here until they go by. We would be too easy a target if they caught us on the plateau."

"A target? You don't really think it's Benedict, do you? It could be anyone."

He twisted to keep the helicopter in sight as it flew overhead. "There are no markings. Whoever it is couldn't be here on legitimate business."

He was right. The helicopter was low enough for her to see for herself that there were no letters or numbers on the black fuselage. It flew past, the wind from its rotors sending a cloud of grit over them. She ducked her head against Anthony's chest.

"That energy I traced was close," he said. "It felt like less than two miles. I should have realized Benedict would have patrols around the area."

"But there were no lights yesterday. I didn't see any sign of buildings."

The chugging of the helicopter engine dropped suddenly, blocked by the rock, but it didn't disappear. The noise seemed to come from all around them. It was impossible to pinpoint where it had gone.

Anthony stepped away from her and looked over the valley. "We should have started back before this. If they spot the Jeep and come looking—"

He didn't have a chance to finish what he was going to say. The helicopter reappeared, swooping past them from the right so close they could see the rivets in the tail. It made a tight circle over the valley, the bubble-shaped windshield mirroring the sky. It hovered above the slope, the nose swinging back and forth as if it were some monstrous animal that was searching, searching…

Something hit the side of the cliff above them, sending a shower of dust and pebbles over their heads.

Anthony hauled Melina down on the ledge, rolled her onto her stomach and flattened himself on top of her.

Seconds later, the place where they had been standing was hit by a barrage of bullets.

Chapter 8

There was nowhere to run. Bullets whined inches above their heads. Pieces of rock pelted the ledge around them. Melina felt Anthony jerk. She realized some of the debris must be hitting him, yet he remained where he was, spread-eagled on top of her, shielding her with his body. She could do nothing but lie beneath him and pray.

The noise of the helicopter rose in pitch as it drew closer, echoing from the cliff wall, mixing with the sound of wind and the ricocheting bullets. The din was painful.

Anthony moved his head so that his lips were beside her ear. "We'll slide farther back on the ledge. Cut down their angle."

She nodded to show she understood.

"Okay. On three. One."

She braced her palms against the rock.

"Two."

She could feel his body tense. She did the same, drawing in her breath, only to choke on the dust that filled the air. She coughed.

He eased some of his weight to his knees so he could slip one arm around her midriff. "Three!"

Keeping their heads down, they scrambled across the rock until they were deep beneath the overhang. There wasn't enough room for Anthony to lie on top of her. Instead, he quickly rolled her into position so that her back was against the wall, then stretched out alongside her so that he was facing outward.

Melina continued to cough, her eyes watering from the dust and grit from the wind of the helicopter's rotors.

"Use your jacket to breathe through," he shouted. "It will filter the dirt."

She dipped her head and grasped the collar of her jacket to yank it over her nose. It helped. The coughing eased. But she still couldn't get enough air. It wasn't the dust as much as the shock.

They were being shot at. Why? By whom?

There was only one answer. Who else but Benedict would dare to act this way? He was ruthless. He wouldn't hesitate to have his men shoot first and ask questions later if someone strayed too close. That was what had happened a week ago in Santa Fe.

But she and Anthony were in the middle of nowhere. They had traveled the area for almost a week and hadn't found a trace of Benedict. This was too improbable, too much of a coincidence. How could they have stumbled onto his location by chance?

Yet Anthony claimed it hadn't been by chance. He had led them here. He had sensed an energy source and had followed it.

Oh, God. She couldn't think about that now.

The gunfire abruptly ceased. The helicopter's engine screamed closer.

"They can't see us anymore," Anthony said. "They're moving in to take a closer look."

With the rock behind her and Anthony lying in front of her, Melina was protected for the moment, but she knew he wasn't. She shoved at his back. "We should make a run for it."

"Don't move."

"But if we stay we'll be trapped here."

"Wait."

She could feel tension hum through his body as he held himself completely motionless. A tremor traveled from his back to her palms. She felt a surge of power, as if she were being sucked into the wind that battered them.

The sound of the helicopter changed. The rhythmic thump of the rotors sputtered.

Melina slid her arm around Anthony's waist and pressed herself full-length against him, her knees behind his thighs, her breasts flattened against his back and her forehead rubbing his hair. She couldn't stop herself. She needed to hold him. She felt…connected.

There was another surge, like a wave lifting her up, carrying her forward. She slipped her hand past the edge of his jacket and splayed her fingers over his chest. His heart beat hard beneath her palm. "Anthony?"

He covered her hand with his and squeezed hard. His palm was sweating yet his fingers were ice cold. "Wait," he repeated.

She heard the helicopter sputter again. The noise that battered her eardrums strengthened. She flexed her jaw to ease the pressure and hung on to Anthony's solid form. The wave continued to build. It was frightening and exhilarating and eerily familiar. "Anthony!"

His chest heaved. Melina felt a sensation of release flash through her. It wasn't sexual. It wasn't even physical. It was on a deeper, more intimate level, on a plane she hadn't known existed.

The sound of the engine cut out, leaving nothing but its echoes and the whistle of the rotors as they sliced the air. The silence lasted no more than a few seconds before the engine roared back to life. The sputter was more pronounced, like a rhythm knocked out of sequence.

The pitch dropped, falling away quickly as if the helicopter was retreating. Melina held her breath, not daring to hope. Could their attackers have given up? The noise continued to diminish until she was able to hear other sounds, the screech of a hawk, the sigh of the wind and the harsh rasp of Anthony's breathing.

She lifted her head, squinting past him through the settling dust. The slice of sky she could see beyond the ledge seemed overly bright. And blessedly empty.

The unexpectedness of the attack left her stunned. So did the sudden way it had stopped. It had seemed to go on forever, but in her head Melina knew the whole event couldn't have lasted more than a few minutes.

Her heart still pounded. Her senses felt heightened. She felt sparks of awareness along every inch of her skin. Now that the danger was over, reaction was setting in.

You felt...side effects of my stray energy.... It mimics sexual arousal.

Anthony's energy. His psychic energy.

"Melina," he said. His voice was hoarse. "Are you okay?"

She pressed her face to his hair. She could smell the dust that had showered them when he'd been lying on top of her.

Her cheek brushed a chip of rock that was held by a tangle at the back of his neck. This was the second time he had saved her life. "I'm fine, you made sure of that. What about you?"

"I'm all right."

"What do you think happened to the helicopter? It sounded as if they had engine trouble."

"It was their fuel pump. It's electronic." He paused. He sounded out of breath. "I couldn't disable it, only disrupted the circuit, but it bought us some time."

The helicopter was a faint, sputtering buzz in the distance now. It was definitely going away. Whatever Anthony had done had worked.

Whatever *he* had done?

But that was impossible, right? He had no tools or weapons. He couldn't have affected anything on that aircraft from here. There must be some other explanation. Maybe the dust the rotor blades had stirred up had been sucked into the engine. Or maybe they had run low on fuel.

Then why had Anthony told her to wait? He had known something would happen. And what about that wave of…power she had felt?

When did skepticism cross the line to denial?

Anthony rolled away, then glanced at the rock overhead. A film of moisture gleamed on his forehead. He clenched his jaw and reached back to catch her hands. "We don't have much time," he said, tugging her out from beneath the overhang. "I wasn't able to short out the radio."

She moved on her knees toward him. Short out the radio. Of course. That would have been another option for someone with the psychic power to manipulate energy fields. Had he used up all his strength wrecking the helicopter's fuel pump? Was that why his hands were cold and his forehead was sweating?

"Benedict's going to send reinforcements." Anthony rocked back on his heels and cupped her elbow. "We have to get to the Jeep and get out of here."

She nodded as he helped her to stand. Right. Benedict would be nearby. Less than two miles to the northwest, according to Anthony's psychic ability. The energy source that he had traced probably powered Benedict's new stronghold. It would be prudent for her and Anthony to retreat before someone else found them.

Melina looked at the bullet-scarred rock and started to tremble. She clenched her hands, trying to stop the cascade of thoughts. She couldn't. They all fit. The truth was right in front of her.

Anthony hadn't lied to her. On some level, she had known that all along. That was the source of those gut feelings she'd been having right from the start. That was why she didn't fear him, and why she had believed all the other things he had told her. His energy, his power, his *difference*…all of it had been obvious for days. She hadn't wanted to admit it. Why not?

Because she liked being able to verify facts. She liked translating everything into black and white. It was the best way to deal with the illogical, irrational, unreasonable feelings that she had managed to avoid for years.

It was so much safer to love her job than to trust her heart.

Things were going well, Anthony told himself as he fisted the towel to swipe the haze off the mirror. He flung the towel over the shower curtain rod, clattering the rings. He should be grateful that Melina was handling his revelations as well as she was. It looked as if she had taken his advice and was thinking like a reporter. She was demonstrating the strength and intelligence he had come to admire. Despite the shocks she had been through, she had managed to regain control of herself and her emotions before they had been halfway back to Antelope Ridge. With her hands clenched tightly in her lap and her jaw set, she had looked just like she had on the night they had met.

He yanked his hair back from his face. The elastic band he used pulled out a dozen wet strands. He clenched his teeth and picked up his can of shaving cream. Yes, Melina had taken the news of his psychic abilities—and their side effects—better than he could have hoped.

Once she had set aside her initial skepticism, she had turned all business. She completely ignored the sexual pull between them and didn't refer once to the intimacy they had shared. He was certain she wasn't as calm inside as she appeared on the surface, yet she hadn't spoken of anything personal for the rest of the day. Instead, she had stuck to the only issue that mattered to her—her story about Benedict.

He should be pleased, he reminded himself as he slapped shaving cream on his cheeks. This was what he wanted. This was why they were together in the first place. It could have become a lot more complicated if Melina hadn't calmed down enough to regard things logically. In fact, she was as focused on her priorities as he was.

Right. Fine. So he was pleased.

He picked up his razor and yanked it along his jaw, hard enough to nick his skin. Blood welled up in a neat triangle and dripped down his chin.

Anthony threw the razor into the sink and met his gaze in the mirror. He wasn't pleased. He was annoyed as hell. He knew he shouldn't be, and that only made it worse.

Now, more than ever, he felt cheated. He still wanted her. How could he make civilized conversation when he'd felt her climax in his arms? How could he look at her speak when he remembered the taste of her mouth and wanted to kiss her until their passion stirred again?

But that wasn't what he was here for, what either of them was here for. He'd had his chance. He'd let it pass. He should be preparing for the next step. His own desires were immaterial. He was too close to success to risk letting anything interfere with what he had to do.

Anthony blotted his chin, finished shaving and put on his work clothes. He gathered the equipment he would need for the night ahead and stored it in a backpack, then went to look for Melina.

She was alone on the patio behind the guest dining room. She stood near the wrought-iron fence, her back to the doors, her face lifted to the setting sun and her hair streaming over her shoulders like molten bronze. Anthony paused with his hand on the knob of the terrace door to look at her, and he was jolted by a wave of longing so strong it stole his breath.

It was the connection, that was all. Now that it had been opened, it was damn hard to close. It was impossible to pretend it wasn't there.

But he wasn't going to let it stop him again.

The breeze was turning cool. Shadows were creeping over the patio. Melina curled her fingers around the fence and pressed the phone to her ear. If she gave herself more time, she would probably be able to come up with a gentler way to do this, but she had waited long enough. This had to be done. It should have been done sooner. "My answer is no, Neil."

"You don't sound like yourself, Melina. Are you sure you're all right?"

No, she wasn't all right. She probably wouldn't feel the same again. Her whole view of reality was undergoing a fundamental shift. The paranormal was real. Psychic powers were possible. Her rational beliefs of a lifetime had been blown apart.

What else had she been wrong about?

Now, more than ever, she needed to regain control somehow. "Please, don't change the subject. I'm trying to do the decent thing here."

The phone crackled. "If I've been pressuring you, I'm sorry. If you need more time to think—"

"I've already taken more time than I should have, Neil. It wasn't fair to keep you on hold for so long."

"I wasn't going anywhere."

Neither were we, she thought. She closed her eyes and pinched the bridge of her nose, trying to stem the tears. She didn't know why she felt like crying. She had been wrong to consider Neil's proposal. She had never been emotionally committed to him. For eight years she hadn't committed herself to anyone. She hadn't allowed herself to get close enough to anyone to release her passion.

Not willingly, anyway.

It was the storm. The energy in the lightning. That's what you felt. It was out of your control.

"I'm sorry, Neil," she said. "You were partly right, you know. I have been using this story as an excuse to keep traveling."

"What happened, Melina?"

That wasn't a simple question to answer. She was still trying to sort through it all herself. "I had to straighten out my priorities, decide what I really wanted."

"And did you?"

"Yes. That's why my answer is no."

"Melina…"

"Neil, I respect you as my editor, and we get along well as friends. Let's not lose that, okay?"

A burst of static drowned out his reply.

Melina moved a few feet to her left, trying to find better reception. She had come outside because of the static in her room. Now it was starting up here. "Neil?"

"I feel as if I should be getting angry or something, but I'm not," he said. "I must be getting used to you turning me down."

"I'm sorry."

"Is it really no this time?" His voice tangled with more static. She wiped her cheek. "It's really no."

"Okay."

Her chin trembled, whether from a laugh or a sob she didn't know. His calm acceptance of her rejection was exactly in character. It was why she liked him. It was why this was the right thing to do.

He didn't love her. He had never claimed to. His proposal had grown out of their friendship, and his realization that he had reached middle age and had been so focused on his career that he had neglected to have a family.

He was a nice man, a good man. Now that she had set him free, he was bound to find someone else.

There was a series of loud crackles.

She put her finger over her ear. "Neil? I can hardly hear you."

"Does this...finished with...Titan story?"

"Titan? Not yet. I'm too close to—" She paused. "Neil?"

A loud hiss came through the receiver. A second later the signal went dead. She looked at her phone. The battery indicator wasn't low. Why would it cut out that way? The back of her neck prickled. She turned around.

Anthony was standing beside the patio doors, his arms crossed, his legs braced apart. He was dressed in a body-hugging black turtleneck and black pants that made him look wickedly dangerous. His hair was damp and slicked tight to his head, accentuating the lean angles of his face. The skin on his jaw gleamed from a fresh shave. His green gaze was so vivid, she could feel it touch her across the distance between them.

Awareness tingled down her spine, quick and carnal. Her breasts tightened, her lips parted. She swayed, her phone slipping from her fingers.

The noise of the phone hitting the brick patio snapped her out of the haze before it could deepen. Wait. That awareness. Had it been enhanced? Had it been a side effect of Anthony's power? She grabbed the fence behind her for support and looked from her phone to Anthony. She thought of the static. The dropped signal. Cell phones used electromagnetic waves. "Did you do that?" she demanded.

He uncrossed his arms and walked toward her. A black backpack dangled by one strap from his hand. He hitched the strap over his shoulder, then picked up her phone, checked to see if it still worked and switched it off. "Do what?"

"You cut off my phone."

"Yes."

She caught a whiff of his soap. She thought of the way his neck smelled, and her pulse tripped. She told herself to ignore it. This was probably due to some stray energy. "Why? You have no right—"

"I told you already, Melina. I'll do whatever is necessary to make sure you're safe." He turned, giving the area around the patio a thorough survey. There was a small nick on his jaw where he had likely cut himself shaving. "You can't let anyone know we're close to Benedict."

"I was talking to my editor."

"I figured that. Your conversation looked intense. Are you okay?"

"I'm always intense about my work."

He held out her phone. "You can't tell him anything."

She took her phone and slid it into her jacket pocket. "I wasn't planning to. Not until I finish my story and call in the FBI. What's in your pack?"

"Just some supplies."

"You're going back to that valley to look for Benedict's stronghold, aren't you?"

He hesitated for a beat. "Yes."

"Not without me."

"Melina, it could be dangerous. Benedict's people spotted us this morning and are going to be on the alert."

"It's even more dangerous for you. You told me Benedict's after your entire family because of your powers. If he discovered you're nearby, you would be handing yourself to him on a platter."

"If he learned who I am, the worst he would do is capture me. He would kill you."

"Don't ask me to stay behind, Anthony. Especially not now. I *need* my work." Now that she had broken up with Neil, she thought, it was all she had left.

"I'll take the Jeep as close as I can, but I'll be hiking the rest of the way on foot. It's going to be rough."

"If you try to leave without me, I'll rent a truck and follow you, anyway. You know I will."

"Yes, I figured that, too. You haven't taken my advice yet."

I warned you. Remember that…. Melina pressed her lips together. There was no chance of her forgetting.

He tilted his head, continuing to watch her, then lifted his hand to her face. He rubbed her cheek with his knuckle. "Why were you crying, Melina?"

The change of topic took her off guard. She had hoped he hadn't noticed, but she should have known nothing would get by him. "The breeze is cold."

He dried her other cheek and smoothed her hair behind her ear. "Did your editor say something to upset you?"

It was hard to keep her mind on the conversation when all she wanted to do was lean into his touch. She wanted to soothe her fingers over that nick in his jaw. He had gentle hands for a large man. Wonderful hands and clever fingers that had worked such magic.

No. It had been a reaction to the lightning, she reminded herself. Anthony had made that perfectly clear. "It was the other way around. He's the one who should have been upset."

"Why?"

"I turned down his marriage proposal."

Anthony caught her chin. "He asked you to marry him? When?"

"Months ago. Considering everything that's happened, I owed him an answer."

He stared at her, an odd, almost eager expression on his face. "Did you turn him down because of me, Melina?"

What could she say? That she couldn't contemplate the prospect of letting anyone else touch her after what she had experienced with Anthony? Should she tell him that those few hours from the night before had probably ruined her for any kind of intimacy with an ordinary man? His hand on her chin was sending tingles through her body. Just the scent of his soap made her knees weak.

Or should she tell him the rest of the truth? That she was scared, confused, and more determined than ever to keep her feelings under control.

She tipped her head away from his hand. "I had already made my decision before we got caught in the storm."

He grasped the top of the fence, beside her waist. "I remember now. That must have been what you were thinking about in the Jeep when you talked about your heart's desire."

"That's right. I realized then that it's my work that I love. I don't want to marry anyone."

"Did you love him?"

She started to ease to the side. "I liked him as a friend."

He put his other hand on the fence, pinning her between his arms. "Then why did you take months to say no?"

Why? Because she had been deluding herself. She had thought that after eight years she might have healed enough to take another risk, and it was safe to take a chance with Neil because he didn't have her heart.

"Are you sure this has nothing to do with our connection?"

With Anthony's arms on either side of her, she felt enveloped by his strength. Protected. But not safe. No, this man was anything but safe. Tears threatened again. "Why should it? You explained that what happened between us was only a physiological side effect of your talent."

"Yes, that's what I said."

"You told me I wasn't responsible. You said it was out of my control."

His leg nudged hers. "Right."

She counted to ten as she tried not to sway into him. "It must be inconvenient."

"What?"

"Triggering a reaction like that with any woman who's nearby whenever you use your talent."

"It doesn't happen every time. And it doesn't happen with every woman."

She looked at his mouth. Her lips tingled. "No?"

"No, Melina." His knee brushed her thigh. "And it has never been as strong as what happened last night."

"Why…" She had to clear her throat. "Why do you think that is?"

"I don't know." He lowered his head, stopping with his mouth a breath from hers. "I wish we had the time to figure it out."

Was he going to kiss her? Did she want him to? No! Yes! Damn, she didn't know what she felt. Was this real?

And did she want it to be?

He pushed away from the fence and stepped back. "But we don't have time, Melina. I plan to be back at that canyon before moonrise. If you want to come with me, you have twenty minutes to get ready."

The conference room in Benedict's headquarters was modeled on the one he had studied years ago at his sister's complex in Oregon. The walls were bare steel that was riveted to layers of concrete and lead sheeting to guard against electronic eavesdropping. The lighting was dim, save for the pools of illumination over each chair that flanked the oval table. The only way in or out was through a private elevator that was keyed by Benedict's thumbprint.

Agnes had been a conceited bitch, but she had understood about power. Yes, she knew how lighting could be used to dramatic effect, and she realized how the echo from the steel walls would lend extra impact to her words. She was smart, no question about that, but not smart enough to stay alive. The law had caught up with her.

She hadn't seen it coming.

Benedict gripped the edge of the table. He wasn't going to share his sister's fate. He almost wished she was still alive just so he could show her. Then she would be the one who had to be grateful to him. Maybe he'd throw her a bone, find her a job to do here, remind her every day that she had been wrong, that he wasn't a failure, that he wasn't the screwup she had always called him.

"We powered up the incubators in the new lab yesterday, Mr. Titan. The backup generator tested out fine. The rest of the equipment should be fully operational by next month."

Benedict swiveled his chair toward the man who had spoken. He was small, bald and had an irritating habit of thrusting out his chin to chew his upper lip. He was one of the junior scientists who had been part of the team Benedict had brought over from Europe. He'd gained his current position in Benedict's inner circle by default, when his predecessor had been killed. "Not good enough, Dr. McNair. It must be ready within the week."

"Impossible. It will take at least two weeks to calibrate the instruments properly."

"Don't tell me it's impossible." Benedict slammed his palms on the table. The noise echoed from the walls like a gunshot. "I've waited more than thirty years for this. I advise you not to try my patience. You, too, can be replaced."

McNair tugged at the lapel of his white lab coat, then shuffled the papers that were on the table in front of him. "I'll redouble my efforts."

"See that you do." He swiveled his chair to the right. "Gus, how are security operations going?"

Gus rubbed his eyebrow, his gaze darting to the floor. "The gadgets are running good, but we could use an extra shift on the surface patrols. We've been shorthanded since last month."

Benedict scowled. He didn't like being reminded how many men he had lost to the FBI's raids. He didn't like the way Gus kept stroking that singed eyebrow of his, either. Why was everyone deliberately irritating him? "Then you should be joining the patrol yourself instead of whining about it. You're not having problems, are you? Was there a security breach?"

"No, no, it's going okay. No problem. The helicopter team spotted two trespassers this morning but they scared them off before they got near the perimeter."

"Where did they go?"

"The chopper had engine trouble and had to come back for repairs. By the time they got back there, the campers were gone."

"Campers?"

"From what I heard, they were a couple of Indians."

Benedict's scowl deepened. Since when did Indians go camping? They didn't need to get back to the land, they *lived* on the land. Could they have been spying? Perhaps they had been hoping to shake him down for a better deal.

He wasn't on Indian land. The nearest settlement, the Antelope Pueblo, was miles to the south. He'd encountered some resistance from a few of the tribe members when he'd started construction here, but that had been easily resolved. He had used the formula that always worked for him in the past: bribe those individuals who could be bought, eliminate those who couldn't. It hadn't been that difficult, since even the ones who were paid to keep their mouths shut had only seen what he wanted them to see.

He waved his hand toward the monitor that hung over the center of the table. "Show me the video from the helicopter," he ordered.

The image that appeared on the screen several minutes later was blurred by motion. Two figures stood on a ledge near the top of the cliff to the southeast. A man and a woman. He appeared to be holding her in his arms. The next view was closer. The couple was visible only for a few seconds before they dove for cover.

Benedict snapped his fingers. "Replay that!"

A man and a woman. He was holding her in his arms. She

had red hair. He had long black hair like an Indian, all right, but he appeared taller than the average native and—*What was that glint at his ear?*

Benedict's mouth went dry. Could it be? He shoved his chair back, got to his feet and leaned over the table. "Again! Slower this time."

The images unfolded in slow motion. He watched the couple dive. He saw the rock crumble under the force of the gunfire. "Who gave the order to shoot?"

"You did, sir. You told us to shoot any trespassers and get rid of the bodies."

"Well, I didn't tell you to shoot *them,* you incompetent bastard!" He strode down the table to where Gus sat, grabbed the back of his chair and spun him around. "Don't you recognize who they are?"

Gus twisted to look at the monitor, his hand stealing to his eyebrow.

At the gesture, Benedict's temper snapped. He backhanded Gus across the jaw, knocking him to the floor. "That's my son and the Becker woman. I've been waiting for them."

Gus got to his knees. Blood welled from a split in his lower lip. He blinked blearily. "But last week you wanted Habib and me to kill that reporter."

"Don't contradict me! I realized I have a use for her, too. Get Habib to enlarge those frames and pass the pictures to everyone on security. These two are not to be harmed."

"Yes, sir."

Benedict stepped back before any of Gus's blood could drip on his shoes. "Have everyone double their efforts on my monitoring network. The next time the woman is located, bring her directly to me. There will be a bonus for the man who carries out this order. I always reward loyalty."

Gus staggered to his feet. He pressed his mouth against his

sleeve and nodded. "What about your son? Don't you want him, too?"

Benedict shook out his knuckles, trying to ease the sting from the blow he'd been forced to give Gus. "Do I have to do all your thinking? She's the weak link. Get her, and we get him. Dr. McNair!"

"Yes, Mr. Titan?"

"Is the guest chamber ready?"

"That isn't really my department. The construction—"

"Are you contradicting me, too?"

McNair glanced at Gus and looked quickly away. "No, sir. I, uh, believe the chamber beside your sanctum was completed before the lab was. Because of your specifications, it was relatively simple to construct."

Benedict nodded with satisfaction, his mood instantly improved. He ended the meeting, walked to the elevator and pressed his thumb to the small lighted pad to activate the controls. As soon as his men had filed out, he returned to his place at the table.

The blurred image of Anthony and the red-haired reporter was frozen on the monitor. Anthony was holding her to his chest, his stance protective. Yes, there would be a use for that woman, Benedict thought. He slid his thumb into the groove between his first two fingers, rubbing rhythmically in and out.

The psychic power of this place was even greater than he had thought.

How much greater would it be once he added the power of his oldest son?

Chapter 9

Anthony sensed the motion detector a split second before Melina would have broken the beam. He grabbed her by the waist and yanked her backward. "Hold it," he whispered.

To her credit, she didn't make a sound. Off balance, with her shoulder against his chest and her weight on one foot, she froze.

Anthony looked around, trying to spot what he had sensed. Through the ghostly green images of his night vision goggles, he saw the detector was less than a yard away, concealed in a fissure in the side of the cliff and aimed across the only clear path through this winding section of the valley floor. It was powered by a low-voltage battery, so it took little effort for Anthony to reroute the circuit back on itself, rendering it useless without breaking the signal.

This was the eighth one they had encountered since they had descended from the ledge where they had spent the previous night. Like the others, it was linked to a live camera. Whoever monitored the security system would be able to tell if the alarm was triggered by a human intruder or by an animal or a stray leaf blowing across the beam. Anthony probed for the camera and found it nestled beside a rock above the motion detector.

He put his mouth beside Melina's ear. "I'll interrupt the video signal for ten seconds to get us out of range. On the count of three. Ready?"

She shivered, her hair brushing his cheek. Her body tensed as he counted. When he reached three, she sprang into action with him, sprinting to the far side of a group of boulders that loomed to their right. "Are we clear?" she asked.

He paused as he opened his mind to check the area. There was nothing, only the sigh of the breeze and the distant howl of a coyote. Moonlight flowed over the canyon rim here, making the goggles unnecessary. He pulled them off to allow his vision to adjust. "Yes, we're clear."

"This is incredible," she said, moving next to him. She had changed into dark clothes before they had left town, so she blended into the shadows almost as well as he did. "It looks empty, but the whole valley must be wired for intruders. We have to be on the right track. How far do you think we've come?"

He checked the display on the GPS unit he had clipped to his belt. "A little over a mile." He slipped his pack from his shoulders, stored his goggles and withdrew a bottle of water. The going had been difficult since they had left the Jeep, but Melina hadn't complained. She hadn't held him up, either. As much as he would have preferred to leave her behind for safety's sake, he couldn't help admiring her determination. He offered her the water bottle.

"Thanks." She took a drink as she looked around. The vapor from her breath floated palely past her cheek. "There must be another way in, Anthony. I can't see Benedict doing this route on foot."

"He could be travelling by air."

"By helicopter?"

"Or by plane if he has a landing strip. It wouldn't be difficult to build a runway on one of these flat-topped mesas. We're going in the hard way because when I scout a location, I prefer to go by ground. There's less chance of detection."

"Only for someone with your talent." She leaned against the nearest boulder. "Being able to sense the detectors before they sense you must come in useful with that troubleshooting work you do for Jeremy Solienti."

"It does."

"You mentioned your sisters had talents, too. What was it you said, telekinesis and luck?"

Even though Anthony was impatient to keep going, he heard the fatigue in Melina's voice and realized she needed to have a break before they started off again. Indulging her curiosity would provide her with an excuse to rest. "That's right. With Elizabeth's ability to manipulate small objects, there wasn't a lock she couldn't open."

"And with Danielle's luck, you wouldn't have been caught. Not that you were doing anything illegal," she added.

"No more illegal than what we're doing now. We used to be an unbeatable team before Danielle moved away."

"I'm sorry, Anthony. I didn't mean to bring up your estrangement. It must hurt."

"It doesn't matter."

"Your feelings are immaterial, right?"

"Of course they are."

She looked at him for a minute, then shook her head and paused to take another drink. "How did you start working for Jeremy, anyway?"

pick up his pack instead. A moonlit-silver cliff jutted into the valley ahead of them. "There," he said.

Twenty minutes later they had reached a small, brush-covered rise at the base of the cliff. The bite of diesel fumes tainted the air. A glow of light came from the other side of the rise. The hum of power was audible now, yet it didn't seem right somehow. Anthony motioned Melina to stay where she was. The slope was lined with vibration sensors. He disabled them carefully, then took his binoculars from his pack and worked his way to the top of the rise.

Against the backdrop of the night-shrouded valley on one side and the looming cliff on the other, the scene that stretched before him seemed surreal. Two banks of floodlights set on tripods illuminated an area of the valley floor half the size of a football field. Power lines ran from the lights to a generator—was that the source of the hum he had heard? There was a small, metal shed, some portable toilets and three boxy trailers like the kind used on construction sites, but there were no pieces of construction equipment, no dump trucks or pickups. The only vehicle in sight was a black helicopter. It had no markings on the side.

"That looks like the helicopter that attacked us."

At Melina's whisper, Anthony lowered the binoculars. He should have known she wouldn't stay behind. She never did. "Yes."

She crouched beside him where he knelt behind the cover of a creosote bush. "Those trailers couldn't be Benedict's stronghold."

"I agree. There must be more to it than this."

The door of the nearest trailer opened. Anthony grabbed Melina and yanked her flat on the ground with him just as two men stepped out. One paused to light a cigarette while the other hitched the strap of a rifle over his shoulder and set off along the edge of the lighted area. A few moments later the second man walked in the opposite direction. Guards, Anthony thought, taking note of their routes.

"That man with the cigarette," Melina whispered. "I think I recognize him."

"Who is he?"

"He looks like the man who was in the passenger seat of the van the night Fredo was killed. He was the one firing at us."

Anthony adjusted the focus of the binoculars. The guard was a heavyset man with prominent jowls. "He's missing an eyebrow. It could have been burned off."

"Okay, so those trailers *must* be connected to Benedict," Melina said. "Do you think he just hasn't built the place yet?"

"He's had months. It would be finished."

"Are you still feeling that energy source?"

"It's stronger than ever. The generator that's powering the lights is too small. The real source is deeper. It feels as if it's coming more from that direction," he said, gesturing toward the wall of rock on their right.

"None of this makes sense. Why would anyone…" Her words trailed off. She caught his arm. "Anthony, what's that on the side of the cliff?"

He rolled to his side and tilted the binoculars upward. The cliff rose smoothly until it curved inward about two-thirds of the way from the ground, forming an enormous shadowed pocket that was covered by a lip of overhanging rock. It was like a giant version of the shallow cave that had sheltered him and Melina the night before.

Yet the shadows weren't empty. There were shapes on the ledge, shapes with square corners and straight edges that seemed to grow from the rock itself.

Too many feelings crashed over Anthony at once. Excitement, anger, dread, rage. And propelling them all, there was an overwhelming sense of purpose. Yes. *Yes!* After months of frustration, after years of waiting, the time had come. Without looking further, he *knew.*

This was it. His search was over.

"Oh, good God," Melina whispered. "Is that what I think it is?"

Anthony passed her the binoculars, his throat too tight for words.

Their theory had been right. Benedict had been drawn here because he wanted the mystical power from Indian artifacts.

They just hadn't guessed how big the artifact was.

The Anasazi village was a marvel of ancient engineering, designed for defense, constructed of sandstone slabs held together with mud, hundreds of feet up the side of the cliff. Seven centuries ago, it would have served as a fortress, sheltering an entire community from whatever danger prowled the valley floor.

Melina had read that there were thousands of sites like this scattered throughout Colorado and New Mexico. Little was known of the people who had built them. They had vanished mysteriously, abandoning their painstakingly built cliff cities to the ravages of time. They were called the Anasazi, a Navajo word meaning "ancient enemies," yet to their Pueblo descendants, they were known simply as The Old Ones.

A shiver went through her as she lowered the binoculars. Now that she had stopped moving, the chill of the night was catching up to her. Yet the chill was from more than that. It seemed that just when she thought the scope of Benedict's crimes couldn't get any bigger, it did. Only he would have the audacity to exploit something like this treasure. Despite its crumbling walls, the place projected a sense of power through its very age. It should be preserved. It should be respected.

Instead, its purpose had been perverted. It was serving as a cover, as window dressing, to hide a criminal's headquarters.

He's in plain sight, but even if you look, you won't see him.

Poor Fredo. Now she understood what he had meant. Benedict had camouflaged his stronghold brilliantly. Melina shifted onto her stomach and turned the binoculars to the floodlit area at the base of the cliff. There was an area of neatly dug shallow pits and piles of dirt near the trailers. It was crisscrossed with a grid made of posts and strings. There were even a few scattered shovels and sieves made of wire mesh nearby, as if someone were excavating a genuine archeological site.

That was probably how Benedict had kept his construction under the radar. He could have ferried in his supplies by air, relying on the site's isolation and his security patrols to keep unwanted visitors away while the stronghold was being built. He could even claim his guards were there to protect the archeological site from looters. And if any authorities should question him, he likely had all the proper permits to justify his presence.

No one would realize there was anything *within* the cliff. No one, that is, except someone with the ability to sense the electricity that powered it. Anthony speculated there was probably a natural cavern system that extended into the cliff behind the village. A large complex of rooms could have been constructed there with only minimal excavation. He had sounded strained when he'd told her. Was he concerned that Benedict might be able to get away?

She should reassure him that her contact at the FBI wanted Titan as much as Anthony did. Liam Brooks had dedicated years to pursuing the man. Once she told Liam where Benedict was hiding—and she wasn't going to let any receptionist put her on hold next time she called—he had the clout to make it, well, a federal case. The FBI had the resources to surround this entire valley. No matter how big the cavern system was, they would eventually hunt Benedict down.

Melina set down the binoculars to study the man beside her. For the past ten minutes Anthony hadn't moved. Not physically, anyway. Yet he was far from still. The energy that always pulsed through him was closer to the surface than she had ever seen it. His body was snapping with tension like a spring being coiled.

What must be going through his head? she wondered. Was he thinking about his family, about the suffering Benedict's actions had brought on them all? Was he envisioning Benedict finally behind bars where he could do no more harm?

She felt a lump in her throat. Anthony had been so matter-of-fact when he'd related that horror story from his childhood, it had been all the more heartbreaking. His strength was amazing, as was his resilience. He hadn't needed to say it in so many words, but his love for his sisters was obvious. Melina had seen it each time he mentioned his family. His wasn't a showy kind of love; it was a bone-deep devotion that colored everything he did.

What would it be like to be loved like that?

As if he felt her gaze on him, he turned his head to look at her.

The fury in his eyes took her off guard. It was naked violence on the edge of exploding.

Instead of being afraid, she felt more than ever like crying. There was so much anger inside him, and it was all linked to Benedict. It was so unfair. A man with Anthony's deep passion would have so much love to give.

He motioned behind them with his head. "It's time to go, Melina."

She nodded. He'd already warned her that it would be safest if they were out of the valley by daylight. Besides, there was no need to stay longer. They had gotten what they'd come for. They knew where Benedict's stronghold was. According to Fredo, Benedict was too paranoid now to leave it. The man known as Titan, who was wanted by every law enforcement agency in the world, was at this moment only a few hundred yards from this spot.

This was what she and Anthony had set out to do a week ago. This was the reason for their partnership.

It was almost over.

She should be pleased.

She was going to get the story of a lifetime.

"This is for your story," Anthony said, switching on a light as he walked into her room. He tossed a thick brown envelope on the bed.

Melina closed the door behind him and followed him to the bed. She folded one leg underneath her as she sat on the edge of the mattress. She reached out to pick it up. "What is it?" she asked, picking up the envelope.

"My files."

It took her a moment to register what he had said. She was still groggy from sleep. She had been so exhausted she hadn't bothered undressing when she had reached her room after they had returned from their scouting trip this morning. It seemed as if she had just toed off her sneakers and fallen into bed when Anthony's knock on her door had awakened her. But the sky outside her window was black. Night had already fallen. She had slept the entire day.

She yawned as she turned the envelope over in her hands. "What files?"

"The records from the fertility clinic and Benedict's notes."

The grogginess fled. Her jaw snapped shut in midyawn. She lifted the flap of the envelope and looked inside. There was a faded yellow file folder that was stuffed with sheets of paper. "Benedict's handwritten notes?"

"Yes." He crossed the room to her window and pulled the curtains closed. He switched on another light.

"Anthony, this is…" She didn't have a word that was adequate. Even without this, she had the scoop to end all scoops. But having these documents was like hitting a journalistic mother lode.

He dropped a floppy disk beside her knee. "Here are some computer files I acquired a few months ago during my last job for Jeremy. They were encrypted, but I managed to decode a small fraction of them. They appear to deal mostly with Benedict's sister Agnes's work, but I couldn't decipher any details."

She glanced at the disk, her pulse racing. "Why are you giving all this to me now?"

"Now that we've found Benedict, I have no more use for this material."

"Why don't you give it to the police yourself? This is evidence."

"My deal was with you, not the police."

"Your deal."

"We agreed to share our information. You kept your half of the bargain. Now I'm keeping mine."

She set the envelope down and got to her feet. She straightened her sweater and brushed at the lingering dust on her pants. She raked a hand through her hair. It was hopelessly tangled. She wished she'd had the presence of mind to clean up before she had let him in. Vain as it was, she didn't want him to remember her this way.

But then, he'd seen her at her worst, when she had been hurting and desperate and crawling over him for relief. It shouldn't matter if he saw a few sleep wrinkles now. She was only thinking about this because it was far easier to focus on the mess she was outside instead of the train wreck that was happening inside.

All right. She had known this was coming the moment Anthony had traced that energy source to the Anasazi village. He was dissolving their partnership.

Couldn't they at least have discussed it first?

Well, why should they? How many times had they both made it clear that Benedict was all they were after?

There. Logical and reasonable. No need to feel upset. This was exactly what she had wanted, the story that would make her career.

"Thank you," she said. "This is more than I could have imagined."

"You worked hard. You deserve to get what you wanted."

"You do too, Anthony. It's only a matter of time now before Benedict is arrested." She hesitated. "But I haven't called anyone yet."

"I know."

Of course, he would know. If he had been anywhere nearby, he would have been able to sense the phone signal as soon as she dialed.

Then why hadn't she done it? Why had she delayed making that phone call? Every minute she postponed it increased the possibility of someone else breaking the story.

Yet once the authorities got involved, she would be swept into the madhouse of deadlines and official statements and scrambling to file copy while it was still hot. And she would have to say goodbye to Anthony.

Was that the real reason she had gone to sleep this morning instead of typing up the first draft of her story? Oh, God. She really was a mess.

"About the cops, Melina," he began.

"I've been thinking about that," she said. "I can't risk calling the Antelope Ridge sheriff, not with the Titan Syndicate's record of corruption. Benedict must have somebody local on his payroll or he couldn't have stayed out of sight so long."

"I agree. He likely bribed some people at the Antelope Pueblo, too. They must have been paid to keep quiet about his phony dig site. Trusting anyone local is out of the question."

"I think it would be best if I went through my contact at the FBI. I trust him."

He looked at her in silence, his jaw twitching with tension. He paced across the room, pivoted and came back to stand at the foot of her bed. He reached into his pants pocket and took out a folded piece of paper. "Here are the coordinates of the site I got from my GPS unit. Make sure you give them to the FBI when you call. I've also marked on our map the route we took."

She took the paper and slipped it into her own pocket. "It would be easier if I guided them myself."

He grabbed her shoulders and jerked her to face him. "No. Absolutely not. I don't want you going back to that valley under any circumstances."

It would be simpler if she could get angry. There he went, ordering her around again. Being the bossy, controlling, overprotective bully.

But she couldn't get angry. She understood why he was wired this way. He thought it was his responsibility to keep everyone he cared about safe from Benedict.

Everyone he cared about?

His grip on her shoulders softened. He ran his palms down her arms to her hands. "Melina, I know what this man is capable of. You can't take any chances."

Her skin tingled under his touch. Tremors chased up her arms. Was this caring? Or just another side effect of his abilities? "All right."

"Good." He passed his thumbs over her knuckles. "I want you to be safe."

"Anthony, I'm not going to use it."

"What?"

She nodded toward the envelope. "The information about your family's psychic powers. I have plenty of material on Benedict already without going into that part of his schemes. You don't need to have the curious invading your privacy. You've all suffered enough."

He squeezed her fingers. "Thank you, Melina. I had agreed to give you my story, so I knew I had no right to ask you to withhold that part, but I don't want the others to be hurt."

Melina felt that pesky lump come back in her throat. The others. He gave no thought to how his own life would be disrupted if people knew about his power. Did his sisters realize what a good man he was?

Oh, she was such a coward. Why didn't she just come out and say it? Why was it so hard to tell him she didn't want their partnership to end?

She wanted far more from him than her story. There was still so much she wanted to learn about him, so many layers to uncover, so many possibilities to explore. Safe or not, how could she let him go?

How many times did a man like Anthony Caldwell come into a woman's life? It wasn't only his power that made him special.

"There's something I want you to do, Melina. It wasn't part of our original deal."

Her heart pounded. Her hands trembled in his. "Yes, Anthony?"

"Wait until tomorrow at dawn before you make your call to the FBI."

For an instant, she felt a surge of joy. He wanted to postpone the end, too. He didn't want to say goodbye any more than she did.

But then she saw the tension in his jaw. She saw it in his gaze next. More than tension. Anger. Rage. It was the same way he had looked before they had left the Anasazi village. He had looked this way in the restaurant a week ago when he'd told her about his mother's murder.

"Melina? All I need is twelve hours."

She didn't have to ask. She knew.

It was the last piece of the puzzle. The final part of the truth that she hadn't wanted to see. But it fit. Oh, it fit so well it should have been obvious from the beginning.

He worked outside the law. He preferred to be in control and didn't trust authority. All along he had never intended to wait for the police. That had been her suggestion, not his. A man who had taken a baseball bat to someone who had tried to molest his sister would never leave his mother's murderer to the courts.

He didn't want justice. He wanted vengeance.

She lifted herself on her toes, looking him in the eye. "You're planning to take on Benedict alone."

"It's the only way to be sure he's stopped."

"That's why you gave me your files now. You were just waiting until it got dark again. You intend to go back there tonight."

"I know where the sensors are. It won't take me as long to get past them."

"You'll be one man against a veritable army in a hidden fortress." She yanked her hands from his and grabbed his head, anchoring her fingers in his hair. She gave him a hard shake. "And you had the nerve to ask *me* to be careful?"

"I have to do this to protect my family."

"Even with all your special powers, you can't stop bullets, Anthony. You're too angry to think straight. Confronting Benedict on your own is suicide. If he doesn't kill you outright, he'll use you. You're playing right into his hands. He'll…experiment on you."

"That's the chance I'm willing to take."

"Well, I'm not." She let go of him and stepped back. She looked around the room for her cell phone and spotted it on the wooden blanket chest where she had left her purse. She ran to pick it up and jabbed Liam's number.

"Melina, no."

She heard two rings before the signal went dead. A sensation of warmth flashed down her spine. She recognized it— it was a tickle of stray power. She tried to ignore the effect, gritted her teeth and walked to the small table that held the room's regular phone. She dialed the number again. This time the phone didn't ring even once before it cut off in a burst of static. Heat pulsed between her thighs so fast, she moaned. She dropped the receiver and whirled on Anthony. "Your tricks won't stop me. You're not going in alone, even if I have to try every phone in town."

"Don't interfere, Melina. I've been preparing for this day for twenty-eight years. I need to do this."

"No, you don't. You've spent your whole life putting your own needs last. You've done enough. It's time to think about yourself."

The lights in the room flickered. "This *is* my life, Melina."

Something sliced at her heart. Her breasts tightened. She grasped a corner of the table for balance. "It doesn't have to be, Anthony. You could have so much more if you put aside your anger."

"You don't realize what you're asking."

"Maybe I don't understand what you've been through, but I do understand what it's like to live your present through your past."

He hesitated, then took a step toward her.

"I understand about needing a goal to focus on so you won't have to think about the pain. That's what you're doing, isn't it?"

His jaw hardened. "Finding Benedict and dealing out justice for my mother and my family is what keeps me going. It's what I live for."

"Yes, I know. It's like my work. That's what keeps me going. It's what I live for. But I've already shown you I'm willing to compromise about this story. I'm not going to publish all the information you gave me."

"Why, Melina?"

"I told you. I don't want you and your family hurt."

"I meant why is your work so important?"

"We're talking about you."

"No. We're talking about you now. What happened in your past? Where did your pain come from?"

For eight years she had kept this inside. She had locked up the pain along with the passion. She had chosen to be safe instead of opening her heart. She had even contemplated entering into a loveless marriage as a way to have part of the dream she had left behind.

Yet how could she expect Anthony to let go of his past if she was unwilling to let go of her own? This could be her last chance. If he left now…

"Melina?" He took another step, closing the distance between them. He tipped up her chin with his knuckle. "You know what happened to me. I want to know about you. What did you lose?"

"I lost my child, Anthony."

Chapter 10

The words hung in the room like a shout, flooding the sudden silence with echoes of pain. Melina felt them return to her, batter her, wash over her, but she held her ground. Now that she had come this far, there was no going back.

"You had a child?" Anthony asked.

"He would have been eight years old this Thanksgiving." She crossed her arms, rubbing her hands over her sleeves. "But he never saw his first birthday."

He spread his fingers over her cheek. "Melina…"

She leaned her head into his hand. "My life has been different from yours, Anthony. I'm not trying to compare what happened to me to the tragedy that you lived through. I just wanted you to know that I do understand how loss can change your life."

A stray strand of energy brushed over her, not so much a jab as a caress. "What happened?" he asked.

"I told you I had a storybook childhood, right?"

"Yes, I remember. You said you had two wonderful parents."

"They were the happiest couple I have ever known. They loved each other with a passion that even a child couldn't mistake. When I think of my home, I think of sunshine. It was filled with love. Nothing bad could happen there. I grew up wanting the same thing for myself."

"But you didn't get it."

"My parents died in a car accident when I was away at college. I had never known loss before. I didn't know how to deal with it, so I turned to a man I thought I loved. I dreamed of starting our own home and filling it with sunshine and children." She moved aside. "I always wanted to have children."

He dropped his hand. "You have deep emotions, Melina. Any man would be lucky to have your love."

Even though Anthony was no longer touching her, she felt a hint of warmth trail down her back. The roots of her hair tingled. She crossed to the bed and picked up the envelope of evidence he had given her—the evidence she wasn't going to use—trying to keep her thoughts focused. "Well, Chuck wasn't looking for love, he was looking for a meal ticket. The day we got engaged, he asked me to move in with him. He used my inheritance to pay his rent and put him through law school." She creased the flap at the top of the envelope. "I was happy to go along. It was easier to let him make all the decisions. I...wasn't as adamant about being in control back then as I am now."

Anthony regarded her closely. She could almost feel him sorting through the facts. "Did you marry him?"

"No. He wanted to postpone the wedding until after he graduated. When I got pregnant, he tried to talk me into an abortion. I refused. Things kept getting worse. It was Thanksgiving weekend when I finally faced the fact I had made a mistake. I had my suitcase packed and was waiting for a taxi when Chuck came back early from a football game."

"What did he do?"

She crumpled the envelope, holding it to her stomach. "We argued. He lost his temper and punched me. In the belly. I went into labor. By the time the ambulance got there I had already given birth."

A mixture of rage and compassion flashed across Anthony's face. He reached her in two strides, took the envelope and tossed it on the floor, then looped his arms around her back and pulled her to his chest.

She leaned into his embrace, soaking in his strength. It wasn't that she couldn't stand by herself—she had been coping with this for years—but being in Anthony's arms took the sting from the memories.

Some of the bands on her heart loosened. The words came easier than she would have thought. It felt good to share this. She wondered why she hadn't done it before. "I had been thirty-one weeks along. My son was so small, and it had taken so long for the paramedics to get there, they didn't think he would make it to the hospital. He did." She inhaled shakily. "He lived three days."

"I'm sorry, Melina." His voice rumbled through his chest.

"I'll never know whether or not Chuck wanted to kill our child. He swore he didn't mean to. I pressed assault charges afterward, but Chuck knew the law better than I did so the case was dropped on a technicality."

"The law doesn't always work the way it should."

No, it didn't, she thought. Yet what had happened to her didn't come close to what Anthony and his family had gone through. "I didn't pursue the case. I realized none of it would have happened if I hadn't been so gullible."

"Not gullible, Melina. You were vulnerable."

"I wouldn't be again. The day I buried my son I took control of my life. I chose a career that dealt in fact instead of fantasy."

"That's why you became a reporter."

"Yes. My job became everything to me. It's how I coped with what I had lost." She took a minute to gather her thoughts, then tipped back her head to look at him. "That's why I recognize how much getting Benedict means to you."

At the mention of Benedict's name, the muscles in Anthony's arms hardened. The tenderness that had briefly softened his face disappeared.

Melina could feel his withdrawal. She gripped his arms, filled by a sense of urgency. She still ached from the pain of her own memories, but she wouldn't let that stop her. That was in the past. Her concern was Anthony's future. She had to get through to him. "I do understand, Anthony, but I still won't let you do it."

"I have to."

"You could be caught. You could be killed."

"Not before I kill him."

She wanted to shake him again, but she knew it wouldn't do any good. "And then what? Did you ever think of that? If you do kill him, are you going to be able to live with yourself afterward?"

His gaze didn't waver. "I couldn't live with myself if I didn't."

"Let the FBI handle it. Please. They won't let Benedict escape."

He moved his hands to her waist. His fingers dug into her hips as if he were on the verge of pushing her away. "Melina, I'm sorry. You're asking too much."

"Damn you, Anthony! Why is it all right for you to worry

about everyone else but the minute someone cares about you, you shove them away?"

The lights suddenly brightened. The air crackled. Melina gasped as pleasure streaked from his fingers to her thighs.

She reminded herself the pleasure was only a physical side effect from his talent. Meaningless. Not real.

When did skepticism cross the line to denial?

The question made her pause. It was the same thing she had asked herself when she had first accepted Anthony's psychic talent.

Maybe these feelings weren't real to Anthony, but her desire for him didn't turn on and off with his power. She slid her hand from his arm to his chest. "I do care about you, Anthony."

Anthony muttered an oath. "Melina..."

"Don't push me away."

Waves of energy shimmered between them. Melina felt his heart beating hard beneath her hand. The rhythm echoed in her pulse, heightening her senses. She slid her palm down his shirtfront and felt the swell of washboard muscles and a line of silky hair.

When had she opened his buttons? she wondered hazily. She pushed the edges of his shirt apart, splaying her fingers on his bare midriff. Tiny shocks burst like bubbles along her palm.

His thumbs pressed into her hipbones, sending shudders down her legs.

She swayed into him and placed a kiss in the center of his chest. Crisp curls tickled the tip of her nose. The scent of soap and Anthony wove through her blood. She tilted her head to lick the hollow at the base of his throat.

Power swept through her like a hot wind, sparking awareness in every nerve in her body. She didn't consider resisting. She couldn't. She yanked his shirt down his arms to bare his shoulders, hearing fabric rip, not caring, not pausing, needing to get closer.

Anthony shuddered, his muscles tensed. "You're upset," he said. "You don't know what you're doing."

Yes, she did, she thought. For the first time in eight years she really had put aside her past. She was reaching out. She was going to trust her heart. And it felt right. She traced her lips along the edge of his collarbone.

"It's my power, Melina. Don't confuse what you feel."

She gave him a sharp nip to show him what she thought of that, leaving the imprint of her teeth on his shoulder.

"Damn it, Melina," he whispered. "We can't do this. Not now."

She met his gaze defiantly. "If not now, then when?"

Desire swirled in his eyes. So did anger. The combination was dangerous, thrilling. Exhilarating. As wild and free as lightning on a cliff top.

I'll do whatever is necessary to make sure that you're safe.

How many times had Anthony said those words to her? Had anyone ever said them to him?

Melina smiled. *Whatever is necessary.* Without another thought, she reached between them and unfastened his pants.

It was her smile that did it. Anthony had seldom seen Melina smile. There hadn't been much cause for it. Since the time they had met, they had been racing from one tense situation to another. The only smiles he had seen were fleeting and half-formed.

She had given him another piece of herself tonight. He knew she hadn't done it lightly. Like her other emotions, her pain ran deep. He had known for some time that it was there, and had wondered about it. It had taken courage for her to reveal her story. He was moved by the trust she had shown in him. But instead of clarifying the situation, it made everything more complicated.

This new level of trust she had brought them to only intensified the awareness between them. It pushed at his senses. She said she cared about him, and he was disturbed by how much he wanted to believe it was true. The connection they shared was infusing his body with cravings that took every shred of his willpower to fight.

Yet it was her smile that reached him. It lit her face with the strength that had allowed her to overcome the blows that had been dealt to her without turning bitter. It crinkled the corners of her eyes with honesty. It put two dimples in her cheeks and stretched her lips into a generous, open, unconditional invitation that only someone made of stone could resist.

If not now, then when?

Damn it, why not? She wanted this. So did he. Whom would it hurt? He had waited twenty-eight years to fulfill his destiny. Would a few more hours make that much difference?

Anthony heard the rasp of his zipper. He caught Melina's wrist and lifted her hand away from his pants.

Her smile faltered.

Holding her gaze, he sent a short burst of energy to the lamp beside the bed. It snicked off. Melina's eyes widened as the backwash broke over them. He brought her hand to his mouth and pushed the tip of his tongue into the center of her palm, the way he had once before, watching her reaction as she realized what he was doing. Slowly, carefully, he loosened the restraints on his power.

She trembled, her lips parting.

"Is this what you want, Melina?" he asked.

Her smile returned, blossoming with pleasure. "Yes, Anthony, but only if you feel it, too."

"I'll show you what I feel," he said. He switched off the other lamp, then opened the connection with Melina, letting his desire flow through. It mingled with hers, swirling as it returned to him, swelling so fast he stumbled backward, off balance.

The back of his knees hit the edge of the mattress. He swept Melina into his arms and fell across the bed. She landed on top of him.

There was no storm to augment his power. The light that filtered through the curtains was from the moon, yet Anthony could swear he felt the tickle of distant lightning on his cheek when Melina kissed his jaw. He grasped the hem of her sweater and tugged it upward. She caught his hands, then sat up with him, straddling his legs. She finished pulling off her sweater and flung it aside along with her bra.

Anthony had never seen a woman look more beautiful. It had nothing to do with the shape of her body. It was because of the way she held her shoulders proudly, her back arched as she offered herself to him. The skin across her breastbone was tinged with a blush, her nipples were swollen, her breasts rippled with each unsteady breath she drew.

The other time, it had been over too quickly. They both had been cheated. This time Anthony was going to make it last. Even when he had looked his fill, he didn't touch her. He held his palms a breath beyond her nipples and sent a pulse of energy through his hands.

Her lips parted in surprise. Her knees tightened against his thighs. He felt her shudder.

He rotated his wrist and did it again. "Do you like that, Melina?"

"Oh!" She wriggled her shoulders. Her eyes darkened. "Oh, my."

He watched her enjoyment—he felt her enjoyment—as he

explored her breasts. Then he moved his hands lower, doing the same thing to her hips, to her thighs, to her knees, showing her other pleasure spots, reveling in her soft moans of delight.

She leaned forward, flattening her hands on his chest, her breathing shallow, her hair swinging over her shoulders. "How do you do that?"

"What?" He gathered the locks in his hands and used her curls to diffuse his energy, feathering the pulse through the ends of her hair over the sensitive skin of her neck. "You mean this?"

"Anthony, that's...oh!"

He stroked a curl from the base of her throat to her chin. "Ahhh..."

He licked his thumb and touched it to her lower lip.

She gave a whispered sob.

"Take off the rest of your clothes, Melina. I'll show you what else I can do."

Her sob turned into a laugh. She didn't argue with his order. She rolled off him and did as he asked. He got rid of his own clothes and pulled her down on her stomach. Starting at her toes, he caressed every inch of her, then turned her to her back and started all over again.

He could smell her perfume and the scent of aroused female, making each breath he drew a burst of pleasure on his tongue. The power built more quickly than he would have believed. He lowered himself on top of her, using his body as he'd used his hands and her hair. Through the layer of dampness that sealed them together, he channeled his energy from his skin to hers in wave after sensual wave.

She tossed her head restlessly. She hooked her ankle behind his thigh, urging him closer.

He tried to ease back on his power. He knew too much

would be painful for her, and he had more sensations he was eager to share. Yet the connection was too strong. He couldn't control it now any better than he had before.

She arched off the mattress, locking her arms around his back. She closed her teeth over his earlobe.

"Melina…"

"Show me more, Anthony," she murmured.

He moved between her legs, tilted his hips and did.

Melina cried out.

Anthony immediately stilled. He drew back to look at her. Had he gone too far? Had she passed out again?

She blinked and moistened her lips. Her pupils were so large, her eyes looked black. She moved her hands over his shoulders and down his arms. Her fingers trembled.

He smiled and did it again.

She clutched his biceps, her body rippling with another release.

He used his knees to nudge her thighs wider apart. "Do you want me to stop?"

In reply, she sank her nails into his buttocks.

The energy that shot through him was stronger than what he'd given her. It eddied around them, drawing them closer, joining them so tightly he could feel her breath in his lungs. He looked in her eyes and saw a reflection of his own. Was she moving? Was he?

"Anthony!"

He rolled them to their sides and brought his mouth down on hers. Sparks glittered behind his vision. He was no longer in control. It didn't matter. He let the passion take them both.

Melina paused at the side of the bed and looked at Anthony. It was difficult to see him through her tears. She hoped that once everything was over, he would understand why she had to do this.

Understand, yes, but there was a good possibility he might never forgive.

Even in sleep he looked intense. Sprawled naked across the mattress on his stomach, one arm flung over the place where she'd been lying, he dominated the bed the same way he dominated the room. His hair was loose, tangled from the play of her fingers. Moonlight silvered the swell of muscle along his shoulders that she had traced with her lips. His back was a long, lean span of male beauty, tapering to tight buttocks that bore the marks of her nails.

Part of her wanted to slip off her clothes and crawl back into that bed with Anthony. Simply standing here looking at him sent her pulse racing. And if she allowed herself to think about what he had done…

Oh, God. Too late. The mere thought of the way he had used his power to pleasure her sent an aftershock careening through her body. He was a generous and creative lover. Sensitive. Responsive. And so unbelievably sexy, he took her breath away.

Each pore in her body was glowing with satisfaction. Every inch he had touched had become an erogenous zone. What she had experienced during the thunderstorm had been merely a taste of what Anthony was capable of. She hadn't thought pleasure like this was humanly possible. She felt so sated she could barely move.

A tear burned a path down her cheek. She let it fall unchecked. Anthony had used his power freely. For four hours straight he had channeled his energy into sex. And that was probably why he'd relaxed enough to fall asleep.

She curled her nails into her palms. *Whatever it takes,* she reminded herself. She had known she wouldn't be able to change his mind about confronting Benedict. She had done this to save his life.

She pressed her lips closed to keep her sob inside. Was she going to lie to herself? She hadn't done this only to save him. Her motives weren't that noble. She had made love with Anthony because she had wanted to. She wasn't going to make excuses.

He stirred in his sleep, his fingers spreading over her pillow. His mouth curved in a sleepy smile.

Concentrate! she ordered herself. She looked away and picked up her shoes. She knew if she didn't leave now, she wouldn't leave at all. Taking care to avoid the floorboard that creaked, she tiptoed to the door. She made her way downstairs, through the darkened house to the guest dining room at the back, unlocked the terrace door and stepped outside.

The temperature had dropped rapidly with nightfall. The brick patio was slick with a thin layer of frost. Melina turned up the collar of her jacket and walked through the gate to the parking area.

Anthony's Jeep was parked at the far end of the gravel lot, almost out of range of the light on the side of the house. She hurried past the pair of other cars, wincing at the noise her shoes made on the gravel, but she didn't want to slow down now. Any minute Anthony might wake up. He would be furious when he learned what she had done.

She knelt beside the front tire of the Jeep, unscrewed the cap over the air valve and depressed the pin in the center. A stream of cold air hissed past her hand. The front fender sagged lower as the tire began to deflate. She looked over her shoulder, her heart pounding. This wouldn't stop him, but it would slow him down and buy more time. With her free hand she reached into her pocket and pulled out her phone.

Naturally, Liam Brooks wasn't answering.

Melina moved to the rear tire, opened its air valve and dialed again. As she had explained to Anthony earlier, she had to be cautious about whom to trust, but she couldn't afford to waste time, either. If she couldn't reach Liam within the next minute, she was going to take her chances with the state troopers. She would work her way up the chain of command from there.

Just as she was about to give up on Liam, she heard a series of clicks as if the call had been transferred. The ringing started up once more with a different tone.

A woman's voice came on the line. "H'lo?"

Melina was surprised to hear the receptionist at this time of night. She brought the phone close to her lips. "Harriet?"

"No." There was a sigh and the rustle of fabric. "Who's this?"

"Melina Becker from the *Daily Journal.* I'm calling for Agent Brooks."

Bedsprings creaked. "Hang on, I'll see if he's available."

"No!" Melina said as loudly as she dared. "This is an emergency. Don't put me on hold—"

Too late. The line went silent. Melina kept the phone pressed to her ear and moved around to the far side of the Jeep. Where was Liam? Who was answering his phone now? If she didn't know better, she would think he had a girlfriend, but Liam hadn't been interested in any woman since his wife had died. He was a by-the-book agent with the personality of a rock. Like Melina, he lived for his job.

The cold was numbing her fingers. She fumbled for a minute before she got the next valve cap off and depressed the release pin. A frigid stream of air hissed into her face. She jerked back just as the phone clicked.

"Brooks here."

At the deep, calm tone, Melina sat down hard on the

ground, her eyes once more filling with tears. Liam Brooks might have the personality of a rock, but he also had its strength. Just hearing his voice steadied her. "Liam, thank God!"

"Melina? Are you all right?"

"Yes, I'm fine."

"Dani said it was an emergency. You're lucky she decided to connect my phone."

Who was Dani? Melina didn't want to take the time to ask. She might only have a matter of seconds to get her message across. "Liam, I need your help."

"What's wrong?"

"Send in everything you've got. Helicopters, SWAT teams, the army if you can swing it, but—"

"Melina, you don't sound like yourself. Take a deep breath. You're not making sense."

No, she didn't sound like herself at all. There was no professional detachment here. She was teetering on the edge of panic.

She checked over her shoulder. She couldn't see the house from this side of the Jeep, only the overgrown yew hedge that surrounded the property. Were those footsteps she heard on the patio? She wouldn't be able to hear Anthony coming over the hissing noise from the deflating tire. She slid along the gravel, pulling herself deeper into the shadows. "I know where he is."

"Speak up, Melina. I can hardly hear you."

"Titan. We found his stronghold."

"Titan's stronghold? Is that what you said?"

"Yes. Titan." While she spoke, she let go of the air valve and shifted to one knee so she could dig into her pocket. "His real name is Benedict Payne. Anthony told me—"

"Did you say Anthony?" Liam interrupted.

She withdrew the paper Anthony had given her with the GPS coordinates. "Yes, I'm with a man named Anthony Caldwell. He's in terrible danger, Liam. So is his entire family. You have to arrest Benedict. Whatever it takes, don't let him get away. He's worse than any of us could have imagined."

The woman who had answered the phone was speaking excitedly in the background, saying something about Anthony. Liam's voice overrode hers. "Melina, you have to focus," he said firmly. "First priority, tell me where you are."

Her hands were shaking too hard to unfold the paper. She tossed it aside. "I'm in New Mexico, Liam. In a small town called—"

A hand slammed across her mouth, muffling her words. Melina struck out with her arm, only to have both of her arms seized from behind.

She threw back her head but couldn't loosen the grip over her mouth. From the corner of her eye she saw two men looming behind her, one holding her arms, the other lifting a gun while he squeezed her jaw. She tried to scream but the sound didn't get past her throat.

Liam's voice, tinny and distant, floated through the air. "Melina! Are you there? What's happening?"

Her phone was snatched from her fingers. There was a sudden crunch of breaking plastic and Liam's voice cut out.

Melina twisted to kick out just as the gun arced downward. Pain burst across the back of her skull. By the time her head hit the gravel, Melina felt nothing at all.

Chapter 11

Anthony came awake with a start, his heart pounding so hard he was out of breath. How long had he been asleep? He moved his hand across the sheet beside him. His fingers found a trace of Melina's warmth and stirred a hint of her scent, but the place where she had been lying was empty.

He jackknifed up. "Melina?"

His voice sounded strange to him. Hoarse and needy. He never fell asleep with a woman. And he sure didn't wake up and think only about wanting her back in his arms.

He raked his hair off his face and scanned the room. The shadows were empty, but then, he had already sensed that he was alone.

Anthony jerked his hand toward the lamp, flooding the room with light. He looked at the clothes on the floor. He could see at a glance that Melina's were gone. He looked at the wooden chest where she had dropped her phone. Her purse was still there, as was her green carry-on bag. Only her cell phone was missing.

It didn't take a genius to put the pieces together.

But he didn't want to believe it. Not after what they had shared. She wouldn't have done this to him. Not Melina.

Hadn't she felt the power between them? Hadn't she realized how rare their connection was? She had writhed in his arms and had moaned his name. She had stroked his face so gently and had whispered that she understood....

How could she have betrayed him?

He slammed his fist into the bed. "Damn you, Melina."

Yet even as he cursed her, he realized his anger was for himself. He knew Melina wouldn't have backed down. That was the way she was. He had known that making love to her was only postponing the argument.

He never should have let his guard down, no matter how warm her smile had made him feel, no matter how much he had wished that the world could have stopped and the night could have gone on and just for a while longer, he could put his obligations aside and forget about his destiny.

He rolled to his feet and yanked on his clothes. He didn't have time to indulge in regrets. Chances were good that Melina had gone outside to make her call. The sheet hadn't cooled down completely, so she could only have a few minutes' head start. It might not be too late to stop her.

Anthony followed a set of small footprints across the frost-covered patio. They must be Melina's. Who else would have come out here? He shut out the discomfort from the cold that stole through his ripped shirt, and opened his mind, scanning for a phone signal.

Nothing. The footprints continued through the gate to the parking lot. At his first glimpse of his Jeep, Anthony broke into a run. Damn the woman, she had guaranteed he wouldn't be going anywhere fast. She had let the air out of his tires. "Melina!" he shouted.

A dog somewhere down the block started to bark. Anthony rounded the front of the Jeep. Only the rear tire on the passenger side was flat. The gravel beside it was scuffed, as if someone had struggled—

Anthony stopped dead, every sense on alert. He probed the space around him. Still nothing. He widened his scan, checking for anything that didn't belong, but he sensed only emptiness. He walked around the other cars and searched the shadows at the edges of the yard, then ran past the house to the street. It was deserted. The houses were dark. It was a quiet neighborhood, which was why he'd chosen it. Few passersby. No witnesses.

A breeze stirred the branches of the tree overhead, clattering them together like bones. Dried leaves whispered past his feet. A hollowness settled in Anthony's gut. Melina wouldn't have gone this far. She didn't have her purse. She hadn't packed her things. She had only come outside on her own because she'd wanted to make a phone call. A phone call she hadn't wanted him to hear.

He should have been more careful to protect her. He shouldn't have indulged himself with her when he knew they were this close to Benedict and this close to the end. And he damn well shouldn't have fallen asleep.

He returned to do another search of the yard, then retraced Melina's steps to the Jeep. He knelt beside the rear tire, running his fingers over the scuffed gravel. His gaze was caught by a white square that was wedged in front of the wheel. He picked it up, recognizing the paper he'd given Melina with the coordinates of Benedict's stronghold. She would have taken it from her pocket so she could tell the authorities where to go, but she hadn't unfolded it.

Why not? And why hadn't she finished sabotaging his

Jeep? The hollowness spread. He looked at the gravel again. A few of the pebbles were smeared with something dark—

No. Oh, God, *no!*

He touched a fingertip to one of the smears. It was sticky. It smelled like blood.

He keeled over, bracing his hands on the ground, fighting for breath. For an instant his mind refused to function. His senses rebelled. He couldn't take this in.

No. Not Melina. He couldn't lose her, too. There had to be some other explanation.

Farther in the shadows beneath the body of the Jeep, he spotted her phone. Or what was left of it. Pieces of plastic and circuit board lay on top of a small, pale rectangle that was the size and shape of a…postcard.

Anthony threw himself flat and reached beneath the vehicle. He knocked the broken phone aside, grasped a corner of the postcard and drew it out.

The picture on the front was familiar. It was a thatched cottage against a backdrop of green countryside. This was Benedict's calling card. The other time Anthony had seen one of these it had been on Fredo's body. That card had been blank. It hadn't needed words. The dead body it had rested on had been message enough.

No. *No!*

He got to his knees. His hands were shaking so badly, it took precious seconds to turn the card over.

This one wasn't blank.

We have the reporter. If you want her to live, come and get her. You know where we are.

Anthony's chest heaved as air rushed back into his lungs. She wasn't dead, he told himself. She wasn't dead. All right. They hadn't killed her yet. That wasn't what they wanted.

Then what did they want? Why had they abducted Melina instead of simply killing her?

Come and get her.

The answer was obvious. Benedict didn't want her, he wanted *him.*

A red haze descended over Anthony's vision. He hadn't thought it was possible to hate Benedict more than he already did, yet the fury that tore through him was unlike anything he had known before.

Benedict had issued a direct challenge. Nothing on this earth was going to stop Anthony from accepting. The game would end tonight. It was the only way to stop the evil. He was going to find and destroy the man he'd once called father, no matter how deep a hole the bastard was hiding in.

He was sorry Benedict Payne would only be able to die once.

Anthony shoved the postcard into his pocket and lurched to his feet.

"You appear to need help."

At the woman's voice, Anthony jerked. He looked past the Jeep to the house.

A small, dark-haired woman was walking toward him from the direction of the patio. Slippered feet poked at the hem of a long, black robe. A blue plaid blanket was draped around her shoulders like an oversize shawl. She held it closed at her throat.

Anthony clenched his fists and strode toward her. "Who are you? What are you doing here?"

The woman stopped and took a step back. "Do not spend your anger on me," she said, freeing one hand from the blanket to wave toward the house. Light shone from a window over the terrace doors. "I was asleep until I heard your cry."

Anthony forced himself to take a calming breath. He looked more closely at the woman. With the light from the house at her back, he couldn't see her face clearly, but he still saw enough. Blanket. Slippers. Hair flattened on one side of her head. She must be Mrs. Rodriguez's other guest. He glanced at the lighted window. "Did you see what happened?" he demanded.

"Your rage is dulling your senses. I have just told you that your shout woke me."

Her words were tinged with an accent—Melina had mentioned last week that the other guest had a foreign accent. He scanned the edges of the yard again, then gestured toward the house with his palm. "Sorry I disturbed you, but you should go back inside."

She didn't move. "You are distressed. Perhaps it would help you to talk about it?"

He shook his head, muttered another apology and returned to the Jeep. He didn't have time for this. He didn't need her help, or anyone else's. He had to fix the tires and get to the stronghold. He opened the tailgate, dug through his tools until he found the emergency air pump, then set it up beside the front tire and crouched to affix the nozzle to the air valve.

The woman's slippers scuffed across the gravel. Her shadow fell over the flat tire. "How did this happen?"

He strove to control his temper. She likely meant well. But his mind was too full of his need for vengeance for him to have patience for idle conversation. "It's cold. You'll be warmer if you go back in the house."

"People often tell me their troubles. They come to me for answers."

He stepped around her and yanked open the driver's door. He started the Jeep's engine, plugged the pump into the cigarette lighter, then went back to watch as the tire began to inflate. It was too slow. He sent a shaft of energy to the pump to give it an extra boost.

The woman tapped him on the shoulder. "This is not the way to get her back."

Anthony turned. Her face was still in shadow, yet there was no threat in her tone or her body language. She had already been at the bed-and-breakfast when he and Melina had arrived last week, so logic dictated that she couldn't be one of Benedict's operatives. Yet that comment hit too close to the mark. "Would you explain that?"

"It is your lady friend with the sunset hair that you seek, is it not?"

"How do you know?"

"It is her name you shouted. And who else would cause such distress in the middle of the night? The disagreement must have been serious for her to do such damage." She tilted her head, looking at the tire. "But your anger will not win her for you. It will push her farther away."

Anthony ran his hand through his hair. This woman probably thought he and Melina had had a lovers' spat. If only it had been that simple. He glanced behind him at the tire. It looked full enough, so he shut off the pump. "Excuse me, ma'am, but—"

"Yes, I see you are impatient, young man. Your worry is not misplaced. But before I go, I will give you one piece of advice. Heed it well." The woman drew herself up. She extended her finger to point at his chest. "Those who walk alone are the first to fall."

An odd silence followed her words. Anthony thought he heard an echo of her voice in his mind, but it was from a different time and a different place, with the noise of a carnival drifting on the spring air....

A carnival? No, there was just a barking dog down the block and a cold November breeze.

Yet those words seemed significant. Why?

She turned and started back toward the house, the edge of the blanket trailing behind her like a cloak.

"Wait," Anthony called after her. "What did you mean by that?"

The woman paused and looked over her shoulder. "Always full of questions. The answers are already in your heart if you but stop to listen."

The terrace door clicked shut behind her. A puff of cold air swirled from the shadows, seeping through his ripped shirt to his chest. To his heart?

Anthony shook his head and turned back to the Jeep. It was nonsense, he told himself. Just the musings of an eccentric and probably sleep-addled stranger. He didn't have time to worry about it.

He moved the pump nozzle to the next tire. While it inflated, he mentally replayed the route to Benedict's stronghold. He hadn't been able to detect the stronghold's entrance on his last time there, but he suspected there was an access tunnel somewhere behind the trailers. There was probably a natural entrance behind the Anasazi village, but he wouldn't waste time searching for it. Benedict knew he was coming. The fastest way for Anthony to get in would be to give himself up. Once he was inside the cave system...

The cave system. Sweat dampened his palms as he thought about entering that dark, closed-in space. He wiped his hands on his pants, refusing to let the dread take hold. Nothing was going to stop him.

Those who walk alone are the first to fall....

The woman's words replayed in his head so vividly, Anthony glanced around to see if she had returned. He was still alone. And alone was the way he wanted it. It was his destiny to face Benedict, to avenge his mother and to protect his family. This was what he lived for. He didn't care what happened to him after he killed the bastard.

Your anger will not win her for you. It will push her farther away.

The anger made it simple. It gave him strength. He couldn't remember a time without it. He was certain he was capable of killing Benedict. The skills he had learned while working for Jeremy, combined with his psychic talent, made him more than a match for an ordinary man. Sure, he hated caves, but he hated Benedict more.

The second tire was full. Anthony shut off the pump and carried it to the third tire. Before he could start filling it, his gaze was caught by the blood spots on the gravel.

Your anger will not win her.

He would be willing to give up his life to stop Benedict.

What would he be willing to give up to save Melina?

Anthony attached the pump nozzle to the last tire, his thoughts whirling. It *wasn't* simple. It hadn't been simple since Melina had burst into his life. She must be terrified. She had bled on the gravel. How badly was she hurt? Was she afraid he wouldn't come for her? What would happen to her if he died before he could get her to safety?

But vengeance was what he lived for. He couldn't change his destiny, could he?

Those who walk alone…

It would be 3:00 a.m. in Philadelphia, but Jeremy Solienti picked up the phone on the second ring. His greeting was as gruff and businesslike as always. "Solienti here."

Anthony was relieved to hear his friend sounding like his old self—the beating Benedict's men had given him months ago might have crippled another man, but not Jeremy. The retired mercenary was too tough to be kept out of commission for long. "Hello, Jeremy."

There was a brief pause. "Anthony, where the hell have you been? I should fire you for dropping out of sight like that."

The sharp comment was typical of Jeremy. So was the warmth beneath the words. Anthony tucked the receiver against his shoulder as he slipped a fresh water bottle into his backpack. He looked around his room to see if he had missed anything. "Sorry to get you up but—"

"You didn't. Danielle did ten minutes ago. She was asking if you had called."

"Dani? Is she all right? What happened?"

"She's fine. She and that nephew of yours are back in Chicago."

He dropped his pack on the floor. "Why? They were supposed to stay on that island in the Mediterranean, where they were safe."

"She got spooked. So did Elizabeth. They're both convinced you're in trouble." His voice roughened. "I've been spooked myself and I don't need any of their woo-woo powers to tell me that. Anthony, what's going on? It's been months since anyone heard from you. We've been worried. A lot has happened since you disappeared."

Anthony had cut himself off from Jeremy, and from his family, in his pursuit of Benedict. He'd wanted no distractions and no interference. He'd thought this was the best way to protect them, that it would be safer for everyone if he kept them out of it.

Yet it seemed that distance hadn't cut off the link he had with his sisters. It hadn't changed the concern that Jeremy had for him, either.

The minute someone cares about you, you shove them away.

He braced himself against Melina's words. But there was no time to think about them. He was already delaying more than he wanted to. He had to stay focused. "I found Benedict Payne, Jeremy."

"That's what Danielle said. Some reporter named Becker called Liam about an hour ago claiming the same thing."

It took a moment for him to process the facts. Melina had called Liam? *Liam* was the contact she had been so vague about?

Liam Brooks was the FBI agent who had been assigned to Danielle's case—and had won Danielle's heart—five months ago. How would Melina have known that Liam was connected to Anthony's sister?

Anthony swore as the truth hit him. Melina *hadn't* known. Out of all the possible contacts she could have had in the FBI, Melina's just happened to be Liam Brooks.

This was no lucky coincidence. It was Danielle's talent at work.

"But the call got cut off before she could tell him where Benedict was," Jeremy continued.

The smashed phone. The blood on the ground. Anthony pushed the images out of his mind. He gave Jeremy a brief but thorough summary of the events of the past week, including his deal with Melina. He finished with a description of how and where they had found Benedict's stronghold.

Jeremy whistled. "That's some defensive position he's got himself."

"That's where Benedict has Melina. The bastard wants to do a trade. Me for her. I plan to be there by dawn."

Jeremy knew Anthony too well to waste time arguing. His reply was terse and to the point. "You'll need backup."

"Yes."

"Liam's a good man. You can trust him. He organized the

raids that shut down the Titan Syndicate drug labs last month. He could get the manpower to handle whatever Benedict can throw at him now."

"A full-scale raid isn't the best way to get Melina out. We need a quick, surgical strike."

"Do you have proof Melina Becker is still alive?"

It was a reasonable question. No different from the other reasonable questions that Jeremy might ask during the planning of any job. Yet it delivered such a blow to Anthony's heart, it was a moment before he could reply. "She has to be. I would feel it if she wasn't."

"*Feel* it? She's not psychic, is she?"

"No. The connection we have is from something else."

Jeremy whistled again, this time slow and soft. "She's more than a business partner to you."

Anthony didn't deny it—his friend couldn't have missed the hitch in his voice. His partnership with Melina had gone beyond business days ago—probably from the first moment he'd touched her. He just hadn't wanted to see it. "She's an exceptional woman, Jeremy. But right now she's a pawn in a game she never should have been involved in. I'll fund the whole job. Transportation, extra equipment, whatever you think is necessary."

"From what you described of Benedict's setup, quick and surgical isn't going to be easy."

"I don't care what it costs. Just help me get Melina out."

"I used to have a team that could handle an assignment like this," Jeremy said. "They were the best I've ever trained. They were unbeatable."

"Jeremy—"

"But they were stubborn as hell. They broke up. The full team hasn't worked together in years."

"Do you want me to beg?"

"No, son. What I want you to do is make a phone call. It's one that's long overdue."

The phone rang six times. It was answered on the seventh. The voice that came through the receiver was high-pitched and slightly breathless. "Hello?"

Anthony grabbed the edge of the window frame and tipped back his head, inhaling fast. He'd thought he'd been prepared, but the sound of her voice scraped open the wound. How long had it been? Over two years since they had spoken. He had been so full of anger at her desertion, he had vowed to let her break the silence first.

"Hello? Is anyone there?"

This was no time for pride or dwelling on past hurts. With Melina's life at stake, everything else was immaterial. Anthony spoke fast before she could hang up. "Dani, I need your help."

There was a stunned silence. Then his sister's voice shrieked through the line. "Anthony! My God. Where are you? We've been so worried. So much has happened—"

"Danielle, I don't have much time. Please, listen to me."

"Anything. Whatever you need. Just tell me."

He felt an ache behind his eyes. It was so easy, as if the arguments and the two years apart had never happened. There was so much he wanted to say and a hundred questions he wanted to ask. Later. If there was a later. "I need us to be a team again. You, me and Elizabeth. Just like in the old days."

"You've got it. And I know I speak for Liz. I just got off the phone with her and she's as anxious about you as I am. When and where?"

"How fast can you two get to New Mexico?"

"Liz told me that Cole has the corporate jet standing by. They could leave Philadelphia within the hour, pick me up here and we'll be there by mid-morning."

Cole Williams was Elizabeth's new fiancé. Anthony had fences to mend with both him and Liz. He had been filled with resentment when his sister had turned to Cole instead of to him, but like his problems with Dani, the issues all seemed irrelevant now. That was part of the past. His concern was the future.

"Is this about Melina Becker, that newspaper reporter?" Danielle asked. "She called here asking for Liam. She said she was with you."

"Benedict abducted her."

"Oh, no! We were afraid something happened. We heard her struggle."

The phone. The blood. *Don't think about it,* Anthony told himself. "He has her at his stronghold. It's northwest of Santa Fe near a town called Antelope Ridge."

"Antelope Ridge?" She drew in her breath. "*Ant*elope! Oh, my God. The postcard!"

Anthony frowned. How could Danielle have known about the postcard Benedict's men had left under his Jeep?

Her next words answered his question before he could ask. "Last spring a medical student who had been mixed up with the Titan Syndicate was killed trying to get a message to Liam. She had written it on a postcard but all we could make out were the first three letters. Ant. It must have been Antelope. She must have been trying to tell Liam where Benedict was building his stronghold. If only we had realized—"

"Dani, we don't have time to go into this. We have to rescue Melina. Benedict wants to trade her for me."

"That son of a bitch." Danielle's voice trembled with sudden vehemence. "Not again. People are nothing but tools to him. What's the plan?"

"Jeremy has the details of the location and will supply anything you need. He'll be contacting Liam to coordinate this with the FBI, but whatever happens, they can't move in on the stronghold until we get Melina out. Benedict expects me to be alone. We can't risk tipping him off."

"Anthony, you're not agreeing to the trade, are you? Benedict won't keep his word."

"No, he won't. He's too volatile. That's why I have to get there before he changes his mind and hurts Melina." He pushed away from the window and retrieved his backpack. "I'm on my way now. That will buy Melina some time and provide a diversion while you and Elizabeth locate her and get her to safety."

"No. That's too risky for you."

"Risky, but within reason. I'll leave the detecting devices disabled as I work my way into the stronghold, to make it easier for you to follow. The central power source is electrical. I intend to disrupt it once I'm inside the cave system, so bring your night vision equipment and be ready to move fast."

"Wait. Did you say cave?"

"Yes. Jeremy has the coordinates."

"My God, Anthony. You're going into a *cave*?"

"Yes."

"You know how that affects you. You won't be able to function. You have to wait for Elizabeth and me."

"I can't. Every minute Melina is there alone increases the danger she's in. It's my responsibility to ensure her safety."

Her voice turned harsh. "Don't you dare pull this noble, self-sacrificing bull again, big brother."

"Danielle—"

"That's what drove us apart in the first place. You were angry because I broke up the team, but you were the one who didn't want to share. You want everything done your way."

"I realize I made mistakes, Dani. I—"

"Can't you understand that you're not alone? You never were alone, even after you cut me off."

His vision blurred. He rubbed his thumb and fingers against his eyes. "I know that now. Our connection was never really broken. You've always been in my heart, I just didn't listen to it."

"Anthony, I—" Her voice broke. "I love you. I never stopped, no matter how angry and hurt I was."

"Same goes for me, Dani. I'm sorry for pushing you away."

"We both did our share of pushing, but it's not too late to change."

God, he hoped not. "I'm trying."

"Then prove it. You think getting Benedict is your responsibility, but you're not the only one who wants a piece of the bastard who ripped our family apart. All six of us have a score to settle."

"All six?"

"Yes, six. Like I said, a lot has happened while you've been gone. The babies Elizabeth and I thought we remembered when we were kids…they were real, Anthony. Liam found the other triplets. Hawk, Darian and Cassandra. They're alive and safe and—"

"He *found* them?"

"It was more like they found us."

"And they're safe? You're certain?"

"Yes. They're fine. Benedict can't hurt them."

He'd been wrong. There were more than a hundred questions he wanted to ask.

The younger triplets were alive! Two brothers. Another sister. Where were they? What kind of people had they become? Had they learned to use their talents the way Dani, Elizabeth and he had? Were they together? Were they happy?

Would he get the chance to meet them?

The elation he should have felt at the news was submerged beneath his worry over Melina. He checked the time. Why did there never seem to be enough? "I've got to go."

"Anthony…"
"Dani, there's one last thing."
"Anything. What?"
"Wish me luck."

Chapter 12

The elevator started downward with a bump. Melina stumbled sideways, her legs still wobbly. The duct tape they had used to immobilize her earlier had cut off her circulation. It was only now starting to come back.

One of her captors, the man with the basset-hound face and the stubbly eyebrow, grabbed her arm and yanked her upright. "Don't try anything cute or I'll tape you up again."

Tears welled in her eyes as he wrenched her shoulder. She bit her lip, refusing to make a sound of complaint. Even if she got away from these two goons, where would she go? She had seen nothing but windowless rooms and stark white corridors since she had regained consciousness.

She lifted her hand to her head. The shallow cut the gun butt had left in her scalp had scabbed over, leaving a crusty line in her hair. How long had she been out? How long had she been here? She didn't know the answer to either question.

But she did know where she was.

These were Benedict's men. The one who had hit her with the gun was the same one who had fired at her from the van last week. She had seen him again yesterday when he'd been patrolling the phony archaeological dig along with his tall, thin companion. So it was reasonable to assume this had to be Benedict's stronghold.

She should have been more cautious. She should have paid more attention to her surroundings when she had tried to make her phone call. More than that, she should have called Liam the instant she and Anthony had found this place.

Anthony. Did they have him, too? Was he hurt?

She felt a stirring of panic but pushed it down. Now, more than ever, she had to stay in control of herself. She would focus on the facts. She would regard this as a story.

The story of a lifetime.

If she lived to tell it.

She breathed in slowly through her nose, striving for calm. The men beside her smelled like cigarettes. Beneath that, the air had a stale, metallic tang, confirming her belief that they were in the stronghold. What else did she know? The corridor she had just left had wound like a maze, the dips and turns likely following the contours of the natural cavern. Anthony had been right. This complex must have been constructed within a cave system. A big one. How far was this elevator going down? They had to be below the base of the cliff by now, but it was hard to tell.

The elevator glided to a stop. She was better prepared this time. She locked her knees and barely swayed, but then the door slid open and she was propelled into a room of riveted steel. Pools of light shone starkly on a huge oval table surrounded by high-backed chairs. A four-sided monitor, like a small version of the display screen at a hockey arena, hung suspended over the center of the table. It was blank. The table was bare. All the chairs were empty save one.

Melina didn't need an introduction. The man who sat enthroned at the head of the table had to be Benedict Payne.

She stared, her stomach slowly folding itself into a knot. She wasn't sure what she had expected, but it wasn't this. He didn't look like a madman. He didn't look like a monster, either.

His silver hair was trimmed conservatively, as was the silver goatee that adorned his chin. His suit was the color of charcoal and had the understated, perfect fit of expensive tailoring. His hands were clasped sedately on the table in front of him, his fingers slender and pale as if he never wielded anything heavier than a pen.

He could have stepped from the pages of a business journal or a menswear magazine. He appeared physically fit, suave and distinguished, more like an international executive than a cold-blooded criminal.

Somehow that made him all the more frightening.

"Here she is, sir." The second man, the tall thin one, shoved her into a chair. He gripped her shoulder, making sure she stayed.

But she already realized she had nowhere to go.

"You've done well, Habib." Benedict rested his elbows on the arms of his chair and steepled his fingers, reinforcing the appearance of a thoughtful executive.

Melina remembered what Anthony had said about The Magician, the figure in the tarot deck that Benedict identified with. He used secrecy and illusion. She disregarded the trappings and focused on Benedict's face.

"He arrived at the perimeter half an hour ago, sir," the first man said. "He's alone. We've been following your instructions."

"Excellent work, Gus. Are the surface patrols ready?"

"Every available man is on duty. We'll let him get to the second-level corridor before we close in."

Him? Melina thought. Were they talking about Anthony? That meant they hadn't managed to capture him yet. She felt a spurt of hope, but it was short-lived. They knew he was out there. They were watching for him.

Oh, God. This was a nightmare.

For the first time since she had entered the room, Benedict looked directly at her.

Melina recoiled at the coldness in his gaze. No, it was worse than cold. Blank. That was it. His brown eyes had the flat, lifeless regard of a reptile.

"You're proving very useful to me, Miss Becker. I'm pleased now that I let you live."

Did he expect her to thank him? Melina wondered. "Why am I here?" she asked.

"At the moment, you are the bait."

The pieces clicked together. The nightmare deepened. They had taken her to get Anthony. Oh, God. She should have been more careful. Not for her sake, for his. "How did your men find me?"

Benedict smiled, miming a phone by extending his little finger and his thumb. "Simple. Through your cell phone."

"I don't understand."

"I've had your whereabouts monitored since you started working on my story. I employed the same technology that emergency services use to locate cell-phone callers. Whenever you phoned the *Daily Journal,* my associate there used the equipment that I provided for her and traced the signal to see where your call originated."

More pieces clicked. She had phoned Neil on her cell twice since she had arrived in New Mexico. Both times Benedict's men had shown up afterward. If Benedict had a *Journal* employee on his payroll, that also explained how he would have known that she was traveling to meet Fredo.

"Who was it?" she asked. "Whom did you pay off?"

"She's just a junior copy editor with high career ambitions. But then, you're ambitious yourself. It was a bold decision of yours to team up with my son."

"Your son?"

"There's no reason to play coy with me, Miss Becker. You've been with him since Santa Fe. You're a professional busybody. Anthony would have told you about our…special relationship."

"You're not his father."

Benedict's smile disappeared. He gripped the edge of the table. "You're wrong. I created him, so I am his father in the only way that's important."

"You murdered his mother."

"It was necessary. She had betrayed me. And unlike you, she was no longer useful to me."

Flat, cold and without conscience, Melina thought again. She pressed farther back into her chair.

"Everything Anthony is, he owes to me," Benedict continued. "I made him what he has become. The anger that drives him is because of me. It's his anger that makes him strong, the strongest of all my children."

Melina knew there was truth in what he was saying. Anthony was driven by his urge for revenge. Yet there was so much more to him than anger, if only he would give himself the chance.

"His anger also makes him predictable," Benedict said, rising to his feet. He brushed the sleeves of his suit and straightened the cuffs. "He will come here intending to rescue you and to kill me. He will be so blinded by his need for revenge that he won't recognize the trap he's walking into until it's too late."

"You won't be able to trap him."

"Ah. Are you referring to his talent?"

She set her jaw, refusing to answer.

"You would have seen it by now. All my children were born with psychic power. Unfortunately, they were lost to me at a critical stage of development, so I wasn't able to guide their talents properly as they grew up."

Guide their talents properly, she thought. Benedict must be referring to those plans he'd had to experiment with his children.

Benedict was still talking, his tone eerily casual. "As a result, their psychic powers have manifested in unexpected ways. It has made them challenging to reacquire, so I knew I had to exercise caution with Anthony. I wasn't certain what direction his power had taken until I observed him in action recently. His particular talent is subtle, but its potential is enormous."

She tried to tell herself that Benedict was bluffing, but his next words dispelled that hope.

"Potential," Benedict repeated, laughing as he stressed the word. "My son has a most peculiar effect on anything electrical. It's an impressive ability, isn't it? Even now my security people are resetting the detection devices he's been disabling on his way through my valley.

"But this mountain has furnished me with the makings of a perfect trap, Miss Becker." He stamped his foot against the floor. "You see, electricity doesn't conduct through solid rock."

Was that true? she wondered. If it was, then why had Anthony been able to sense the stronghold's electrical power source? Yet what did she really know about how his talent worked? Sensing power wasn't the same thing as manipulating it. There had been nothing but air between Anthony and the helicopter that had attacked them, yet wrecking the helicopter's fuel pump had seemed to drain Anthony to the point that he had been pale and sweating when he'd rolled from beneath the overhang that had sheltered them.

"My men have been cautioned to watch for his tricks. They'll give him plenty of space," Benedict said. "But once he's inside my stronghold, he's mine. And I have you to thank for it."

"No. You're wrong. He's not coming. We're just business partners. He doesn't care about rescuing me."

"You had better hope for your sake that he does, Miss Becker. Your real usefulness will only begin once he's here."

The knot in her stomach tightened. Her *real* usefulness? "What does that mean?"

Benedict walked down the length of the table to stand in front of her. He picked up a lock of her hair and rubbed it between his thumb and his fingers.

She tried not to flinch. She told herself she had no nerve endings in her hair. His touch would wash out. If it didn't, she could cut her hair short.

He moistened his lips and rubbed harder, as if he was deriving some kind of stimulation from the motion.

She fought off a wave of nausea. If he kept that up, she was going to be sick.

"Come with me." Benedict released her hair and walked to the elevator. He pressed his thumb over a panel beside the door. "I'll show you my lab."

Benedict wanted her to be afraid, Melina thought, clamping her jaw shut to keep her teeth from chattering. He was a showman, a self-centered sociopath who fancied himself a tarot-deck magician. He was deliberately taunting her to make himself feel more powerful. She wouldn't give him the satisfaction of seeing her fear.

Think of it as a story, she reminded herself again. Regard the facts logically. Absorb as much information as possible. That way she might be able to help Anthony.

Despite her resolve, it took all her strength to keep the whimper from escaping her lips as she studied the room Benedict called his lab.

It was mercilessly bright, with floors that were the lifeless white marble of a tomb. The flat panels of lights that were recessed into the ceiling left no shadows to soften the equipment that was arranged along the walls. There were banks of computers and benches of glassware. Several wheeled carts that held clear, rectangular boxes the size of small refrigerators were connected by cables and hoses to a row of machines. The purpose of most of the equipment was unrecognizable to her, except for the item at the far end of the room.

It was a table. It had stainless-steel legs and wheels like a hospital bed. It was topped by a thick pad covered with black plastic. Straps of the type of fabric used in seat belts hung from various points on the sides. There were cuffs with buckles on the ends of the straps. Obviously, they were meant to be used as restraints.

And at the foot of the table there was a gleaming set of stirrups just like the kind at her gynecologist's office.

She swallowed hard and forced herself to look away.

Even without any scientific background, she could tell this wasn't a drug lab.

But she and Anthony had already reasoned that the Titan Syndicate's drug business had been a means to an end. A moneymaking scheme. The prelude to Benedict's bigger agenda.

Now that she was seeing this lab, she wasn't sure she wanted to know what that agenda was.

A door at the side of the room opened. One of the guards they had passed on the way here entered and spoke quietly to Benedict.

Benedict snapped his fingers at Gus and Habib. "Immobilize her."

Before Melina could resist, the men had bound her wrists behind her with duct tape and set her in a straight-backed wooden chair in the center of the floor.

Benedict came to stand beside her, his gaze flicking over her from head to toe. "Perfect," he murmured. He rubbed his thumb against his fingers. "With your arms out of the way like that, you remind me of my favorite woman. But she's much…older."

She didn't ask what he meant. She wasn't sure she wanted to know this, either.

He turned to the guard who had entered. "Bring him here."

Through the open door, Melina heard the sound of heavy footsteps and a sliding, scuffling noise, as if someone was being dragged.

No, oh please, let him be all right.

Two more guards entered the room. Anthony drooped between them, held upright by their grip on his arms. His black turtleneck and pants were streaked with dust. His head lolled forward, his hair hanging loose over his face.

Dear God. What had they done to him? Melina strained to rise from the chair. At her movement, Gus pulled a gun from his belt and laid the muzzle against her temple.

She froze.

Benedict swore at the guards. "I told you not to harm him. Is he dead?"

The guard on Anthony's right spoke up. "No, sir. You

warned us to watch out for his tricks. I got a shock from my radio when we frisked him, so we had to defend ourselves. He didn't do it again."

"Fine. Let him go."

The guards released their hold.

Anthony's legs buckled. He fell to the floor in front of them, his palms smacking hard against the white marble. He breathed hard for a moment, then pushed himself to his knees and shook the hair from his face.

Blood trickled from the corner of his mouth. A long red scrape darkened his cheek. The skin around his right eye was purple and swollen, but the rest of his face was so pale, he looked ashen. His gaze zeroed in on Melina. His throat worked as he looked at the gun that was pressed to her head. "Are you all right?" he asked.

She felt every one of his injuries as if they were her own. The words wouldn't come. She nodded instead.

He studied her, as if he was looking for wounds, then wiped the blood from his mouth with his knuckle and shifted his gaze to Benedict. "I'm here. Let her go."

Benedict laughed. "What? After all these years you have no greeting for your father? 'I'm here. Let her go,'" he mimicked. "You're in no position to make demands, Anthony."

Anthony braced his hand against the floor and got his feet beneath him. Slowly, he straightened up until he was standing. He took a staggering step sideways before he regained his balance. "Let Melina go," he said. "This is between you and me."

"Wrong, son. She's—"

"I'm not your son!"

Benedict pointed to Gus. "If he raises his voice at me again, shoot her."

Anthony lurched forward.

One of the guards who had brought him kicked the side of his ankle, knocking his legs out from under him. Anthony went down hard.

"If he threatens me," Benedict said, "shoot her. If he dares to lift a hand at me, shoot her. If the lights in this room so much as flicker, shoot her." He paused and looked at Anthony. "Do you understand your position now? *Son?*" he added.

Anthony repeated the laborious process of getting back to his feet. When he looked at Benedict again, his gaze was so filled with hate, the air around him appeared to luminesce. "What do you want?"

"Why, you've already given it to me. You are what I want. My firstborn, my strongest child. You will help me achieve my destiny."

Melina kept her gaze on Anthony, trying to will him to remain calm. She could see how much this was costing him both physically and emotionally. Sweat beaded on his forehead. He was swaying where he stood. But unlike Benedict's other victims, she and Anthony were still alive, and as long as they were alive there was hope.

At least, that was what she had to keep telling herself.

She tipped her head to the side to ease the pressure of the gun barrel on her temple. "You're not going to gain anything by keeping us here," she said. She cleared her throat, hating the weak sound of her voice. "The police—"

"Don't be stupid, Miss Becker," Benedict said. "I pay well to have people in every level of law enforcement, and would know the instant someone tipped off the authorities. My son is here alone. He wants to kill me, not see me arrested.

"But I digress." Benedict moved to the side of the room where the carts were lined up. He ran his hand down the corner of one of the clear plastic boxes and looked at Anthony over his shoulder. "Do you know why you and your siblings were created?"

Anthony's jaw twitched. "I read your notes in my mother's file. You wanted to possess our psychic powers."

"Not simply possess. My ambition went beyond that. Through you, I was going to control the future."

"What does that mean?" Melina asked. She wanted to draw attention away from Anthony. She worried how long he would be able to restrain himself. "No one can control the future."

Benedict glanced at her. "One can control it if one can foresee it. You have as limited an imagination as my sister."

"I heard about your sister. Agnes Payne is dead."

Benedict gave a grunting laugh. "That's because she never saw it coming. Agnes didn't recognize the potential of the genetic-engineering work she was doing. She thought only of breeding a genius. She succeeded in breeding six, but I took her work to the next level. I combined the special genetic material she had engineered with material from my Gypsy wife and—"

"What special genetic material?" Melina asked.

His mouth pursed. He drummed his fingers on the side of the plastic box. "Don't interrupt me again. You can be replaced."

Gus rubbed the gun barrel against Melina's ear. She gritted her teeth, which were beginning to chatter again.

Benedict returned his gaze to Anthony. "You have me to thank for the strength of your abilities, Anthony. You and your siblings have the DNA of a genius by the name of Henry Bloomfield. He was my sister's boss. It was Bloomfield's capabilities that amplified the psychic component from your mother's genes. My plan was a success. All of you, even the infants, exhibited remarkable power, but you were lost to me just as I was about to begin your training process. Otherwise, I would have had six children under my control who could look into the future."

A bead of sweat snaked its way over Anthony's cheekbone. "Your plan wouldn't have worked. I can't foresee the future. Neither can my sisters."

"That's because you weren't *trained*. Only one of the younger triplets learned to look into the future, but her talent is too raw to be useful. Because of your mother's interference, the gifts that I made sure you were born with were wasted. Squandered. None of you reached your full potential. Next time I won't make the mistake of acquiring a wife. I won't allow my children the distraction of a family." He rapped his knuckles on the box. "Next time my children will grow up under my complete control."

Melina took a fresh look at the row of carts with their boxes. Those carts. They were like the carts in a hospital nursery, only the boxes were much larger than bassinets.

The truth crashed over her. They weren't bassinets, they were *cages*.

Cages big enough to hold a child.

Horror locked the breath in her throat. No. It couldn't be. It was too terrible even to contemplate. Benedict had done some monstrous acts in his life, but surely no one could be *that* despicable.

"Everything is in place to begin the ultimate phase of my plan." Benedict waved his arm to encompass the room. "The next generation of my children will be perfect. They won't be weakened by sentiment. With my guidance, they will become my personal team of psychics, able to foresee trouble before it happens." His voice rose. "My wealth will have no bounds. I will exist above the law. There will be no limit to what I can do."

Melina wrenched her gaze from the cages and looked at Anthony. He was watching Benedict, his fury so intense, he was trembling.

"That is my destiny." Benedict pointed at Anthony. "And you have brought it to me. All my work is present in your DNA. It is your DNA that will father the next generation. And you." He swung his arm toward Melina. "You will serve as its mother."

The stainless-steel hospital bed. The restraints. The stirrups. The empty cages. Melina gasped for air. She wanted to scream. It came out as a croak. "No."

"Be honest, Miss Becker." Benedict moved his gaze to her breasts and then to her stomach. His thumb squeaked across the plastic box. "Haven't you always wanted to have children?"

Chapter 13

The rage was like a living beast inside Anthony. He could feel it gnawing at his gut. It hardened his muscles, making him tremble with the urge to smash something. It sent blood rushing to his brain, hazing his vision with crimson. His jaw ached from clenching his teeth, and his body pulsed with the need for action.

The fury was so strong, it allowed him to stay upright despite the tons of solid rock that he knew were pressing in on him from all sides of the corridor. It let him walk without staggering as the guards led them to a room with a raw stone ceiling that arched less than a foot overhead and windowless gray-brown walls that were painted with shadows. But then the door clanged shut and the air suddenly became too thin to breathe and was filled with the smell of gardenias and panic and his sisters' sobs....

No. It wasn't his sisters. It was Melina who had sobbed.

The sound yanked Anthony back from the brink of his nightmare. Melina. She was all that mattered.

Before she could draw breath for another sob, he reached out and pulled her into his arms.

She stepped between his legs, pressed her face to his neck and wrapped her arms around him so tightly he could feel the edges of his broken rib grind.

He didn't protest. The pain from the beating Benedict's guards had given him wasn't as strong as his urge to hold Melina.

This was what Anthony had wanted to do from the moment he had seen her in the lab. Only the gun that had been pressed to her head had kept him from going to her. Eagerly, he absorbed the feel of her body next to his. The emptiness that he'd sensed when he'd awakened in his bed and found her gone retreated. Some of the crimson lifted from his vision. His thoughts began to steady.

He cupped her head. His pulse was beating so fast, his hands felt clumsy. His fingers brushed a patch of dried blood on her hair. "They hit you. Does it hurt?"

"No, not anymore. They knocked me out when they grabbed me—" She gasped and released her grip on him. "Oh, Anthony, I'm sorry. I didn't think. You're so pale. I must be hurting you."

"It hurts more when you let go." He looped his arm around her shoulders. "Stay here. I need to hold you."

She hesitated, then returned her hands to his back, her touch light, her fingers shaking. "I need to hold you, too. I can't believe what's happening."

"I'm sorry you got dragged into it."

"I was wrong, Anthony. I thought I understood how you felt about Benedict. I couldn't have. Now I do." She spoke fast and low, her voice quavering with fury. "He's a monster. He doesn't deserve to live."

He heard the terror beneath her anger. It was true, she finally did understand.

He wished she didn't.

It was a measure of her inner strength that she had held herself together throughout Benedict's obscene revelations. The bastard hadn't realized how deeply his words had struck, but Anthony did. He knew now how important children were to Melina. He wasn't the only one who was facing a personal nightmare. She must be going through hell.

"We can't let ourselves be part of his plans."

He pressed his lips to her temple and tried to sound more confident than he was. "We won't be."

"Oh, God. I pray you're right."

Anthony turned his attention to the room. Panic lurked on the edge of his consciousness, but holding Melina kept it contained enough for him to take his first thorough look at their surroundings.

The room was nothing but a hollow in the natural rock, a space large enough to contain a narrow cot, a stool and a small table. The lock on the door wasn't electronic. It was a low-tech steel bar that had clanged into place as soon as the door had shut behind them. The lights weren't electric, either. There were no wires or sockets anywhere in sight. The only illumination came from a kerosene lantern that flickered in the center of the table.

The significance of the design hit him all at once. These primitive conditions were no oversight. They served a practical purpose. This room was a prison cell, one Anthony realized was designed for him.

He closed his eyes, trying to calm himself enough to extend his senses and continue his inspection, but it didn't do any good. There was no electricity in the room, no power source of any kind, not even the battery of a surveillance device. That part was good—he wouldn't have to worry about Benedict overhearing them—but even a battery would have been better than nothing.

There were no lines of force he could latch on to and follow. He couldn't feel any current through the stone. No stirrings. No pulses. Not even a tickle. They were locked in. Trapped. Helpless. In a windowless room under tons of rock where they couldn't breathe, couldn't move, couldn't scream....

Anthony buried his nose in Melina's hair, inhaling her familiar scent to keep the claustrophobia under control. His reaction to the cave was dulling his abilities. So was his anger. Danielle had guessed this would happen. That was why she hadn't liked his plan.

He had to have faith in his sisters. Along with him, they were the best operatives Jeremy had trained. They would follow the trail of the detectors he'd disabled. They would find a way into the stronghold.

But if he couldn't feel any current, how could he knock out the central power source? He channeled power, he didn't produce it. And here, underground, he couldn't draw on the ambient energy of the atmosphere. Unless he could get close to an electrical conduit, or unless there was another thunderstorm nearby to provide a boost, he might not be able to gather enough energy to get to Benedict let alone get out of this room.

Damn, he had to concentrate. Try harder to clear his head. It was their only hope.

"Did you see those boxes in his lab?"

His heart turned over at Melina's question. There was no way to clear his head when she was in such pain. He glanced at the cot. The slope of the wall it was set against was low enough to make cold sweat bead his forehead, but the cot was the only place they could sit together. He stooped to walk over to it, lowered himself to the edge of the mattress and pulled Melina onto his lap.

She drew her feet onto the mattress and curled up in his embrace without hesitation. A shudder worked its way down her spine. "There were hoses and wires. And holes in the top. They must be for air."

"Don't torment yourself by thinking about them, Melina."

"I can't help it. Benedict wants to keep children in there. Innocent children."

"It won't happen."

"Not just any children. Our children. He wants to use my body the way he used your mother's and take my babies and put them—"

"Shh. No one's going to use you."

She glanced around the room, then looked at him. Despite her fear, her gaze was lucid. Terror hadn't dimmed the intelligence he had always admired.

It would have been easier for her if it had.

"There's only one cot here, Anthony. One stool. This place is meant for you, not me. They're going to keep me...somewhere else."

She was right. And the reason was chilling. Benedict probably intended to keep her under constant medical supervision once the embryos were implanted.

He tightened his embrace, rocking her in his arms, hardly noticing how the top of his head brushed the sloping rock. "I'm not letting you out of my sight, Melina. We'll find a way out of this."

"It's all so twisted. Children are gifts. They deserve to be cherished."

She had said the same thing last week. He hadn't realized then how much it had meant to her. He rubbed his hand over her back. "Yes, they do."

"A baby should be conceived in love."

"Melina…"

"In love, Anthony, not forced inside me while I'm strapped to a hospital table and my feet are in stirrups and my body is spread open by instruments—"

Anthony caught her chin and turned her face to his. The desire to kill Benedict was never as intense as it was at this moment, but he strove to keep his grip gentle. His anger wasn't going to help Melina. "It won't come to that, Melina. I swear it."

Her chin trembled in his fingers. The tracks of her tears gleamed in the lantern light. "But that's not the worst of it, Anthony. It's not only my body he wants to violate, it's the dream from my childhood. He's taking my beautiful dream of a home filled with love and children and perverting it into something ugly."

"Benedict's mind is warped."

"But he spoke the truth. I have always wanted children."

He moved his fingers to her cheek and wiped her tears. "You told me."

"That's why I stayed with Chuck as long as I did."

"I know."

"That's why I took so long to turn Neil down. I didn't love him, but he would have made a good father. For eight years I tried to convince myself that my job was enough, that I had given up on that old dream, but it wasn't enough. I hadn't given up. I do want children. I just didn't want to give my heart to anyone again."

"Anyone would be cautious after what you went through."

"I was afraid of giving up control. I wanted children but not love or passion." She gave a sobbing laugh that was painful to hear. "It's ironic, isn't it? Being impregnated in a lab by a madman is about as far from passion as anyone can get. It's as if I brought this on myself by my own wishes."

"Melina, you did nothing to deserve this."

"Didn't I? It's my fault you're here."

"That's not true."

"Yes, it is. Benedict's men found where we were staying because of the cell phone calls I made to Neil."

"I was going to confront Benedict, anyway."

"And by trying to stop you, I made it worse." She touched her fingertip to the scrape on the side of his jaw. "I'm sorry, Anthony. I'm so sorry. I never should have left you."

"It's all right."

"No, it isn't." She moved her finger to his swollen eyelid. More tears surged down her cheeks. "What we did last night was incredible. It was wonderful. I only left because I wanted you to be safe. This is my fault."

"Stop blaming yourself."

"Why not? If I had been honest with myself about why I drive myself so hard, if I hadn't been so fixated on getting this story, neither of us would be here right now."

"If you hadn't been tracking Benedict, we wouldn't have met."

"That's right. We wouldn't have met."

"Are you sorry about that, too?"

Her chest heaved, her breath catching. She shook her head so fast, her tears splashed on his chin. "No, Anthony. Are you?"

"I should be. For your sake."

"That's not what I asked. Are you sorry we met?"

What could he say? If he had the power of foresight, if he had known what would happen, would he have chosen a different way to pursue Benedict if it meant he would never have known Melina?

Yes. He wanted her to be safe. His feelings were immaterial.

No. He could no longer imagine his life without this woman in it.

How could both answers be true?

"Anthony?"

He leaned forward and answered the most honest way he could.

The moment Anthony's lips settled on hers, Melina felt the last of her control crumble. The hell with being brave. The hell with being logical. She needed this kiss more than she needed air.

Terror still awaited her outside this room. It was so huge, so overwhelming, it made all those other fears that had shaped her life seem ludicrous.

How could she have been afraid of love and passion? There was nothing to fear in Anthony's kiss. His taste flooded her senses, setting off a wave of warmth, driving out the chill that had crept into her bones. It made her feel alive. It made her feel as if she were part of him.

He licked a tear from the corner of her mouth, then slicked his tongue over her lower lip in a caress so tender her eyes misted again.

She had once thought this man wasn't safe. She couldn't have been more wrong. She had let him see her weakness, she'd had every defense and illusion stripped away, but he had taken her pain and was giving her strength. She trusted him. Completely.

She caught his cheeks in her palms, holding his mouth to hers as she shifted to straddle his lap. The cot creaked beneath them. The wool blanket that covered it bunched under her heels.

Anthony's lips firmed. His kiss changed, grew harder,

bolder. Melina felt her breasts tighten. Heat pulsed between her legs.

But it wasn't the blinding flare of the last time she had kissed him. The spark that made her catch her breath hadn't traveled through his skin to hers.

He grasped her thighs, easing her more securely against him. There was no tickle of sensation to mask his caress, only denim sliding over denim, yet she felt his touch more clearly than when they had been naked.

She slid her hands to his hair. Pleasure flowed over her as she felt his wild, thick locks against her fingers, but the pleasure didn't come in sharp bursts. It was unfocused. Not stronger, not weaker, but…different.

She drew back her head. Her lips throbbed, her heart raced, but it wasn't from his power.

Different. Yes, something was definitely different.

She caught his hand and brought it to her mouth. She moistened his thumb and pressed it to her lip. There was no jolt, no crash of awareness. Just a simple, basic sensation of contact.

There was nothing paranormal about it.

She glanced at the wall behind Anthony's back. Their joined shadows floated against bare rock. She remembered what Benedict had said about the mountain—solid rock didn't conduct electricity.

Anthony's power must be gone. It didn't work in this room.

Oh, God. How long had he known? He hadn't said anything. He probably wanted to protect her from that, too, but it was easy to see they were in worse trouble than she had thought.

The terror that his embrace held at bay threatened to return once more, but she tightened her grip on Anthony's hand and refused to let the fear win. If she did, she would fall apart.

There was more to Anthony than just his psychic power. Far, far more. There was his strong will, his loyalty to his family, his determination, his compassion, his tenderness, his intensity. There were so many other aspects to this complex, fascinating man, she would focus on them instead of the horror. Who knew when she would have the chance to kiss him again?

So she did, and the feelings that bloomed inside her made the stone walls fade. She memorized the texture of his lips, the warmth of his breath, the soft giving and the frank taking of the kiss. She reveled in the intimate exchange of man and woman, in its own way more magical than anything he had shown her the night before.

For the first time since they had met, what was happening between them wasn't enhanced by his talent. There was no power behind it.

The thought made her break off the kiss and look at his face. The bruise beside his eye was purple and the stubble of his beard darkened the scrape on his jaw, but the rest of his skin was still pale, even in the golden light of the lantern.

Yet his gaze was as vibrant, as potent, as compelling as when he had held her in the thunderstorm.

No power?

She still held his hand. She turned it over. Keeping her gaze on his, she lowered her head and touched the tip of her tongue to the center of his palm, deliberately echoing what he had twice done to her.

His eyes darkened. His breathing quickened.

Oh, there was power. It wasn't supernatural. It came from the most basic force on earth.

Melina had felt it for days. Yesterday she hadn't had the courage to name it, but her old fears were meaningless. They would no longer hold her back.

She loved this man with all her heart.

It wasn't fair. It wasn't the right time. They were at the mercy of a madman who wanted to use her body to breed children.

Anthony's children.

Her heart's desire.

She blinked against another spurt of tears. Yes. *Yes!* That was what she wanted. *That* was her heart's desire. A life with Anthony, a home filled with their love and their babies.

But Benedict's ugliness was going to taint this, too. She couldn't bear Anthony's children, only to see them caged and used—

Her mind wouldn't complete the thought. She couldn't go there. Somehow they would escape. She had to believe that. Together, she and Anthony would be able to find a way out of this.

But how could they? Without his talent to help them, how could they get out of this room? They were trapped and helpless.

Anthony tipped her face to his and kissed the tears from her cheeks.

His tenderness zinged right down to her toes.

"Anthony," she whispered.

"What?"

The words caught in her throat. She didn't know what new nightmare tomorrow would bring. How could she tell him?

But if she didn't tell him now, when would she? "Anthony, I know your psychic power is gone."

He didn't deny it. "It's this place."

"You didn't want to worry me."

"I'm sorry, Melina."

"It does prove one thing." She laced her fingers with his and brushed her lips over his knuckles. "It proves your stray energy isn't causing what's happening between us. We are. The two of us together."

He glanced at their joined hands. "Melina…"

"So don't try to tell me that I'm confusing what I feel." She pressed his hand over her heart. It was beating so hard, she could hear her pulse in her ears. "Do you feel this?"

"I'll protect you. I promise. I'll take care of you."

"All I want you to promise is that you'll take care of my heart. It's yours, no matter what happens to the rest of me."

He splayed his fingers over her breast. "No one will hurt you. I'll do whatever it takes."

"Anthony, stop. I don't expect your protection. I'm not asking anything, I'm giving. That's what love is about. I love you."

Joy flashed across his face. He looked younger, lighter, as if the shadows around him were lifting. But then his jaw tensed. His gaze turned fierce. "Melina…"

"I realize this isn't the best time to talk about this, but I don't know how much time we have left before they take me back to the lab. I do love you, Anthony. Whatever happens to us, I want you to know that."

He was silent for a while. When he spoke again, his voice churned with emotion. "You asked me if I'm sorry we met."

"Are you?"

"I'm only sorry we didn't meet sooner." He pressed his forehead to hers. "For most of my life I started each day thinking of how I would kill Benedict. Today I woke up thinking about making love with you."

"Oh, Anthony, I wish I hadn't left. I wanted you so much."

He wrapped his arms around her and fell backward, pulling her down on the cot with him. "Do you want me without my power?"

She stretched out to face him and fitted her body to the

length of his. "You're the same man. It's not what you can do that I love, it's who you are."

"The connection between us—"

"The connection?" She kissed his chin. "That's what you've always called it, but I call it love, Anthony. Ordinary, everyday love."

"No, Melina. Not ordinary. There isn't another man on this earth who could love you as much as I do."

She tucked his words away in her heart. This wasn't fair. Why here? Why now? Oh, damn, it wasn't fair at all. If they didn't make it out of here…

She never knew who moved first. One minute they were clinging to each other, the next they had opened zippers and pushed aside clothing, sliding their bodies together in an urgent affirmation of love.

There were no sparks to dazzle her, nothing but love to enhance the touch of his hands. It was more than enough. More than she'd dreamed of. It was what she hadn't known she was seeking.

Anthony held her as the last of the shudders faded, then helped her straighten her clothes. He stroked her hair back and placed his lips over her ear. "I didn't believe I could feel anything stronger than my hate, but I do. I love you, Melina."

She smiled despite the lump in her throat. How could she feel happiness and despair at the same time?

"If I could change anything about the way we met," he said, "I would change the reason."

"Maybe we would have met anyway, Anthony. Maybe *that* was our destiny."

"All I know for sure is that you've shown me there's more to live for than vengeance…."

His words trailed off to silence.

"Anthony?"

He exhaled slowly, carefully, as if he didn't want to disturb the air around them. "Melina," he whispered.

"What is it?"

"I can sense the light in the corridor."

Chapter 14

Melina slid her hands to Anthony's shoulders. She could feel tension hum through his body. A tremor traveled from his shoulders to her palms. The hair at the nape of her neck prickled.

"It's high-voltage. I can trace the line."

Her pulse thudded. "How?"

"I don't know. It just came back. The energy's flowing into me."

The hope that shot through her was so strong, it was painful. Yes. Oh, please, yes! She flattened herself against him, holding him as close as she could.

A tickle of sensation ran down her spine. Through the layers of their clothing, she felt tiny shocks against her skin. A wave began to build. "What should I do?"

"You're doing it, Melina." He hooked his leg over hers. "Just hold me. Stay with me."

"Always, Anthony," she vowed.

A breeze swept through the room, bringing the scent of dust and damp rock, making the flame in the lantern flicker. And along with the smell of the cave, there was the scent of pine, of sunshine, of wide open spaces...and perfume.

Anthony locked his arms around her back. "They made it. They're here."

"Who?"

"Danielle and Elizabeth. I can feel their presence."

"Your sisters? Where?"

"They're outside. On top of the cliff."

"How did they know—"

"I asked them for help."

Another shock went through her, but it wasn't only from the power Anthony was gathering. He had asked for help? Anthony? The original lone wolf?

The lantern flared, sending shadows dancing over the wall. Anthony grunted. "They're adding their power to mine."

The wave changed. It became richer, higher, rocking her the way Anthony had rocked her in his arms. It flowed through her body and into her heart, carrying her upward. She squeezed her eyes shut and clung to him. Sparks burst inside her eyelids.

"There's the electric cable. It's going deep."

On the threshold of her hearing, Melina caught a rumble. Like thunder, only slower. Vibrations traveled through the stone floor, making the cot creak, shaking the table, rattling the door. Pressure built behind her eardrums. She flexed her jaw, but the pressure grew along with the wave.

"Have to knock out the main generator." Anthony's voice was hoarse, almost unrecognizable. "Hang on, Melina."

The breeze gusted into a wind, tangling Anthony's hair with her own. The rumble turned to a roar. His body went rigid, straining against hers, with hers, lifting her into a whirl-wind of light beyond vision, sound beyond hearing for a quiver-ing, endless heartbeat.

With a grating moan, Anthony unleashed the energy he had gathered.

Release smashed through Melina's senses.

Steel clanged in the corridor.

And the door of their cell swung open to total and utter blackness.

Anthony rolled to the edge of the cot, put his head between his knees and gulped for breath. The energy he'd channeled had left him drained. The force of it was unlike anything he'd experienced before. But he didn't have time to recover. Every second counted. They were a long way from freedom. They had to move now.

Melina understood. She fitted her shoulder under his arm and clasped his waist to help him to his feet. She was feeling the aftereffects of the surge almost as much as he was, her cheeks flushed, her hair corkscrewed wildly around her head, her breathing as ragged as his. But together they managed to stay upright. She snatched the lantern from the table as they staggered past, and extended it toward the door.

The two-foot long piece of steel that had barred the door was lying on the corridor floor. Anthony had never known Elizabeth's telekinesis to work on anything this heavy or at such a distance. That energy wave he'd felt must have ampli-fied her power along with his. It must have enhanced Dani-elle's talent too, because though he could hear the voices of Benedict's guards in the distance, luckily, this section of the corridor was deserted.

But there was no time to puzzle over it, much less to mar-vel. While Melina held the lantern, Anthony closed the door behind them and fitted the steel bar back in place, hoping it would gain them a few more minutes before their escape was discovered.

"Which way?" she whispered.

He looked around. Outside the circle of lantern light, the darkness was total. No speck of daylight would seep this far into the cavern system. Although they were only on the second level of the stronghold, they were still a hundred feet from the top of the cliff. He was suddenly aware of the weight of a mountain pressing in from all sides, closing them in, stealing their air....

He sucked in a deep breath. No. Not now. He had to hold off the panic. The glow of a flashlight appeared at the bend in the corridor to their left. Anthony squeezed Melina's shoulder and turned to their right.

It wasn't the way they had come. The floor sloped downward here, taking them deeper into the cave system. The entrance Anthony had used when he'd arrived was concealed behind one of the trailers at the base of the cliff, but it was heavily guarded, so he didn't want to risk it. As Melina had once told him, he couldn't stop bullets. He had to find some other way out and get her to safety. That was his top priority.

The thought made him stumble. He smacked his hand against the wall to keep his weight off Melina. This route was taking them away from the guards, but it was also taking them farther away from the lab and from Benedict. Anthony knew the chances of getting this close to Benedict again were slim. There might never be a better opportunity to kill him.

But Anthony had meant what he'd told Melina. He had more to live for now than vengeance. He would never regret choosing this woman over Benedict.

Anthony took the lantern from Melina and straightened up, the strength returning to his limbs. The corridor branched into three here. Acting on instinct, he again turned to his right, but they went only ten paces before the branch of the corridor ended in a door.

"That's like the lock on Benedict's conference room," Melina said, pointing to the electronic pad beside the doorframe. "I think it scans his thumbprint."

Something flickered on the edge of Anthony's consciousness. It was a sensation more than a thought, drawing him forward like a candle in a window on a starless night. There was no threat here. The room behind this door wasn't a dead end, it was an entrance. He sent a pulse of energy to activate the tumblers of the electronic lock, then put his fingertips against the door and pushed it inward.

Four steps led downward into the blackness. Unlike the marble of the corridor, the floor here was natural stone, as were the walls. The room was empty except for another door at the opposite end.

He took Melina's hand and opened the other door. A puff of incense-laden air rolled over them, along with a musty, ancient scent. Anthony extended his senses and scanned the darkness. There was energy here, yet its source wasn't electrical. It was older and deeper, droning through the very stone that surrounded them. It wouldn't harm them. He led Melina inside, closed the door and lifted the lantern high.

The walls of the room were lined with treasures representing every major culture in the history of the world. Artifacts of all sizes were displayed on pedestals, in cases, or rested on the floor. Some Anthony could identify, like the Hopi medicine doll and the Toltec ceremonial dagger. Some he couldn't, like the weathered block of granite near the door and the wooden table and chair that rested on a platform in the center of the floor.

"Oh, my God," Melina whispered, pressing close to his side. "What is this place?"

"It looks as if we found Benedict's trophy room."

"These must be priceless."

"I doubt if he paid for them."

"Why would he keep these things in a room like this? It's all bare rock, like the one…"

"Like the room where he wanted to keep me," Anthony finished for her.

"Oh, God. And those display cases are like the boxes in the lab where—"

Anthony grasped her chin and gave her a hard kiss. For her sake as well as for his. There was only so much horror that either of them could take.

She shook his arm. "We'd better go back and try another branch of the corridor. It doesn't seem as if this is a way out."

He looked around. On first glance, it appeared as if she was right. The walls were shadowed with alcoves, but none appeared to lead to an exit. The ceiling arched higher than the one in his cell, yet it was still low enough to make his hands sweat. He was about to turn away when his gaze was caught by a large circular shadow in the center of the ceiling, directly over the platform that held the wooden table and chair.

The flicker in his consciousness that had led him here flared from a candle to a beacon.

Anthony climbed on the table and hoisted the lantern. It wasn't a shadow, it was a natural chimney, wide enough for a man to climb through. Steps were chiseled right into the rock sides, forming a spiral staircase.

He stacked the chair on top of the table so he could get a closer look. The wood made an odd, chuckling sound as it took his weight, but it held. With his head and shoulders inside the chimney, he extended his hand to the first step. The stone was worn as smooth as satin, and emitted the same energy he'd felt when he'd entered the room. This staircase was old, perhaps as ancient as the village that was nestled into the cliff somewhere above them. It must be an escape route built by the Anasazi, a secret path through the cavern to the exit at the base of the cliff. The exit was blocked by Benedict's men, but what about where the route started?

His pulse raced as he looked into the blackness overhead. The corridors of the stronghold had been tiled in white and they had been bad. The cell had been worse. But the thought of willingly climbing into that tunnel...

"Anthony, what do you see?"

He lowered the lantern and looked at Melina. The answer was easy. "I see the woman I love."

Her smile put the lantern to shame.

Anthony dried his palm on his pants, took a deep breath and held out his hand. "Are you up for another hike?"

At any other time, Melina would have marveled at the history she was passing through. The Anasazi had fashioned their escape route with care, carving steps into the rock where the way was too steep, and smoothing out the cave floor like a sidewalk. They had marked the correct path through the winding maze of short tunnels and interconnected chambers by painting the outlines of their hands on the walls. Racing through this without pausing to pay her respects felt as wrong as running through a cathedral.

But she knew there was no time to spare. She hoped the spirits of the ancient builders would understand.

Had Benedict explored this route? Had he discovered their escape? Was he following them? Or was he already at the other end, waiting to take them back to that cell in the rock?

Anthony didn't seem to think so. His grip on her hand was confident as he led them upward. He was certain the passage would end at the cliff village, and had assured her there was no danger there. She trusted him. She did. But she was worried about his lack of color and the clamminess of his skin. At times he had trouble catching his breath. He was probably in pain from the beating the guards had given him, as well as exhausted from that phenomenal burst of energy he'd channeled, but he brushed off her concern.

He was the most stubborn, maddening man she knew.

If she didn't love him so much, she would probably grab him and shake him silly, but that would have to wait until—

"Anthony! Are you going to take all day?"

The woman's voice was faint, echoing from the blackness ahead of them.

Anthony staggered against the wall, the lantern slipping from his fingers. It crashed at Melina's feet before she could grab it. Fire licked across the rock as the remaining fuel ignited, but there had only been a few drops left. It died in a matter of seconds.

Yet the blackness wasn't complete. Light came from the bend in the passageway ahead.

"Anthony?" It was a different woman's voice, softer than the first one. "Please, answer me."

Before the echoes of either cry could fade, Anthony pushed away from the wall, threw his arm around Melina's shoulders and propelled her toward the light. "Dani! Elizabeth! We're here," he called.

The beam of a powerful flashlight suddenly filled the cavern, along with the sound of running footsteps. Within seconds she and Anthony were engulfed by a pair of women. Although their embrace was meant for him, Melina was in the middle of it for the simple reason that Anthony wouldn't let her go.

She didn't need an introduction. During the hike, Anthony had explained to her in more detail how he had asked Jeremy

Solienti and his sisters for help. He'd also revealed Danielle's connection to Liam Brooks, a lucky coincidence that Melina still found hard to grasp. Yet even if he hadn't told her anything, she would be able to guess who these women were. They had the same gypsy-black hair as Anthony, and they wore the same kind of body-hugging black "work" clothes as he did. They carried the same mixture of sunshine, fresh air and perfume that had swept into the stone room.

And it was clear to her that they loved Anthony almost as much as she did.

The taller of the two women pulled back to study his face. "My God, Anthony! You look like hell."

"Gee, thanks, Dani."

The second woman patted his arm gently. "We're not far from the surface, but I brought some medication if you need it."

"I'm fine, Elizabeth."

"He's not fine," Melina said. "He's exhausted and I think he has a broken rib. We have to get him to a doctor."

"I don't need a doctor," Anthony mumbled. He firmed his grip on Melina and started forward. "By the way, this is Melina Becker, the object of our rescue mission, in case you forgot."

Danielle clasped her in a quick embrace, then moved ahead to light the way. "It sounds as if you'll keep him in line. I like you already, Melina."

Although the passage was narrow here, Elizabeth fell into step on the other side of Anthony, slipping her arm around his waist. She leaned past him to smile at Melina. "Ditto. You must be someone special if you got my brother to go into a cave."

"Did you secure the entrance to this passageway before you came in?" Anthony asked.

"Give me some credit. It hasn't been *that* long since we worked together," Danielle said over her shoulder. "We found an easy path straight down from the top of the cliff to the ledge where the village is, so we didn't need to rappel. The area is not only secured, it's crawling with feds."

"We left our night vision gear there," Elizabeth said. "We thought the flashlight would be better for you. This cave must be—"

"What's the situation with Liam?" Anthony interrupted. "How's he doing on the warrants?"

"Red tape's no match for that man," Danielle replied. "He's got the place surrounded and is just waiting for the word that you two are out before he gives the signal to move in. Which reminds me…" She unclipped a radio from her belt and thumbed a switch. "Darling, we've got them both."

Even though she wanted to hear more about Liam and his plans for the raid, Melina realized Anthony had changed the subject twice. She looked at Elizabeth. "What's the problem with a cave?" she asked.

Elizabeth's eyes widened. Her gaze was a more mellow green than Anthony's, yet it was just as perceptive. "Good, heavens. You don't know, do you?"

"Know what?"

"My big brother is seriously claustrophobic. He can't stand enclosed spaces. He breaks out in a cold sweat if he has to get on an elevator."

"It's not that bad," Anthony said.

"Are you kidding? Dani and I have been worried sick, especially when we saw this cavern. I've seen you pass out on a subway car. I'm surprised you got this far on your own."

Melina moved her gaze to Anthony. She had seen that he was in distress but hadn't realized why. She had thought there was another explanation for his pallor, his unsteadiness, his periods of difficulty breathing. But if he was claustrophobic...

She glanced at the rock around them. The flashlight that Danielle held gave far more light than the lantern had, but still, there was no mistaking where they were.

Little facts that she had wondered about fell into place: Anthony's pallor when he'd mentioned the cave system behind the village, the look on his face when he glanced at the overhang the night of the storm, even the way he'd been unwilling to set foot in the tiny motel bathroom the night they had met.

"It's because of the night our mother died," Elizabeth told Melina. "Anthony got us to hide in a closet to keep us safe. We were only three. It...affected him."

Anthony tipped his head close to Melina's. "I didn't want to worry you."

Oh, she wanted to shake him silly again. Right after she kissed him into tomorrow. All this time, she'd been letting him comfort her, but he was living through fears she couldn't even imagine. If only she had known how difficult this must have been for him...

Then again, if she had known, she wouldn't have been able to stop Anthony from putting aside his own needs to see to hers. She sighed, rubbing her cheek against his shoulder. She had once wondered what it would be like to be loved by him. She was finding out.

Danielle clicked off the flashlight and ducked beneath a low archway. With surprise, Melina realized the passageway had flattened out. Daylight streamed across the rock floor. A few steps later, they emerged onto a small, sunlight-filled square between walls of red-gold brick.

After the confinement of the stronghold and the darkness of the cavern, the scene that opened up in front of them took

Melina's breath away. Against a backdrop of blue sky, the Anasazi cliff village spread across the ledge on either side of them like a collection of giant building blocks. Some of the mud and brick walls had crumbled, but others were still intact, soaring two stories high in places, reaching toward the lip of rock that curved protectively overhead. Wind sang through the empty windows and gaping doors, carrying with it the screech of eagles…and the pounding of heavy boots.

A dozen men carrying automatic weapons and wearing dark blue caps and bulletproof vests emblazoned with FBI squeezed past them, heading for the cavern. The rhythmic chug of helicopters echoed from the top of the cliff above them while the tinny noise of a loudspeaker rose from the valley floor. The raid Liam had organized was underway, and judging by the volume of noise, he had sent in everything he had, just as Melina had asked.

After the terror of the past day, it was hard to grasp that it was over. But it was. They were safe. She stepped into Anthony's embrace once more, not for comfort but in celebration. "I love you, Anthony," she said.

Danielle clipped the radio back on her belt. "I'm glad to hear that, Melina," she said. "Because Dare already assures us that Anthony loves you."

"Dare?" Anthony asked.

As more armed men hurried past, one man separated from the others and stopped in front of them. He wasn't wearing a vest or carrying a gun, yet he moved with a fearless confidence. He had the build of an athlete, midnight-black hair and a green gaze as intense as that of Anthony and his sisters.

"Meet Darian Sabura," Danielle said. "Our little brother."

He wasn't little, was the first thing Melina thought. He couldn't be more than an inch shorter than Anthony. His skin was bronzed from the sun, and his face bore the lean, hard lines of an adventurer, yet there was a touching sensitivity in his expression. He put his hand on Anthony's shoulder. He stared at him in silence for a moment. "And I'm glad you're alive, too, Anthony. Welcome back."

Elizabeth raised herself on her tiptoes to kiss her little brother's cheek. "Dare's an empath," she explained. "He knows what you're feeling."

Anthony clasped his brother's arm. "Was it you I felt?" he asked. "Did you lead me to the tunnel?"

"What?"

"I followed a feeling of safety. It helped give me strength. It made me feel as if I were coming home."

Melina felt a lump in her throat as she looked from one man to the other. She didn't need to be an empath to see that neither of these men was accustomed to sharing their emotions. Two tough-guy loners with hearts of gold. Did it run in the family?

"That wasn't me, Anthony. That was all of us."

"All?" Anthony looked at Melina and then at Danielle. Now that he was out in the open, his pallor had disappeared. So had the rest of the shadows. "You said you found them all."

Danielle beamed. "I realize you only asked for Elizabeth and me, but we knew the rest would want to be in on this."

"It was because of their help we were able to pinpoint your location," Elizabeth said. "Once we did, we sent you our love along with our energy." She wiggled her fingers. "That was some power we gathered, wasn't it? Imagine what a good team the six of us would make."

"Come on," Danielle said, linking her elbow with Dare's. "Cassie would know by now that we're coming."

Dare laughed. "You're right. She told us about it five minutes ago."

Danielle led the group around a heap of crumbled brick to

where a chest-high wall ran along the edge of the cliff. A tall man and a petite, black-haired woman stood near the wall, watching the activity in the valley below. The woman was the first to turn toward them. The wind flattened her jacket over her stomach, revealing the gentle swell of early pregnancy. She tugged at the arm of the man beside her. "Hawk," she said. "They're here."

He pivoted fast, his gaze zeroing in on Anthony. He had the rugged demeanor of a cowboy, from his wind-tossed dark hair to his chiseled jaw. Yet, like Darian, there was a sensitivity in his expression that transformed his face when he smiled. He held out his hand and stepped away from the wall. "Hawk Donovan," he said. "And this is my sister, Cassandra." His smile turned lopsided as the woman pushed him aside to give Anthony a smacking kiss on the cheek. "*Our* sister," he corrected.

Melina slipped out of Anthony's embrace to make room for Cassandra. In the past two days Melina had shed more tears than she had shed in years. She hadn't thought she would have any left, but as she watched Anthony get reacquainted with the siblings he had lost, she realized her cheeks were going to stay wet for a long time.

But these were good tears. Healing tears.

"Are you all right, Melina?"

At the familiar voice, Melina turned to look to her right. A man was approaching them from a sloping pathway where the village melded into the overhanging cliff. "Liam!" she said, wiping her face. "Oh, it's good to see you. I'm fine. I'm just…" She hiccuped. "This family reunion. It's overwhelming."

Liam Brooks was outfitted with an FBI vest, like his colleagues, but he held a radio instead of a gun. He said a few words into the mouthpiece, then did something she had never seen him do before. The by-the-book agent with the steady personality of a rock actually grinned.

And for the first time Melina realized with a start that he was a very handsome man.

"Those six are going to take some getting used to," he said.

"That's for sure. They're truly unique."

He seemed about to comment on that, but before he could, a police helicopter swooped past the ledge, stirring up a cloud of dust. He waved the dust away. "Well, Melina, it looks as if you'll get what you want, after all."

At the thought, she had to wipe her eyes again. "Anthony and I haven't had the chance to make plans, but—"

"I was talking about your exclusive." He nodded his head toward the valley. "I'm coordinating the raid from here. You've got a front row seat to witness the end of the Titan Syndicate."

He meant her story. She had forgotten all about it. She crossed her arms over her chest. "All I want is to see Benedict Payne stopped. He's evil, Liam. He's—"

"He's finished," Liam said. "My men have already breached the lower entrance of the stronghold. He won't get away this time."

"You'd better believe it." Danielle came over to give Liam a kiss, then pressed close to his side as another helicopter buzzed past. She coughed and looked at Melina. "If we hadn't needed to rescue you and Anthony, Elizabeth and I would have gone in after him ourselves. That monster has caused so much misery."

"What you should have done is stay where it's safe, the way Cole and I asked you to," Liam said sternly. "There are already too many civilians here. Until the bastard's in custody—"

"Agent Brooks! We have a problem."

The shout had come from the direction of the sloping pathway that Liam had just used. He turned toward it and thrust Danielle behind his back. A second later, Anthony and his brothers had joined him, aligning themselves with Liam to shield Melina and their sisters.

Melina found herself between Cassandra and Elizabeth. She met Danielle's gaze over the petite Cassie's head. All three sisters had a flare of terror in their eyes. It was mixed with rage. The combination was familiar. It was shared by all of Benedict's victims. Melina tried to tell herself she was safe—after all, she was surrounded by agents and sheltered by four very determined men. Yet the horror of Benedict's plans for her and Anthony wasn't far beneath the surface. Would it ever truly go away?

"I warn you again, young man, you are making a mistake."

It was a woman's voice, her words almost drowned out by the noise of the hovering helicopters, but Melina was certain she had heard that voice before. She pressed close to Anthony's back and stretched to see past his shoulder.

Three of Liam's men were struggling with a small, dark-haired woman. They had her by her arms, but their grip was slipping in the shawl she had wrapped around her shoulders and the gold bracelets that gleamed at her wrists. "We found her on the ramp from the top of the cliff, sir," one of the men said. "I'm sorry, sir. I don't know how she got past the perimeter. She isn't armed."

"I have more right to be here than any of you," the woman said. "Let me pass."

Melina gasped as recognition dawned. She tapped Anthony's arm. "That's the woman from the bed-and-breakfast. Mrs. Rodriguez's other guest. What on earth is she doing here?"

"Liam, that's the fortune-teller we met at the carnival, last spring!" Danielle exclaimed. "Remember? She gave you that tarot card."

"I've met her, too," Cassie said. "She knew I was pregnant."

"That's the woman who tipped me off about my birth mother," Hawk said.

It was Anthony who was the first to step forward. "Let her go," he ordered. "This woman means no harm."

"He's right," Dare said, moving with him. "I sense no threat in her."

The FBI agents looked to Liam for instructions. He dismissed them with a nod, his expression confused. "Who are you?" he asked. "How did you get here?"

The woman straightened her shawl. Sunlight glinted from the silver in her hair. "I followed the children as I always do. They gathered here, so I came." She looked at Anthony. "You were wise to take my advice," she said. "Alone, you would have fallen, but there is no strength like that of a family united."

He stared into her eyes. Her gaze was the same piercing green as his own. "How did you know what to tell me?"

"I saw the paths in front of you. That is *my* power." She moved her gaze from Anthony to Hawk and then to Dare. "I am so proud of the men you have become. Your lives were filled with challenges, but you have made the right choices." Her face creased into a smile as she looked at Danielle, Elizabeth and Cassie. "And you three make my heart exult. You have indeed inherited the good soul of your mother."

"Our mother?" Elizabeth asked.

"All of you look so much like her, especially you, Cassandra."

Cassie gave a sharp cry and pressed her knuckles to her mouth. "I saw myself standing with you. All seven of us were together. Right here in the village with the wind blowing around us."

"If you have foreseen it, too, then the time must be right." The woman's smile broadened. "For twenty-eight years I have tried in my own way to watch over you and keep you away from the monster who stole Deanna's life. I foresaw you would discover each other when you were ready. Now you have, and my wait is over." She touched her fingers to her chest. "I am Magdalena Falaso, your mother's sister."

"Aunt Maggie?" Danielle said. "You're Aunt Maggie?"

"Yes, my darling, I am your aunt. There are so many things I wish to tell you." Magdalena's chin trembled with emotion. Her smile faltered. "But forgive me, it has been so very long since I held you, I find I cannot wait another instant—" Her voice broke. She held out her hands.

Without another word spoken, all six of Deanna's children converged on Magdalena at once.

Melina had to use her sleeve to blot her eyes. Had she thought this was done?

She glanced at Liam. His eyes were suspiciously moist. Before either of them could speak, his radio crackled. As he returned his attention to his job, Melina stepped back to better take in the scene, shutting out the sound of the choppers and the bustle of Liam's men, holding to her heart the warmth that filled the air around her.

For the first time since that horrible night Fredo had died, she wished she had a camera. She wanted to capture this moment and preserve it, not for a story—this had gone far beyond a story—but for Anthony.

Like her, he'd found much more than he'd known he was seeking.

Two men in FBI vests jostled her shoulder as they brushed past her. She blotted her eyes again and backed out of the way, her mind still on the touching reunion. But as the men continued past Anthony and his family, one of them glanced back and Melina couldn't help noticing that the skin around his jaw drooped like a hound's, and one of his eyebrows was missing.

Melina felt a chill. She tried to ignore it. She couldn't let the fear come back and spoil this reunion for Anthony. This place was secure. The FBI were all over the stronghold.

So what better disguise for someone who was bent on escape? Especially with everyone relaxing after the false alarm of Magdalena's dramatic appearance.

"Liam!" she yelled, pointing at the two men. They were heading for the pathway that led to the top of the cliff. They must have come from the cavern entrance at the back of the village. "Stop those two. They're—"

Before she could finish her warning, her elbow was caught in a crushing grip from behind. Something hard and metallic was jammed against her temple. It was a gun. She recognized the feel of it. She recognized the smell. And the terror it evoked. She twisted her head.

Like an image from a nightmare, Benedict Payne loomed behind her. He was dressed in the same dark blue uniform and vest as the rest of Liam's people. He had shaved off his silver goatee and hidden his silver hair underneath a baseball cap with FBI on the front, but the shadow of the cap's brim couldn't conceal that flat, lifeless stare of a reptile.

Oh, God. No. Please. He didn't belong here in this place of sunshine and happiness. He wanted to store Anthony like a trophy and keep their children in cages....

"Stay back!" Benedict shouted.

Melina whipped her gaze in front of her. While several of Liam's FBI agents subdued the two men who had jostled her—Gus and Habib, from the look of them—the rest had halted where they were, their weapons drawn and pointed toward Benedict. She heard a series of metallic clicks from behind them and realized all the agents in the area must be doing the same.

"Let her go," Anthony said, stepping forward. He had no weapon, but the look on his face was so deadly, he was undoubtedly the one Benedict had spoken to.

Benedict wrenched Melina's arm behind her and jammed the gun harder to her temple. "Get out of my way," he ordered. "Or I'll shoot her."

Anthony came to a halt ten feet away. He braced his legs apart and folded his arms over his chest, looking as immovable as the cliff. "It's over, Benedict."

"You fool. I'm not finished. I—"

"My brother is right," Dare said, moving beside Anthony. "It is over. You are finished."

Benedict raised his voice. "I want guaranteed safe passage to the airport. I want a jet fueled and ready."

"It ends now," Hawk said. He moved to stand with his brothers, his stance echoing theirs. "You're not going to hurt anyone again."

One by one, Danielle, Elizabeth and Cassandra joined them so that they formed a line, shoulder to shoulder, blocking the way.

"Agent Brooks, get me a helicopter," Benedict shouted.

Liam took a pistol from one of his men, clasped it between both hands and straightened his arms, pointing it at Benedict. "There's no way out this time, you bastard."

Benedict moved his gun from Melina's head and aimed it at Danielle. "Get on the radio and do it now, Brooks. It makes no difference to me which one I shoot."

Danielle didn't flinch. She looked at Liam over her shoulder and spoke calmly, her tone as immovable as the men's stance. "Let my family deal with him."

Liam fumed. "Dani—"

"Trust me. Please." She held out her hand to her aunt. "Aunt Maggie?"

Magdalena went to stand beside Danielle. She clasped her hand and looked at Benedict. "You shall reap what you sowed, Benedict Payne. That which you wanted to control will defeat you."

Benedict twisted Melina's arm, forcing her wrist between her shoulder blades as he pointed the gun at Magdalena. "You! You're the one who stole the babies."

"Deanna loved her babies enough to give her three youngest to me because she feared what you would do when she told you she was leaving you. I found them homes where you could not hurt them. And you shall not hurt them now."

A gust of wind moaned through the village. It wasn't from the police helicopters. The sound of their engines had faded; the air beyond the ledge was empty.

Bracelets tinkled as Magdalena lifted her arm to point at Benedict. "Like a jackal, you prey on the solitary, but we stand united against you. You are no match for the power we wield. Justice will be done."

The sky was clear, yet Melina felt thunder rumble through the stone beneath her feet. The roots of her hair tingled. She blinked and returned her gaze to Anthony. Despite the pain from her twisted arm and the fear that froze her thoughts, the moment her gaze met his she felt a thrill flow through her body, sparking every nerve to awareness.

She had never seen him look so…alive. So vital. So powerful. His hair streamed in the wind, the gold gypsy ring at his earlobe glinting in the sunlight. Energy shimmered around him, as well as around his brothers and sisters, making the ancient walls and the sheltering cliff waver like a heat mirage.

"Enough!" Benedict shouted. The gun slammed back against Melina's temple. "You have three seconds to move aside or I'll shoot her. One."

The thunder in the stone spread to Melina's pulse. It gathered force, becoming a rhythm in her bones. She kept her gaze on Anthony's. Even across the distance that separated them, she could feel the caress of his love.

"Two."

That was the key, she realized. The real source of power. Benedict was not going to win. She smiled into Anthony's eyes and waited for the wave to break. She knew it wouldn't take long. There were six of them. Seven. Standing united, just as Cassie had foreseen.

"Three."

An eagle dove from an empty window in one of the structures, swooping so close that its wingtips slashed Benedict's face. He released his grip on Melina's arm and staggered toward the edge of the cliff. The gun tore away from his fingers and crashed into the wall there, knocking loose a shower of crumbled brick. He spun twice, his feet slipping on the debris, his arms flailing for balance. A nimbus of blue-white light crackled around his face. He screamed and covered his eyes.

It all happened so fast, Melina had barely realized she was free when Anthony caught her in his arms. Sensations too intense to name burst everywhere they touched, leaving her breathless, quivering, gasping for air.

He clasped her to his chest. "Hang on, Melina."

She anchored her fingers in his shirt. Before the wave could retreat, a new one built. It was broader than the last, deeper, darker, more primitive. Melina felt as if the very mountain was vibrating, channeling the power of these ruins, the painted handprints and the storehouse of stolen treasures that had been hoarded deep inside.

"This one isn't ours," Anthony said against her ear. "We're not controlling this."

A surge of cold howled through the Anasazi village, racing past the empty windows, darting around the crumbled walls, gathering the ancient dust until it formed itself into a writhing whirlwind.

From the safety of Anthony's embrace, Melina stared in awed disbelief. The whirlwind tilted, whipping streamers of dust toward Benedict, ripping off his stolen hat and vest, tearing away his shirt, his pants and his shoes, stripping him of his magician illusions.

In less than a heartbeat, Benedict was naked and cowering. The funnel of dust turned black as it swallowed him. The force lifted him off his feet and carried him over the side of the cliff, leaving nothing behind but the fading sound of his scream.

Epilogue

Thanksgiving, one week later

It was lucky that Liam and Danielle's new house here in Chicago was large enough to hold this family reunion, Melina thought, gazing at the crowd that had gathered in the living room. The reunion in New Mexico last week had only been the start. If Anthony's family kept expanding at this rate, by next year they would need to rent a hall.

Deanna Falaso Payne's six children weren't as unique as Melina had thought. Henry Bloomfield, the man Benedict had named a week ago during that nightmare in the stronghold's lab, had fathered six other genetically engineered children with a woman named Violet Vaughn. Like Deanna's children, Violet's had been scattered by tragedy during their childhood, but they had found each other once again.

Although Liam and the others had suspected there was a

blood link between Deanna's children and Violet's for almost half a year, the official DNA test had confirmed the relationship only a few weeks ago. Suddenly, Anthony had four more brothers—Jake, Connor, Marcus and Gideon—and two more sisters, Faith and Gretchen. The six tall, dark-haired, blue-eyed men and women were a fascinating group of individuals, each with stories as heartrending as Anthony's. They had overcome tremendous obstacles; every one of them understood how powerful the love of a family could be.

And since these newly discovered half-siblings of Anthony's were all married and deeply in love—and doing their best to add to the family tree—Liam and Danielle's snowy backyard was overflowing with nieces and nephews.

Melina turned to the window and wiped the condensation from the glass with her palm so she could look into the backyard. It was fortunate that they had served the turkey before the snow had started. Corralling the children long enough to sit them down for Thanksgiving dinner had been difficult, but the minute they had seen the snow, they had disappeared in a cloud of coats, hats and giggles.

She shifted her focus to look at her hand where it rested against the glass. A diamond glinted from her ring finger. Anthony had put it there before they had left his apartment in Philadelphia this morning after a night of loving that neither of them would ever forget. Maybe by next Thanksgiving…

Anthony came up behind her, slipping his arms around her waist. "Are you okay?"

"I'm fine. I just wanted to watch the kids."

He leaned down to rest his chin on her shoulder. "They're really something, aren't they?"

"They're the future." She put her hand over his and moved it to her stomach. For the first time in eight years, this day didn't make her think about the child she had lost but about the love she had gained. Never in her life had she had so much to be thankful for. "I love you, Anthony."

A soft pulse flowed from his palm to her stomach, then curled gently around her thigh. "I've heard a rumor to that effect," he murmured.

"I love your family, too. They're…extraordinary."

His chest rumbled with a quiet chuckle. "I have to admit, it's hard to keep everyone straight without a program. Jake and Gideon pointed out that the number of my siblings has doubled twice in less than a week."

"Jake and Gideon are the math geniuses, right?"

"Uh-huh. I doubt if even those two know how many kids are out there. They don't stand still long enough to count."

She laughed. "I'm just starting to get the first names straight. It's going to be a challenge to sort out all the last ones."

"And speaking of challenges…" He kissed her cheek. "Elizabeth told me Cole offered you a job on one of his Philadelphia papers. Are you going to take it?"

Cole's offer hadn't been the only one that had come in during the past week. From the moment her exclusive story of the fall of the Titan Syndicate had hit the *New York Daily Journal*'s front page, she had heard from practically every major paper on the continent, as well as three television networks.

Yet there were facts that hadn't made it into her story, facts that had been left out of the official police report. How could anyone explain the way Benedict had disappeared? Cause of death—a whirlwind?

Still, no one could deny that justice had been done.

"I probably will take Cole's offer," Melina said. "I'd like to work closer to home."

"Are you going to miss the traveling?"

"Nope. There's nothing I want to run away from anymore." She folded her arms over Anthony's, leaning back into his embrace. "I already told Neil I'm resigning. He'd been expecting it. He sounded genuinely pleased when I told him I'd moved in with you." She smiled at Anthony's reflection in the glass. "It seems he's already dating the new copy editor they hired to replace the one who had been working for Benedict."

He smiled back at her, his eyes sparkling. "It must be something in the air."

"Mmm. You might be right." She tipped her head toward the window. Beyond the melee of children, a middle-aged couple stood arm in arm beneath the snow-dusted boughs of a birch tree. "Have you noticed Magdalena and Jeremy? They went outside to help build the snowman, but they're watching each other more than they're watching the kids."

Anthony whistled softly. "Something in the air, all right."

"And just when I thought things couldn't possibly get better."

He drew her away from the window and turned her to face him. "What would you think about a honeymoon in Florida?"

"Why Florida?"

"The weather."

"Don't you like the snow?"

"It's not that." He stroked his knuckles along the edge of her jaw, sending a whisper of sensation to her lips. His gaze glowed with a private smile. "I heard there are regions in Florida that have a higher incidence of lightning strikes per square mile than anywhere else in the country."

Melina didn't need to be able to foresee the future to be certain that things were going to keep getting better for a long, long time.

* * * * *

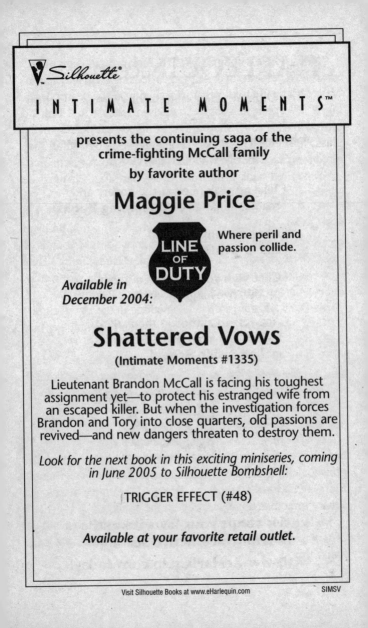

Silhouette®

INTIMATE MOMENTS™

presents the continuing saga of the
crime-fighting McCall family

by favorite author

Maggie Price

LINE OF DUTY

Where peril and
passion collide.

*Available in
December 2004:*

Shattered Vows

(Intimate Moments #1335)

Lieutenant Brandon McCall is facing his toughest
assignment yet—to protect his estranged wife from
an escaped killer. But when the investigation forces
Brandon and Tory into close quarters, old passions are
revived—and new dangers threaten to destroy them.

*Look for the next book in this exciting miniseries, coming
in June 2005 to Silhouette Bombshell:*

TRIGGER EFFECT (#48)

Available at your favorite retail outlet.

**Bestselling fantasy author Mercedes Lackey
turns traditional fairy tales on their heads
in the land of the Five Hundred Kingdoms.**

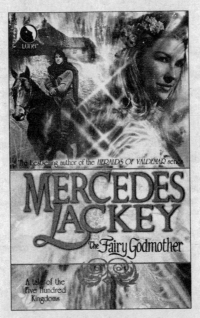

Elena, a Cinderella in the making, gets an
unexpected chance to be a Fairy Godmother. But being a
Fairy Godmother is hard work and she gets into trouble by
changing a prince who is destined to save the kingdom,
into a donkey—but he really deserved it!

Can she get things right and save the kingdom?
Or will her stubborn desire to teach this ass
of a prince a lesson get in the way?

*On sale November 2004.
Visit your local bookseller.*

If you enjoyed what you just read,
then we've got an offer you can't resist!

Take 2 bestselling
love stories FREE!

Plus get a FREE surprise gift!

COMING NEXT MONTH

SIMCNM1104

INTIMATE MOMENTS